PRAISE FOR

'Be warned: Mitchell k   ain
mystery is solved for mc

                                                              ews

'Mitchell's . . . macabre stand-alone thriller tantalises with a diabolical closed-room mystery slowly sloughing its secrets . . . With cagey plot twists, nuanced characters, and a pleasant young romance thrown into the mix, Mitchell's thriller warms the heart as it tingles the senses.'

—Library Journal

'A creepy read that ramps up the chill factor all the way to the end.'

—Tariq Ashkanani

'For me, this book had everything – an excellent police procedural with tension, pace and a compelling storyline. With the added psychological element, there was nothing more I could have asked for.'

—Angela Marsons

'Fast-paced, twisty, and chilled me to the bone . . . I loved every minute of it!'

—Robert Bryndza

'The writer's conflicted heroine and twisted villain are superb characters.'

—*Sunday Express* magazine

'Heart-thumping moments that left me desperate to read more.'

—The Book Review Café

'The very definition of a page-turner.'

—John Marrs

'The tension built up and up . . . I devoured every page.'

—Mel Sherratt

'With her police officer experience, Caroline Mitchell is a thriller writer who knows how to deliver on plot, character, and, most importantly, emotion in any book she writes. I can't wait to read more.'

—*My Weekly* magazine

THE
ISLANDERS

ALSO BY CAROLINE MITCHELL

Individual Works

Paranormal Intruder
Witness
Silent Victim
The Perfect Mother
The Village

The DI Amy Winter Series

Truth and Lies
The Secret Child
Left for Dead
Flesh and Blood
In Cold Blood

The DC Jennifer Knight Series

Don't Turn Around
Time to Die
The Silent Twin

The Ruby Preston Series

Love You to Death
Sleep Tight
Murder Game

THE
ISLANDERS

CAROLINE
MITCHELL

Text copyright © 2023 by Caroline Mitchell
All rights reserved.

No part of this book may be reproduced, or stored in a retrieval system, or transmitted in any form or by any means, electronic, mechanical, photocopying, recording, or otherwise, without express written permission of the publisher.

Published by Thomas & Mercer, Seattle

www.apub.com

Amazon, the Amazon logo, and Thomas & Mercer are trademarks of Amazon.com, Inc., or its affiliates.

ISBN-13: 9781662513053
eISBN: 9781662513046

Cover design by The Brewster Project
Cover image: ©mbond77 / Shutterstock; ©Nic Skerten / Arcangel;
©Johner Images ©Mike Hill / Getty Images

Printed in the United States of America

This book is dedicated to my beautiful Irish sisters,
Ann, Louise and Bridie. With love.

The Selkie

Soft black eyes
Silvery skin
Breath of seaweed and salt
As dark waters pull you in
Sharp white teeth
Flash in the night
The last thing you see
Is a flick of a fin

PROLOGUE

MARY

1 October 2003

I'm going to drown today. My thoughts are morose as I fight a rising sense of dread. I think it every time we cross to the mainland, but tonight I *know*. *Éireann Rose*, our barnacled half-shell, has served us well, but the little boat will not make a safe crossing tonight. My cheeks burn from the wind, and my shoulders inch upwards as waves lap against our boat. I cradle the tightly swaddled newborn close to my chest. The eye of the lighthouse glares at us, and I stiffen beneath its beam. Gabriel, my husband, sits at the stern. His hand grips the tiller of the outboard motor as he negotiates the choppy Irish Sea. He is a handsome man, but not a good man, and I wish he hadn't roped me into this. Gabriel has the innate ability to take something from every person he meets. But life was a darkened room until he came to Selkie Island, which is why I will do anything to stop him from leaving me.

My nameless charge is a wee thing, no more than six pounds in weight. The rocking motion comforts her. But there are five of us in this boat and her twin fusses in Isla's papoose. Isla, with her almond eyes and trusting nature. She stares at me unblinking, the tip of her tongue in its usual resting place between her slightly parted lips. Shame washes over me because I do not deserve her trust.

The storm has come in quickly and we're stuck between the island and the mainland, bobbing to and fro. Gabriel raises his voice over the noise of the engine.

'It's rough, but we'll get there soon enough.'

So we hold on, because our cargo is precious, and the twinkling lights of the mainland are in view. I turn to Isla to reassure her, but I quickly drop my gaze because I cannot bear for my beloved daughter to see my guilty face. The strobe of the lighthouse reveals a boat in the distance, and it becomes hard to breathe. I think of the people I've left behind. Of the baby in my arms. Suddenly the waves sound like thunder in my ears. Each one crashes like an accusation – *traitor, traitor, traitor* – the spray of angry spittle hitting my face. I taste the salt on my tongue and my emotions rush upon me like the swell of the sea.

This is wrong. I cannot do this. This must end. I peer down at the baby, her little cherub nose barely visible beneath her cocoon.

'I'm sorry,' I whisper.

But the rising winds steal my platitudes. Soon I will come to realise that it's too little, too late.

I never make it to the mainland alive.

CHAPTER 1

CLAIRE

Friday 10 June 2022

The award lies against the wall of our London apartment, a fine layer of dust coating the once shiny glass. The words still burn on my memory: *For outstanding excellence in the field of paediatric research and achievement.* For months it has rested there, untouched since that day. So many times Daniel tried to hang it on the wall, and I barked at him to leave it be. Its presence is a constant reminder, not of my successes but of my failures. I do not deserve the award. It is a reminder of my vanity. How ironic that I was on-stage accepting it the night my patient succumbed to the illness that would claim her young life. An illness that could have been avoided if she hadn't been misdiagnosed. I can still see my sister Susan's waxy face, staring but not seeing as she tries to comprehend the news. I can still hear the screams – the animalistic howl that could come only from a mother who has lost her child. They'd rebounded in the hospital corridors that day, and now they play in a loop in my mind. For once I was powerless to make things right. Too wrapped up with my award, I'd let my family down in the worst possible way. It is my fault that little girl died.

A swirl of warm night air curls around the nape of my neck and plays with my hair. I lean forward from my vantage point on the window ledge of our fifteenth-storey flat, my shoe balancing on the tip of my toes as I sit. Somewhere from inside a hollow voice tells me to climb back inside. As always during times of stress, my husband's Irish accent has become more pronounced. Shaky with panic, he reaches out his hand.

'Please. You're not thinking straight. Come inside. I can't do this on my own. Not again. We can talk things through.'

He looks so handsome tonight, the scar from his cleft lip only adding to the character of his face. I should feel guilty. I know this is wrong. Daniel's life has been touched by tragedy. He lost both his parents at an early age. What sort of monster am I, leaving him like this? But my pain is insufferable and relief so close.

The warm breeze tickles the sole of my foot as my shoe dangles on my toe.

'Stay there,' I say in a level voice. 'Take one more step and I'll jump.'

I cannot unbreak the broken. There is no sliding back to normality. Such overwhelming guilt and loss are impossible to dismiss.

London looks beautiful tonight. The air feels thick and warm, and black cabs beep while pedestrians mill on the streets below. I inhale a deep breath, the smell of street food and petrol fumes enveloping my senses.

Daniel gestures at me. 'Please, darlin', just . . . just come back inside. I can help you. Please. Come in.' He is fighting hard to stay calm but a sheen of sweat glazes his forehead.

I edge forward on the thick ledge. We live high enough for me not to survive the fall. A familiar depressive blackness is closing in on me as a physical weight on my chest. I can't do this anymore.

'For Christ's sake, will you listen to me . . . ?' His gaze locks on to mine. 'Just . . . just come back inside and we can talk about this . . . OK? Are you listening? Because I love you, Claire. Do you hear me?'

His pleading is laced with urgency. He knows his words are having little effect. His eyes are wild with panic as he fights an internal battle. I can almost read his thoughts. If he lunges for me now, he will never reach me in time. My shoe slips from my foot on to the streets below. I kick off the second shoe and feel a sense of freedom as the breeze skims both my feet. Soon the pain will be over. But my husband edges closer, and I cannot risk him pulling me inside.

'Step back, or I'll chase them all the way down,' I threaten.

Below us, life goes on as normal, but our world is ripping apart at the seams. I watch him retreat, analysing him one last time. Deep down, he knows these moments are important, but everything is moving too quickly and he is powerless to stop it. I imagine his heart beating with the force of a steam train in his chest. If I ever doubted that he loved me before, I have my answer now. This man loves me more than anything in the world.

But my suffering is eating me from the inside out. This is not a cry for help. This is me, wanting out from this world. I'm not strong enough to shoulder the burden of my actions another day. Daniel had smiled at me tonight, not realising that I was brighter only because the end was in sight. But now he is home early, standing behind me as he tries to buy enough time for the emergency services to save my life.

'Please . . . I can't live without you.' My husband continues to plead.

'Then come with me,' I whisper, but he looks so horrified at the prospect that I quickly regret my words.

'I . . . I can't.'

5

I sigh. The wind that swirls around me whispers that the time for talking is over. I am drawing out the inevitable and the heavy stomp of boots in the hall means the emergency services are here. Daniel must have called them. By the way he is holding his phone, they are probably still on the line. I feel the sting of betrayal. This was a private, intimate moment, now being played to the outside world. Pedestrians have noticed and are being directed away. I whisper a silent thanks as I don't want to hurt anyone on the way down.

'Claire . . . look at me, will you?' Daniel steps forward and I move towards the edge.

'No!' he screams, his eyes brimming with tears. 'Please! Come back inside!'

'Sorry,' I whisper. 'I love you.' Tears blur the edges of my world. 'But I can't do this anymore.'

I must make this quick. I close my eyelids, having decided I do not wish to see the ground rushing up to greet me as I fly.

'No!' Arms outstretched, Daniel lunges, but we both know he'll never make it in time.

I push myself forward and jump.

CHAPTER 2

Daniel

I thought my wife was getting better. I fooled myself into believing she had turned a corner. I should have seen the clues. Despite the smile she had painted on, her award still lay against our apartment wall. She had been unable to even think about returning to her job. I knew she loved me, but not enough to live through the pain she must have been feeling when she climbed on to the window ledge. I honestly believed she had managed to drag herself out of the black hole that had claimed her. She looked so beautiful tonight. The hollows beneath her eyes hadn't seemed quite so pronounced, and her smile had made a welcome return. But the second I stepped inside our apartment, I knew there was something wrong. Perhaps it was the kiss of the outside breeze, or the sense of despair which hung thick in the air. My heart flipped an extra beat, my senses heightened, my body taut. I stepped inside the living room, and my attention was drawn to our floor-length net curtains swirling in the breeze. I blinked at the sight of Claire sitting on our window ledge. My brain tried to comprehend the vision before me, trying but failing to reject the thought that she could fall to her death.

'Claire!' I called, the words a shriek on my lips. I was shocked into sobriety, gripping the back of our leather sofa. There was no point in asking what she was doing. It was plain to see. 'Please,' I said, my heart hammering in my chest. 'You're not thinking straight. Come inside, we can talk things through.'

She glared a warning. If I ran at her, she'd jump before I reached her on the window ledge. During the chaos that followed, I activated the emergency call feature on my iPhone. Cold dread rose inside me as I begged my wife to come in. There was nothing in her expression. No fear, just quiet acceptance. Tears rose in my eyes as I watched my wife give up on the life we shared. It was like speaking to a statue. Each time I tried to inch forward, she did too. It was a battle I was going to lose. I could feel her slipping away as she warned me off. For a fleeting second, her eyes brightened.

'Come with me,' she whispered, and the flicker of hope inside me died.

'I . . . I can't,' I instantly replied. What kind of madness was this?

She stood up on to the ledge, ignoring my screams to come inside. Then she closed her eyes and jumped. I lunged towards her, stumbling as I grasped the air. I was too late.

There was a sudden flurry of movement. A flash of fluorescent jacket as the firefighter abseiled from the apartment above. Then a scream, a firm voice. I clung to the window ledge as my legs became weak. Thank God.

Claire was safe.

CHAPTER 3

CLAIRE

Friday 17 March 2023

I inhale a breath of salt-rich air, trying to feel hopeful as we cross on the ferry to Selkie Island. I am a city girl in every sense, having lived in London, New York, Tokyo and Mumbai. Saint Patrick's Day seems like the perfect time for my first trip to Ireland. My baby is asleep in her papoose, her pink woollen hat poking out of the top as her head nestles close to my chest. Out here, in the wilds of the Irish Sea with nothing but the cry of gulls and steady chug-chug of the ferryboat engine, a sense of calm descends. Perhaps I have a connection. Somewhere in my family tree there is Irish blood. When I first met Daniel in the hospital where I worked, I never thought I would end up here. But the clouds have finally parted and I'm feeling stronger every day.

I wonder if I'll ever be able to return to my job. When I think of the sacrifices that I've made to progress my career . . . and now my award still lies in storage, in a thick layer of bubble wrap.

Guilt surrounds me on many levels, but I'm learning to keep it at bay. For so long, all I've wanted is for the ground to swallow me up. Moving to the remote Selkie Island is the next-best thing. I sense my husband's reluctance to return to his childhood home.

'As long as it makes you happy,' he'd said with a sigh. 'I'll do whatever it takes.'

My colleagues, family and friends say they understand, but I can barely look them in the eye.

Moving to Daniel's birthplace feels right. I like the sense of detachment from the outside world. For the last fifteen years, I was consumed by my career, until it came to a juddering halt. Being together twenty-four/seven feels like we're starting over again. My tongue touches my lips, and immediately the taste of salt makes itself known. My mouth is dry. I stand beside Daniel as waves batter the ferry. There's an elderly man nearby and just one family sitting inside the cabin as we cross. In their scarves and hats, they seem more prepared for the weather than me. Up the ferryboat bobs, and my stomach lurches in response. Daniel groans, clutching the side of the ferryboat. He's as white as a sheet, and sweat is beading on his forehead. I grab his hand and give it a reassuring squeeze. 'It's OK. Take deep breaths and keep your eyes on the horizon.'

He nods weakly, trying to keep it together. I pass him a bottle of water from my bag, and he takes a sip, grimacing at the taste. 'I can't believe I'm seasick,' he mutters. 'I grew up here, for God's sake.'

'Well, it happens to the best of us,' I say with a grin. 'At least we're almost there.'

As if on cue, the ferryboat lurches once more, and Daniel doubles over, retching into the water. I rub his back in circles to comfort him while Kitty sleeps peacefully.

The elderly man rustles a small paper bag and shakes it in our direction. His false teeth appear too big for his mouth, and I try not to stare as he speaks in a thick Cork accent, saying something about liquorice being good for seasickness. People talk so fast here, although my husband's sing-song accent has mellowed from living in London over the years.

'No, thanks.' Daniel smiles in gratitude, as he offers him a sweet. The man's eyes twinkle as he peeps at my daughter, who's snug beneath her layers.

'You one of dem tourists?' he asks, seemingly determined to strike up a conversation while Daniel takes a few deep breaths.

'Visiting family,' I say, feeling guilty for the short reply. 'In Árd Na Mara.'

I utter the words with pride. From what I've seen of it online, it's the most impressive building on the island. I grip the side of the ferry as a wave lifts us. I'm about to say more, but the man's face has grown slack. He looks from me to the baby. He is a stranger, yet he backs away from me, as if I'm carrying an airborne disease.

'No . . .' he whispers on an intake of breath. He's shaking his head, his bushy eyebrows rising in alarm. 'Not with the wee one. Not if you want her to live.'

'What?' I must have misheard.

But now Daniel is taking me by the elbow, guiding me away. 'Look, over there – can you see the seals?'

I follow his gaze into the distance to see three grey heads bobbing between the waves. I recall his stories of the legend of the selkies – half seal, half human; Ireland's very own brand of mermaids.

'That man,' I say, glancing over Daniel's shoulder. The stranger has retreated but his warning remains. 'He said something really odd, about Kitty not being safe.'

But Daniel waves my concerns away. 'Don't mind that auld fart. It's Paddy's Day. He's had his fill.'

I catch Daniel's wistful gaze as he stares out at sea, and I try to read his thoughts. It can't be easy for him, given his parents drowned making this crossing. The last thing he needs is me getting antsy about some inebriated old fellah who I can barely understand.

I know I can acclimatise. We could grow to love it here. I gaze at the lighthouse as the island draws near. It stands majestic on the cliff edge, a pillar of white and red. An ivy-covered building looms tall nearby, bordering the eroding cliffs. A black wrought-iron fence marks out its generous plot. Is it? It is. Árd Na Mara – Daniel's childhood home. It's big, but not quite as beautiful as it looks online. A thin blanket of fog hugs the shoreline, obscuring the view of what lies beyond.

'It's one of the few working lighthouses left,' Daniel informs me, pointing at the giant watchtower which stands on the highest peak. 'The red stripe makes it stand out, although most boats rely on radar now.'

His tousled brown hair peeps from beneath his woollen hat, his North Face jacket zipped up to his chin. I regret wearing my thin designer coat as the wind feels like knives on my skin. I should have realised there is no place for it here. But my clothes feel like a uniform, and I'm not ready to give up my individuality just yet. At least Kitty is dressed for the weather.

I inhale the salty-fresh air as gulls scream and swoop overhead. We are nearing the island. Our time there will be a tonic for us all.

An elderly man in a flat cap waves at my husband from the short pier where boats dock, as he seems to recognise us both. He's got big ears and a mop of snow-white hair.

'Is that Mossie?' I feel a tinge of excitement.

Mossie is short for Maurice, and he and his wife Teresa run the business side of Daniel's family home. It feels strange that I've never met him in the flesh. Mossie and Teresa virtually reared Daniel after his parents drowned. Little has been said about the death of Daniel's parents, whose boat capsized as they crossed to the mainland. Mossie appears happy to see us. The elderly couple rarely leave the island, apart from occasional trips to the mainland for supplies.

'Oh, that's Mossie alright.' Daniel waves back. 'And he's not changed a bit.' He turns to me, a hint of trepidation in his voice. I make out some of his words as the wind whips them away. 'There are ghosts . . . island . . . Claire. Promise, whatever . . . we'll face . . . together.'

I'm keen to offer reassurance and tell him that we will. I rest my hand on our daughter's back. My husband is talking metaphorically, of course. He is an artist and has a way with words. Up until recently, I knew little of his childhood, apart from the fact his parents died twenty years ago, when he was just fifteen. Returning to the island is hard for him, but we all need to reconcile our past. My existence here today is down to split-second timing. Had I jumped from the window ledge of our flat a second sooner, I may not have survived. I owe my life to the ingenuity of the firefighter who grabbed me as I let go. When you're caught in the choppy seas of anxiety and depression, it's hard to imagine calmer times. Yet here I am, with my three-month-old daughter, ready to begin again.

I give my husband a reassuring smile. At least I'll be able to fill the gaps and I look forward to learning more about his past. I know that Mary, his mother, was born on the island. His father, Gabriel, was a French photographer who arrived to photograph the wildlife. He met Mary and decided to stay. They married, had Isla, then Daniel and Louis followed. Daniel said the island was like that, if you gave it a chance. People became enamoured and couldn't leave. But from what I read, its population is dwindling. Sometimes, when Daniel speaks about the island with a strange glint in his eye, I wonder why he left.

CHAPTER 4

DANIEL

When I asked Claire to come to Selkie Island, I masked my concerns with a smile. The whole thing was my idea, but I had every reason to be concerned. Had she known of its dark history, she would never have agreed.

'Are you sure?' I'd said softly, being as honest as I could about the island itself. 'It's a big move. I mean, if you'd prefer a holiday, Bere Island is its sister island, and it's not as cut off from the mainland.'

To be honest, I didn't think Claire would opt to stay at my birthplace. The people who live on Selkie Island are unlike the locals anywhere else we've been. They frown on consumerism and modern-day living. Some homes don't even have electricity. As for Wi-Fi signals – they're intermittent at best. I relayed all of this to Claire, but she dug her heels in.

'It's *because* it's cut off that I want to go,' she'd insisted, but I needed her to be prepared. I told her about the irregular ferry and the local shop, which also acted as a café and pub for the visitors who stayed on the island. It seemed to endear her to the place even more. Then she said the one line guaranteed to diminish my concerns.

'Isla is there. Don't you want to see your sister?'

And I did, more than anything in the world. Isla hated leaving the island, but she had managed a few visits to London, and Claire had always been tied up at work when I went to see Isla in return. I hate returning to my childhood home, but Claire's therapist agreed that time away from the pressures of the outside world would clear her mind.

I formed a plan. We would stay in Árd Na Mara, seeing only the people I trusted. I couldn't risk Claire discovering the truth. She will never look at me the same way again.

My old home needs renovating and it's an opportunity for Claire to channel her energy into something more positive. Being back on the island will rejuvenate my art too. My work has lost its essence, and my motivation has taken a nosedive. Returning to my roots will regenerate the passion that has dissipated over the last year.

Given all these justifications, why am I so nervous? My feet feel rooted to the spot as we cross from the mainland. I'm trying to contain my emotions, but I cannot help but think about my parents, who drowned making this very crossing. It pains me to imagine it, and it was once the talk of the island, because their deaths made no sense. My father was an expert swimmer, and they'd all worn lifejackets on the night they died.

It was days before Da's body was recovered. He was unrecognisable, battered from crashing into the rocks that edged the mainland. Mossie and Teresa found Mam that night. The couple became step-parents of sorts, keeping us going as we dealt with our grief. As a teenager, I was too young to parent my younger brother, and although Isla was twenty, she still needed support. I don't know what I would have done without Mossie and Teresa, as none of our relatives wanted to know. It amazes me how some people glide through life while others experience tragedy and pain at every turn. I try to shake off the feeling and focus on the beauty of the island. The sun is shining, and the sea breeze is refreshing. It's been too long since I've felt this close to nature. But the feeling of unease doesn't go away.

I halt my darkening thoughts and turn to my wife. Things could be a lot worse. My need to protect my family makes my heart swell. I guide her away from Sean Hennessy, a craggy old man with liquorice on his breath. I remember him from my youth when he was our parish priest. Even then his hands trembled and the smell of whiskey was thick on his breath. He seems to have been around as long as the island itself.

The sea is abundant with seals, and I fight my nausea and point to a trio that watches our small ferry boat with interest. Selkie Island gets its name from folklore, and I recall my mother telling me the story of the seal people who turned into humans when they reached dry land. They were said to occupy these parts until an islander killed one of the pups. A curse was placed upon the island, bringing misfortune to any human infant who ventured on its shores. The fable inspired poetry, art and even short films and animations, which encourages tourists to this day.

The island looms closer, an oppressive force that ties my stomach up in knots. I shove my clenched fists into my pockets. Claire is smiling now, one hand on the papoose strapped around her shoulders and waist. I feel another wave of protectiveness. It's up to me to keep it together. Dark waves slap against the rocks as the ferry pitches back and forth.

Mossie is waiting on the pier, ready to drive us the short distance home. Teresa will be in the kitchen, the fire stoked, the fridge full. Everything is planned in a regimented fashion. I called ahead, explained what was needed. They know I can't take any chances. There's too much at stake.

CHAPTER 5

THE ISLANDER

They're here. Everything I've heard about their arrival is true. Island gossip is not difficult to pick up, if you're listening in the right places. Much has been made of the return of the 'famous artist' Danny and his 'English wife' on Saint Patrick's Day. I watch her gracefully step off the ferry, moving like royalty among peasants. Her designer clothes are impractical for island weather, but she walks with her head held high. Her artificially blonde hair billows on the sea breeze, and her cheeks are slapped red from the cold. She may appear confident, but she's holding on to her baby as if she's entering the heart of a storm. She's too engrossed in her little one to notice me amongst the body of people shuffling about. Many of us wear a sprig of shamrock, having been to Mass this morning. Some are getting the ferry to celebrate Paddy's Day on the mainland, while others have come to buy fish fresh from the boats. The smell of the seaweed overwhelms my senses. A few people gawk at the newcomers. There was quite the flurry when word spread about Danny's return. The island is usually quiet, but this is big news.

There has been lots of renewed storytelling about Árd Na Mara as a result. They only have half the story, but I know it all.

Danny has changed since his youth. His light beard masks the scar over his lip, and the brown hair that once skimmed his shoulders has been cut short. He's a good-looking man, and wealthy, from what I've heard. But his blue eyes carry an intensity, and he appears on edge. He has every right to be. I wonder whose idea it was to come to Selkie Island. Are they running away from something, or perhaps towards something? Has he come back to reclaim his birthright and settle into island life with his wife and child? But he doesn't understand the danger that awaits them. The island has a way of bringing out the worst in people, and there are things here of which even I dare not speak. His wife should have stayed where she was. This isn't a place of safety, certainly not for the likes of her. That baby she's carrying is in danger, just like the ones before.

My layers of clothing offer me anonymity in the small crowd, and I keep my head down. I'm established with the locals. Part of the furniture, so to speak. They think I'm harmless. They don't know what I've done.

I steal another glance at Danny, noting the growing trepidation on his face. Perhaps my perception is tainted, given what I know. Is his wife aware that when he comes to visit he stays on the mainland? His family go to him because he's unable to cross on the ferry to visit home. Why has he returned now? The past may have a strong hold over us all, but Selkie Island is not the place to face your demons head on. They'd better not outstay their welcome. I'll be watching them.

CHAPTER 6

CLAIRE

The air smells amazing, so fresh and salty compared to the smog-burdened streets of London. I love its cleansing smell, and the sounds of the gulls as they circle the fishermen bringing in their catch.

'Welcome to Árd Na Mara,' Daniel says, as his childhood home looms into view.

It stands high near the cliff edge, a short walk from the towering lighthouse, which is striking against the marble sky. Mossie, Teresa and Isla live here, taking in visitors who book through Airbnb for a secluded getaway. Sometimes they host yoga, painting or writing retreats to bring in some extra cash. But their online reviews have taken a nosedive, which is where we come in. Planning the renovation is a big project and will help keep my mind off things.

The place is bigger and more imposing than it looks online, but also tired and worn. There are twenty bedrooms in Árd Na Mara, with five set aside for family and staff, ten for residents, and five in the basement which haven't been used in years. From what Daniel has told me, those are locked and forgotten, growing damp from a mains pipe which burst a few weeks ago. We plan on renovating those when the business is back up and running. It's too much to take on at once.

'I've never seen a house with so much ivy,' I say, and guess the online images of a clean whitewashed building were taken years ago. The trees planted in the sloping lawn are bare, sleeping giants not yet awoken by spring. Ivy leaves move in unison as we approach the grand old house. It feels like the place is alive. I hug Kitty in my arms. She's due a feed soon and I'm grateful she has been awake but content for most of the journey over.

'The old place has been let go alright,' Daniel agrees, out of Mossie's earshot as he grapples with our bags. 'We'll have to have that all trimmed back. It does the stonework no good.'

I smile at the sound of his Irish accent, which has grown stronger in Mossie's company as they chat about his island home.

I cast my eyes over the windows, which are barely visible beneath the choking vines. The sagging roof is green with moss, the chimney belching out a thick plume of smoke. Daniel's home is so close to the cliff edge that the waves thunder as a constant backdrop. The tall, wooden, paint-chipped door creaks open as we approach, and a wide-hipped woman with wild frizzy grey hair greets us both. A silver shamrock brooch is pinned to her green cardigan, and she wears it with a polo neck and a navy pleated skirt.

'Teresa,' Daniel says, as she beams at us both.

'Nice to meet you,' I say, shaking the woman's hand. She squeezes my fingers in a firm grip.

Daniel has told me about her. She was like a mother to them after the death of his parents, but he doesn't like to dwell on the past.

'This is Kitty,' I say, and Teresa's gaze flicks to Daniel before peeping down on our sleeping baby.

'Sure she's the spit of you, Danny,' she says.

It's their first time to meet and I couldn't be prouder, but I see a hint of concern in her eyes. She knows. I don't need to ask Daniel.

I can see it on her face. But I don't see judgement, just sadness. It seems that my problems have become her problems too. She raised Daniel and wouldn't want this upset for him.

'Isla!' Daniel calls, as his sister joins us on the doorstep.

Within seconds, he has enveloped her in a hug. Her smile is wide, her eyes twinkling as he lets go. She is dressed in a tie-dye blue jumper and a pair of jeans, and looks much younger than her forty years.

'Lovely to see you again, Isla,' I join in.

She glances again at Kitty before giving us both a gentle hug. Her chin rests on my shoulder and I inhale the smell of the sea from her damp strawberry-blonde hair. She has a warmth to her that instantly relaxes me. Teresa ushers us all inside.

'Come in, come in,' she urges. 'The range is blasting the place out of it. We got a good lot of turf home this year.'

'Turf?' I ask, needing a reminder of my husband's Irish ways.

'It's fuel. Like coal.' Daniel smiled. 'From the bog.' And then I remember, turf is harvested for fuel from their peat bog every year.

I glance around Daniel's home. There are pictures of his parents hung on the wall, and I notice his mother has an identical shamrock brooch to Teresa's pinned to her dress.

We wander through the hall, our footsteps echoing in the vast space. In the corner stands an old grandfather clock whose ticking echoes through the halls of the empty house. To the right is a huge living room and I peep in through the open double doors. The furniture is mostly from a bygone era; heavy mahogany sideboards and armchairs with thick brown leather that look like they were once expensive but are now worn. There's a musty smell, like dust and age mingling together. Even though it's midday outside, inside it feels like dusk.

'Have you got the changing bag?' I follow my husband as he goes the other way. 'She's due a feed.'

Teresa smiles with a matronly face. Her hands are on her hips, a half-apron tied around her generous waist.

'Hand her here to me. We're all set up. I'll feed her and put her in the cot upstairs so she can have a stretch.'

Daniel sees my hesitation. I catch him and Teresa exchanging a smile.

'It's OK, Teresa's basically a baby whisperer,' he reassures me.

We unbuckle Kitty from her confines and she's soon in Teresa's arms.

'Her room's all set up, with a baby monitor and everything.' She points to the left of the staircase. 'Head on into the kitchen. There's tea in the pot, you both must be parched.'

Reluctantly, I watch her hold Kitty, totally at odds with my feelings. I've always embraced travel and meeting new people, but motherhood has awoken insecurities that I didn't know I had.

Mossie busies himself, bringing in our belongings to the hall. He's sixty-eight, weatherworn and muscled from labour. He's short but broad, with a deep-lined face that is a testament of time spent outdoors.

Lunch awaits us in the spacious kitchen. A huge oak table sits in the middle of the room and I sense Daniel and his siblings spent a great deal of time here. He speaks little of his younger brother Louis, who lives on the mainland. They haven't seen each other for years.

'I love that you're here.' Isla regards Daniel warmly as she pours the tea.

I enjoy how Isla uses the word 'love' to describe how she feels about things. It must have been tough after lockdown, trying to keep the business afloat. Árd Na Mara is rough around the edges, a far cry from our swish city apartment. I gratefully accept a cup of tea, bone weary from the journey. It's been a long day. I relax when Teresa re-joins us and tells us Kitty is settled in her cot. I stop myself from getting up and checking. Separation anxiety, Daniel calls it. It stems from the death of a patient – a reminder of the fragility of life. It can't be good for Kitty, being the focus of all my attention. I need to learn to accept help when it's offered. Daniel takes off his coat, then gets the baby monitor from the sideboard and switches it on. I mouth a silent thank you as he places it on the table before me and I hear the soft chimes of a mobile being played above Kitty's cot.

'Let me help you with that,' Daniel says, as Teresa lifts a metal bucket next to the range.

'Get away with ya,' she chides. 'I've been filling this range since before you were born, I'm not going to stop now.' But she walks with a slight limp, and I make a mental note to question her about it later on.

My shoulders relax and I begin to feel at home. 'Have you been swimming today, Isla?' I ask, helping myself to a ham sandwich.

'Yeah.' Isla smiles, finger-combing her damp auburn hair. I admire her porcelain skin, dotted with biscuit-coloured freckles granted by the fickle Irish sun. It's fortunate that Isla doesn't suffer from the congenital heart defects common with Down's Syndrome. According to Daniel, she's in excellent health.

'Fair play to you,' I say with genuine admiration. 'I can't even stay in the bath when it turns lukewarm.'

Isla has been cold-water swimming since childhood. It provides many health benefits, and her ability to swim well undoubtedly saved her life the night her parents drowned. A quietly spoken woman, she contributes to the running of the household and lives a full life. Daniel once told me that Árd Na Mara is kept open as a job for Isla as much as anything else. But while bookings have gone down, utility bills have risen, so it's a perfect time for us to step in and help. We're not short of money and can afford to contribute to its upkeep, so it's a win-win for everyone. I don't know exactly how long we're going to stay, but we're starting with a timeframe of six to nine months.

Teresa switches on the light and glances upwards as the bulb flickers overhead. 'The electrics need updating – they don't always work as they should.' It's not just the electrics that need looking at. The kitchen units will need replacing, and then there's the roof to contend with, but for now we'll start with new furniture, wallpaper and paint.

As he steps into the kitchen, Mossie removes his cap to smooth back his white hair. He reiterates that bookings have tailed off, before helping himself to a chunk of soda bread. Looking around, I can see why. Daniel follows my gaze to the peeling paint on the wall, to the door not quite hanging right on its hinges. I doubt that he sees it the same way as I do, with the stern judgement of a stranger. I remind myself not to be harsh.

'It's a lovely place, and so big compared to what I'm used to. We'll soon have it right.'

I'm confident we'll get Árd Na Mara back on its feet. It's not fair to leave it all to Isla, Teresa and Mossie – and Aoife, the woman from the island who handles the bookings online. We've blocked out April and May so we can start work in peace.

Daniel knocks back the dregs of his tea. 'Island tradesmen don't move in English time. The pace is a lot slower here.'

He turns to talk to Isla about how she's been getting on. Her name means Island, and as she speaks about the weather and the wildlife, I can see how attuned she is with the place. But someone is missing from this happy get-together. Daniel's brother, Louis. Not one of them has mentioned his name. Daniel knows everything about me. In the five years since we married, my family have welcomed him into the fold. But each time I ask about Louis, the barriers go up. Louis has never met his niece, and it doesn't look like Kitty is going to be acquainted with him any time soon.

Isla gives me a curious eye and I wonder if she knows about my breakdown. Teresa's mood feels forcefully cheery, so I've no doubt that she's aware. It's not as if I'm going to jump off the top of the lighthouse. I've too much to live for. They've nothing to worry about.

CHAPTER 7

CLAIRE

I feel better now my feet are on solid ground and my stomach is full. Once upon a time I would have checked my phone, but since my suicide attempt, I've slowly weaned myself off. My work colleagues meant well but the constant stream of calls and updates were stressing me out. I don't miss social media, or emails, or the endless WhatsApp notifications. But I do miss my older sister and I vow to call Susan as soon as I settle in. I take Daniel's arm as he escorts me into the hall towards the central staircase, which is wide enough to walk side by side. I try to imagine it in grander days, but the smell of rising damp lingers in the air.

'The first thing we'll do is get a proper heating system in place,' Daniel says, reading my mind.

It's not like London, where our heating could be set by an app on our phone. In Árd Na Mara, the radiators work off the range in the kitchen and an old boiler in the basement. It's a big ask for such a huge house. Daniel tells me about the open fireplaces that are in each of the upstairs bedrooms.

'Da had most of them blocked up after the place was converted, and installed safety glass in the windows, but we've managed to change them all back.'

'Then there was the outside exercise yard,' he continues. 'The high fencing was ugly so we had it taken down.'

I know little of the institution Árd Na Mara was once used as. Mary and Gabriel made a good income taking in what was deemed 'disturbed' young women and caring for them. According to what I found online, the twenty-bedroom house was a privately run rehabilitation centre contracted by the state. It was somewhat like Shelton Abbey in Wicklow, an open prison for men who required lower levels of security. But unlike Shelton Abbey, Árd Na Mara was privately owned, and the women who stayed weren't allowed out to work. Judging from what I had gleaned, the rooms were more homely, but the women were still criminals and confined to the grounds.

'This place comes alive at night,' Daniel explains, looking around the grand old hall. 'But it's only the pipes. And don't forget about the wildlife outside. Owls screech, foxes cry, and then there are the rats . . .'

'Rats?' I say, my eyes widening.

But Daniel is laughing. 'Just checking you're listening.'

I slap his arm. 'You know I draw the line at rats.' The stairs creak as we climb.

'So what do you think? Will you like it here?' He looks at me in earnest. I'd been wondering the same thing about him.

'Of course we will.' My reply is instant. 'We've got the whole summer ahead of us. It'll be lovely.'

'C'mon,' Daniel says. 'I'll show you to our room. It's been, what, a whole twenty minutes since you checked on Kitty?'

He is being good-natured, but he has a point. I need to claw back some time for myself. The landing is long and wide, and as I pass door after door, I note the upstairs is in need of modernisation too. The décor carries the same dark theme throughout. A hint of dampness lingers, but in a building with ceilings as high as this, it must take a lot to keep it warm. I admire the decorative coving, although it's in need of a lick of paint. Daniel opens the door at the end of the gallery landing.

'At least the room is warm,' he says, his face quietly apologetic. 'We'll soon have the décor up to date.'

The house has a strange vibe, and as I follow him in, I feel like I'm being watched. I check myself. My imagination is running away with me. But Daniel's movements are stiff, and his gaze flickers to the shadowy spaces as a breeze howls outside. The room is dim, the window clouded with ivy. A bare bulb hangs overhead, but the place is mercifully clean and cobweb free. A double bed has been made up, with red cushions plumped. The room is warmed by a roaring fire burning in the hearth. I glance at the black, flowery wallpaper with blooms of red and pink.

'Was this your parents' room?'

'Yeah,' Daniel says. 'Is it too weird? It has the best sea views. Once we clear the ivy away, that is.'

'No, not at all.' I smile. I've stayed in all sorts of places since my backpacking days. I look to the square patches of wallpaper that are a different shade than the rest. 'What pictures hung there?'

Daniel shrugs. 'Teresa probably took them down when she was cleaning up. All the walls will need to be stripped.'

It seems like a plausible explanation.

'Where's Kitty?' I was expecting her cot to be here.

Daniel rests his hand on my arm. 'She's in the room next to ours.'

'But—' I begin to complain.

'A little space will do you both good,' Daniel interrupts. 'Lots of parents have a separate nursery, and if it makes you feel any better, you can keep the monitor next to the bed.'

He slides his arm around my waist as he leads me to the room next door. It's warm, with a fire in the hearth. This room is nicer than ours. A sturdy-looking cot stands at the centre, with a rocking chair in the corner and a deep blue rug covering most of the wooden floor. The room is filled with soft toys of every size and shape: teddies, dinosaurs, plush dogs and cats, each one worn but clean. There's a beautiful wooden rocking horse in the room with a real mane and tail. I know instantly that it belonged to Daniel.

'It's my old nursery,' he confirms, a sad smile on his face. 'Isla and Louis slept here too.'

'And now it's Kitty's,' I say softly, watching her sleep.

She's been awake for a lot of our travels and looks so peaceful in the cot. It strikes me as strange, how the room seems to be kept as a shrine to days past. But then I remind myself that guests with children would have access to this room too.

Daniel doesn't stay long. 'I'll help Mossie with our cases.'

I can't work my husband out. Until now, I could read him like a book. But there's something about this place that unnerves him. He gives me one last, uncertain look before walking out into the hall.

CHAPTER 8

DANIEL

Claire thinks I'm happy to be home, but she could not be further from the truth. Already I sense the ghosts of my past waiting to reacquaint with me. It took a lot of soul searching before I made the decision to return. I was a different person in London. England had not just gifted me success, it gave me peace. The ability to begin my life again. To fit in. But the monsters in my paintings are not born from artistic flair. They are symbols of my past. I've spent the evening chatting to Isla and Teresa, who are pleased to have us here. Now the doors are locked and the windows shut tight against the impending storm.

I climb the old, creaking stairs, each step invoking memories I closed the door on years ago. Claire's soft voice carries as she reads a bedtime story in my old room. It feels strange not to have the interruption of ringing telephones or computer screens. I've reinvented myself since leaving the island, but I never realised just how much until now.

I listen at the open bedroom door, feeling a sense of relief at the sight of her. She is the one bright spot in my life, the one person who makes me feel like everything is going to be OK. The rain taps against the window, just as it did when I slept there as a child. I look around the rafters as the past envelops me in a chill. But I won't tell Claire what took place beneath this roof. I almost lost her. She doesn't need the burden of my past. She's sitting on the rocking chair and will be up checking in the night, whether she hears crying or not. Her long blonde hair shadows her face as she takes a break from the story to peep into the cot. I step back from the doorway, family secrets bobbing to the surface of the dark waters of my past.

I shudder as I enter my parents' bedroom. There are no photos of them here. I asked Teresa to take them down before we arrived. I asked her to do a lot of things. It'll be hard enough trying to sleep without having them staring at me from the wall. I poke the open fire, feeling a sudden need to infuse some warmth into the room. The burning timbers crackle and hiss beneath the heat. It's the dampness that makes them squeal. Turf is a smoky fuel, now banned in many parts of Ireland due to concerns over it being carcinogenic. I've planned the renovation to be in keeping with the house. I also need to employ someone to fix the leaky shed roof. At times, I wonder if it's worth keeping this old place on. Everything is either damp, leaky, crumbling or in need of repair. But then I think of Isla, who has spent her life here, and wouldn't be content anywhere else. Then there's Teresa and Mossie, who we owe so much to. Besides, it's not as if anyone would want to buy this old place now.

'Everything alright?' Claire interrupts my chain of thought. I ramble on about the roof and the weather. Days without rain in Ireland are like a church without prayer. I need to acclimatise to the inclement weather, or the rain will drive me insane. I check the clock resting on the fireplace. A part of me wants to tell Claire that this island is not our home and we need to return to where we belong. I swallow back the words.

'Did you fall asleep?' I say instead.

'I dozed off for a few minutes,' Claire admits, masking a yawn with the back of her hand. 'It must have been lovely, growing up with so much space to run around in with your brother and sister.'

She unbuttons her blouse, looking at me with a question on her face. She wants to ask about Louis, but I'm not ready for it. I want to stay in our little bubble for now. Claire is content, Isla's reading a book in her room across the gallery landing, and Mossie and Teresa are banking turf in the range to keep it going overnight. I don't want to think about my parents, or the brother Claire wants to ask me about. Here, in the warmth of the bedroom, it's just me and my perfectly imperfect wife.

'Fancy a game of chess?' I ask, hoping it will distract us both. The windows rattle as the wind picks up. Outside, trees creak and groan in the wind, as if protesting our presence.

Claire reaches for the chessboard. As she busies herself with the pieces, my hands become clammy. Today has taken its toll. First travelling on the boat from the mainland, then returning to Árd Na Mara, and now the storm. My stomach is still churning and I'm not even on the ferry.

'Set up the board,' I say quietly, before turning away from my wife. 'I'll bring up a pot of tea to the room.'

And then I'm out on the landing, feeling breathless as the storm continues to beat down outside. Claire is wrong. Árd Na Mara was not a happy place. All the times I visited Isla in the past, I lied to Claire about where I'd stayed. I've never made it further than the mainland. I've always stayed in a hotel and had her come to me. It's more than seasickness that makes me vomit. It's the memory of the night of the storm, when my parents took the boat out and only Isla returned alive. The night was lost in a haze of horror and fear, but now I shut my eyes and relive it all. I can still see my sister's chalk-white face, clutching the waterlogged baby in a papoose attached to her chest. My dearest and only sister almost drowned trying to save the babies my parents had sold. Their sins finally caught up with them.

The hairs prickle on the back of my neck and I wonder if that's the end of it. I can't shake off the feeling that there is more to come. I don't like who I am when I'm here. This was a big mistake. I lean across the landing banister, trying to steady my breathing. We'll stay until Claire is strong enough to go back to work. Back to the life we had before the undiagnosed illness that brought our world crashing down. But I've not even spent one night on the island and its hold is strong. When we leave, things won't ever be the same.

CHAPTER 9

MARY

Then

I never realised that I was living in darkness until Gabriel came into my life. At the age of twenty-one, I was naïve. I was an only child, and my parents had done me no favours by shielding me from the outside world. The furthest I had got on my travels was the occasional visit to Cork or Dublin with my old schoolfriends, but I hated public transport and felt overwhelmed by the pace of city life. My circle of acquaintances was so small. Young people left the island as soon as they could for work. My mainland friends married, and we fell out of touch. The population had halved in recent years. Nobody was interested in spending time on Selkie Island anymore. Nobody except Gabriel. I remember the first time I saw him. It was early morning, and I was walking the island with my collie, Skye, trying to make sense of my world. Kieran and I had been going steady for four years. Everyone expected us to marry, and I knew he'd made a trip to the jewellers on the mainland. My best friend, Orla, had been going on about it all week, saying how lucky I was. But I didn't feel lucky. I felt suffocated. Kieran was honest, hardworking and kind. He loved the island as much as I did and was everything I could have wanted in a husband. My parents adored him, and he wasn't short of a bob or two. But he bored me half to death. His idea of excitement was attending the ploughing championships every year. It was my own fault. I should have spread my net wider. But I loved living on the island. I was a 'home bird', as my mother called me, and according to her, what I lacked in looks I made up for in loyalty and dependency. Which is why the thoughts roaming through my mind that day weren't like me at all. Perhaps I'd felt a change in the air. Or maybe I'd been reading too many romance novels. Either way, as I walked towards the cliff, the question loomed large in my mind. *When Kieran proposes, should I say yes?*

Oblivious to my discontent, Skye bounded ahead in the undergrowth of wild grass and ferns. I took pleasure in my surroundings, breathing in the sweet aroma of fresh rain and wildflowers as the island eased my troubled mind. It came to life in the spring, a canvas of countless shades of green. A recent heavy rainfall made the foliage even more vibrant than before. I admired the pretty red lantern flowers peeping out between leathery green leaves, and the delicate flowers of the hardy fuchsia in abundance this time of year. I looked beyond them to the sandstone mountains, and the goats that grazed on its peaks. I knew every inch of the island, but it still had the ability to mesmerise. The chatter of birds and the harmonies of insects were music to my ears. I snapped out of my thoughts at the sudden sound of Skye's excited barks.

I was not prepared for the expletives that emitted from beyond the cliff edge as a flock of birds burst forth. At least, I think they were expletives, because they were spoken in French. Given the annoyance of the person uttering them, that was probably a good thing.

'Hello?' I said cautiously, edging towards the undergrowth. Skye yapped and barked with enthusiasm, her shiny black fur glistening in the sun, tail high as she returned to me.

It was wild and isolated on this side of the island. Anything could happen and nobody would hear me scream. But my curiosity was stronger than my suspicion as I approached the cliff edge. It didn't jut out sharply, but rather descended gradually into the sea. If you were careful, you could climb down towards the rock pools if the tide was out.

'*Zut alors!* Your hound has ruined my shot!' the young Frenchman shouted as he climbed to the cliff edge, telescopic camera in hand.

I opened my mouth to speak but as I caught sight of the man before me, the words would not come. It was not often I found myself lacking in conversation. I had heard about the artist who was visiting the island. According to local rumours, he photographed all forms of wildlife and had his work published in guidebooks, calendars and nature magazines. He also kept some of the photos to paint later on. Some of the locals had even been photographed, much to their amusement. Nothing happened without everyone on the island knowing about it. According to Orla, he was handsome. She had not been wrong. Broad in stature, he was at least six feet tall, with a strong jaw-line and looks that appeared exotic in this part of the world. With his wavy black hair skimming his shoulders, he could have stepped out of the pages of any one of my Mills and Boon books.

'She was only being friendly,' I said, calling Skye to heel. 'You're the painter, aren't you?' I couldn't help but ask as my inquisitive nature returned. My mother said I'd chat to the devil himself if he reared his ugly head. But the photographer's head was far from ugly, despite his abrupt nature.

'How long are you here for?' I continued, as he ignored my question and bent to pick up his rucksack.

'I've booked the B&B for two weeks but I'm playing it by ear.' He paused to check his watch. 'You live on the island?'

'All my life,' I said proudly, as if it was some great feat.

'Good. You can be my guide. Where can I get the best view of puffins around here?'

I realised it was a command, not a request. 'I suppose I could spare half an hour,' I said. 'But then I've got to get back to Mam and Da. You'll find the puffins near the lighthouse, where I live.' I turned to walk away and realised he was still standing there. 'This way!' I said cheerily, as he grabbed his rucksack and caught up.

'You live in a lighthouse?' His eyebrow arched, and a strange fluttery feeling made me catch my breath. I smoothed back my hair, all thoughts of Kieran gone.

'No,' I chuckled. 'I live in Árd Na Mara, the building next to it. It's a . . . care home.'

'Ah, *oui*!' he exclaimed. 'The place where the naughty girls go.' His lips curled in a smile. 'You're not the only one who listens to gossip around here, no?'

'It's a care home for young ladies unable to enter into society.' That was the line my parents rolled out when people asked. In reality, Árd Na Mara was a privately run institute for female criminals deemed too mentally ill for prison. A spate of prison suicides led the government to find an alternative and sticking them on an island where they could be forgotten seemed the answer to everything. The women were all quite different and their crimes varied. Some had been found guilty of arson, while others had committed assault, or even infanticide. Some poor souls had been forced into solicitation. Coming to Árd Na Mara was a luxury compared to their previous life on the streets. Their sentences varied, and by the time they left us, many would not reoffend. Árd Na Mara provided us with a living, although I hadn't had the most conventional of upbringings being reared in an institute. But it never felt like an institute to me. The scent of vases of wild flowers filled the air instead of disinfectant. There were no prison bars on the windows, just impenetrable safety glass and thick, heavy doors. There were no long, clinical corridors, just the generous top gallery landing, which provided access to most of the bedrooms. Of course, there were the basement rooms, the ones with no windows and strong metal doors. They were equipped with extra security for the women hell-bent on hurting themselves. I sighed at the thought. I didn't like venturing down there.

'There's lots to see on the island,' I said, deciding to change the subject. 'If you're free tomorrow, I can show you the bays where you'll get pictures of fin whales and dolphins. The water's full of them if you know where to look. Then there's the basking sharks and seals. I know where to find them all.'

'I would like that very much,' he said, pulling the strap of his rucksack up.

'What age are you?' I said jauntily, calling my dog to heel.

'What age do you think I am?'

'Older than me.' I blushed as he looked me up and down. 'I'm twenty-one.'

'Then you are seven years younger than me. Um . . . a simple, starry-eyed girl.'

He seemed pleased with his English description, but being called 'simple' was hardly a compliment. Undeterred, I pointed towards the lighthouse.

'You'll see gannets, fulmars and guillemots up here, as well as the usual seabirds.' When it came to the island, I was a walking encyclopaedia. I stopped in my tracks. 'I don't know your name.'

'Gabriel,' he said.

'I'm Mary,' I replied, another flush rising to my collarbone as he gracefully shook my hand.

It was not the hardy handshake of a calloused hand that I was used to. Instead, he gently curled his fingers around mine, his skin soft and warm. I didn't realise it back then, but my question had been answered. I was not going to marry Kieran. Not when I could feel like this about another man.

CHAPTER 10

CLAIRE

I've faced my rocking chair towards Kitty's cot so I can watch her fall into slumber. She's been fed, changed, and thanks to an extra layer of clothes, is comfortably warm. Yet I cannot leave her side. I'm in my pyjamas and dressing gown, my blonde hair skimming my shoulders, thick socks on my feet. The ivy quivers on the window outside as it is pelted with rain. A cold, thin sea breeze screeches through the gaps in the timber window frames. It's a comfort, knowing Kitty is safely tucked up, and as my breath falls in line with hers I monitor the rise and fall of her chest.

Already I feel at home in the rugged landscape we have found ourselves a part of. I sit back in my rocker and search my mind for a lullaby. What was the one that Daniel used to sing? The low, haunting melody used to fill the air of our nursery after she was born. I take a breath as the words flow naturally.

'My bonnie lies over the ocean, my bonnie lies over the sea. My bonnie lies over the ocean, oh bring back my bonnie to me . . . bring back, bring back, oh bring back my bonnie to me . . .' After

Kitty was born, I'd find Daniel so overcome with emotion that sometimes he'd sing this, his eyes moist with tears.

'M-Martina?'

My singing stalls as Daniel stands over me, wearing nothing but his boxers, looking pale and confused.

'What . . . what are you doing?' His eyes are glassy. He's looking right through me. I should have expected this as change can be a trigger, but he hasn't had one in a while. I reach for his hand. His skin is cold. How long has he been out of bed?

'It's OK,' I whisper in the half-light, guiding him to our room.

I've told no one this, but Daniel's night terrors creep me out a little. When he's like that, he feels like a different person. Sometimes he shouts, other times he stands quietly in the room, and I awake to discover I'm being watched. He must have put Kitty in a separate room so he wouldn't wake her up. Yet he has found us just the same.

'Who's Martina?' I say, knowing he's asleep but unable to help myself.

'What . . . ?' He blinks three times. I wait for him to come back to himself as I switch on the bedside lamp and get into bed beside him.

'You were sleepwalking,' I say, although there's more to it than that. But he tugs on the cover, mumbling to himself, his eyes now closed.

I was wrong. He's still asleep. The general guidance is not to disturb him. I listen as his breathing regulates and I smooth back his hair. His eyes may be closed but the muscles on his face are tense, and I reassure him in quiet tones that he's at home, safe in bed. Within minutes, he's gently snoring, but I'm uneasy with the sounds around me and I shift restlessly as I try to get back to sleep. The sound of the waves crashing against the rocks is a constant, eerie background noise.

A gentle knock on the door wakes me up. Teresa carries the teacups on a tray while I scoot up in bed.

'I thought you might be tired, so I've made you breakfast.'

I nudge Daniel awake, grateful I wore my pyjamas.

'You shouldn't have,' I say, but Teresa has already laid mine on my lap. She goes to take the second tray from Isla, who is waiting in the hall.

'It's just this once.' She smiles, handing Daniel his tray. She catches me checking the time as I take my Apple watch from the charger on my bedside table. 'Kitty's fed, changed and dressed, so don't you go worrying about her.' She pauses. 'It's a grand day outside. Is it still alright to take her out?'

I look at Daniel. This is news to me.

'It's just a little walk,' he says, before giving me a look to suggest that I should trust his judgement. We discussed this before we came here. When it comes to Kitty's care, I need to hand over the reins.

'Sounds lovely,' I say, but it doesn't sit comfortably. I thank Teresa for the food before she leaves. I return my attention to my tray. It is laden with home-made brown bread, a pot of tea and a full Irish breakfast. The smell is making my mouth water, and Daniel gives me a smug grin. 'You set this up, didn't you?' I smile. 'So we can have some quality time together.' It feels like a second honeymoon, and I can't complain.

'Busted,' he says, pouring some tea. 'I'll be out all morning, finding a suitable location to paint. I thought it would be nice if we have breakfast together.' He follows my gaze as I take in the sight of the plate laden with food. 'I got her to grill everything, just as you like it. So make sure you eat it all.'

My stomach growls in response. Breakfast in bed is a treat, but there's something I need to know first. 'You had a night terror last night.' I butter a slice of bread.

'Did I?' Daniel cuts up a sausage. 'I don't remember.'

'You've not done that in ages. You were probably overtired.' I mirror his actions and dip my sausage in my poached egg.

'Probably,' he said, chewing. 'Want to try some black pudding? I'd forgotten how good it is.'

'No, thanks,' I decline. 'Has it happened before? When you've stayed here to visit Isla?'

Daniel shrugs. 'I wouldn't know, would I? I rarely wake up.'

'Only that . . .' I sigh, not ready to drop the subject just yet. 'You mentioned someone called Martina. Who's she?'

Daniel stops chewing, his knife and fork hovering over his plate. A beat passes before he resumes eating. 'No idea. Could be anyone. I don't know what I'm saying when I'm asleep.' He glances at my plate. 'Eat your breakfast. It's going cold.'

He races through his food now, and I give him a comical look. 'There's no rush.'

'Isn't there?' Daniel pats his mouth with the napkin Teresa has provided. 'How often do we get the chance to be in bed together undisturbed?'

'Oh,' I say, returning his wicked smile. 'In that case . . .' I slice off some bacon and chew. Intimate moments with my husband are rare these days. I push away thoughts of Martina and focus on finishing my food.

CHAPTER 11

DANIEL

I've forgotten what it's like to walk through morning dew, the taste of salty sea air on my tongue. I feel like a different person since coming to Selkie Island. Or perhaps I'm returning to who I used to be. My memories are frighteningly strong. Everywhere I look, I see my parents wandering the island. I gaze out to sea from my vantage point on the jagged cliffs. I see my father crossing to the mainland in his boat as he confidently negotiates the frothy water. A private man, he left after dark because he didn't want people to know about his business. He was the talk of the island just the same. Why did he leave us so often? If he loved the mainland so much, why did he settle here?

I see my mother, in her old-fashioned long dresses and sensible boots, strolling through the grassy clifftops, picking wildflowers to fill the many vases in our home. Wisps of dark hair dance around her face as they escape her headscarf, and she closes her eyes as she raises her face to the weak winter sun. I can almost smell her scent, a flowery moringa perfume which my father brought back from the mainland as a peace offering for being away for so long.

She loved us all dearly, which is more than I can say for Da, but it was glaringly obvious that Louis was her favourite child. Louis, who looked so like him, with his tousled dark hair and moody expression. I find it hard to imagine his presence. In fact, I'm not sure what he looks like now. It's been years since we've spoken, but I wouldn't know how to rebuild our broken bridges. We've had enough disruption without having him back in our lives. Thank God for Isla. My beautiful sister, with her quiet ways and warm hugs. She has always been a silent watcher. She takes in more than we know. I hope she's happy with her life. I've been waiting to talk to her properly. We had a general chat this morning, but I don't want to rush things. She's just happy that I'm back.

I stand at my canvas, my ideas taking shape. It may be Saturday, but there isn't a tourist in sight. They know better than to come here off season. This time of year, the wind could batter them mercilessly, the waves too high to make a trip worthwhile. The cold doesn't bother me today, because I'm lost in concentration. My paintbrush works as an extension of my hand as the images come to life. There is a monster hiding in this rugged landscape as seagulls divebomb the water. The sea is the pulsing heart of this island, and I bring life to the ebbing tide. My brush moves quickly on to the image of a scaly green dragon climbing the craggy cliffs. But there is another figure, small and cowering, on the rocky beach. For hours, I am lost in my creative world. It is only when my stomach rumbles and my limbs ache from stiffness that I step back and survey my creation. I view it with a critical eye, taking it in from every angle as I move right and left. The best of the daylight has dissolved behind slate clouds rolling overhead. Only then do I realise who the young woman huddling in the picture is.

'Martina,' I whisper, wanting to touch her. To climb into the painting and right a wrong. But while I have brought her to life on canvas, I cannot reach her now. To think that Claire heard me

43

whisper her name. This merging of my past and present lives makes me uncomfortable enough to want to leave. I start to pack up my things, feeling guilty for being gone for so long. But Claire knows what I'm like, and this painting feels different and fresh. The gallery is going to lap it up. A part of me wants to keep it to myself and hide it away from the world.

I carefully carry my canvas while my art supplies are in the pack on my back. A dormouse rustles in the undergrowth, scampering before my feet. My old life in London seems like a million miles away. I think of my wife and baby, and what we've been through to bring us here. How will Claire feel when she discovers the truth? Will we ever be the same again?

CHAPTER 12

THE ISLANDER

Last night's storm is evidenced by debris and leaves along the cliff path. Today the island is at peace, but I feel smothered by my thoughts. I need time alone to come to terms with Claire's presence, which looms like a guillotine over my head. I close my bedroom door and turn the key in the lock. I need time to decompress. This is my private place, a haven from a chaotic world. To an outsider, it would seem that the chaos is within these four walls. My bed is unmade, my sheets rumpled from a night of fretful dreams. A book lies on the floor, its spine cracked. A half-empty bottle of sleeping pills sits on the bedside table next to a glass of water, which is coated in dust. The walls smell of damp and the limp curtains hanging over my window are permanently closed. Once, it may have bothered me, but I have bigger things on my mind. I switch on the light, open my dresser drawer, and cast an eye over my stash. To an onlooker, they are worthless random objects: a paperclip, a small blue button, a tiny silver shell – to name a few. To me, they are something else entirely. I feast my eyes on my selection, then I pop a small grey pebble between my chapped lips and roll it around on my tongue. The stone is a fossil from my past. It carries its own special meaning. I like the hard, unforgiving texture against the roof of my mouth. It comes from a handful that I picked from the beach when I first swam in the sea. I can still taste the salty water, see the bobbing heads of seals as they regard me with curiosity. I wanted to die that day, but the cold water sharpened my senses, and I found the strength to keep going.

I touch the small clear bag of dirt with the tips of my fingers. This treasure originates from the island graveyard. The crumbles of dirt have dried up, but memories linger on. Before, I could contain my anger, but now there's a threat on my horizon. Claire is an intelligent woman, the type of person who won't be content to let things lie. How long before she starts asking questions? What happens then? I roll the stone from left to right in my mouth, recalling the community once united by grief. This is *my* island, and outsiders aren't welcome. Their presence brings nothing but trouble. If the Englishwoman discovers the truth, the island will never be the same again. I imagine the news as it hits the papers, or, God forbid, national TV. What if Ryan Tubridy discusses us on *The Late Late Show*? Or Pat Kenny on Newstalk radio? We would never live it down. I picture our small Catholic church and the troubled parishioners within. It has taken decades to repair the harm inflicted upon us. I will not allow our people to be put through that again – all in the name of satisfying an outsider's curiosity. My anger rises as I imagine the shame bearing down on us all. I swallow, briefly closing my eyes as I wait for the pebble to lodge in my throat. My own private game of Russian roulette. I exhale as it clears my airways. My mind is heavy with the weight of my secrets. It's only a matter of time until my risk-taking catches up with me. But not before I deal with the problem on my doorstep. I pace the room, the steady clop of my boots echoing on the creaky floorboards. The Englishwoman has no place here. If she thinks she can set down roots, she can think again.

CHAPTER 13

CLAIRE

I awake with a start as I find myself alone. I must have fallen asleep after breakfast in bed. Daniel has left to explore the island, leaving me to acquaint myself with the house and make plans. The baby monitor has gone, but I can hear the radio playing and I know Kitty is safe with Teresa downstairs. I shower and make myself presentable, plucking my cable-knit Ralph Lauren jumper from the wardrobe and tugging it on along with jeans and thick socks. The radiators are warm, but I can't dress lightly like I did in my London flat. There are so many crevices in this house, no matter where you stand you'll feel the cold slice of a draught.

I quickly tidy up our bedroom and a napkin falls from Daniel's trouser pocket on to the floor. I smile at the sight of his scribbles. It's amazing how he can press so lightly with his pencil and not tear the delicate tissue. My husband is a doodler and quite often has a pencil tucked behind his ear. I find his drawings everywhere. On shopping lists, on napkins and sometimes on the tablecloth when he's wrapped up in a telephone conversation and the right side of his brain gets to work. But his real passion is art. His works are known worldwide and fetch more money than I could imagine ever paying for a picture myself. His landscapes feature colourful mythical characters that appear real. Some of them are created in his mind, others from the world of folklore. It's a gift to be able to make them fit into the settings he has chosen. Others try to imitate, but they're a shadow of Daniel's art. I remember the first time I saw *The Drowning Man*, the painting that catapulted him to success. It had a different quality to his subsequent work. It was raw and disruptive, and lingered in my mind. When he gives himself to a creation, he becomes totally enveloped in its world. He is married to his work as much as he is to me.

It was a leap of faith for Daniel, leaving the island. He was just eighteen when he packed his bags to move to London in the hope of being discovered. It took years, but he persevered. We met when he came to the hospital to visit a friend. He'd looked so lost that day as he'd asked me for directions. I'd just come off my shift, so I walked him to the ward. It was funny how we kept bumping into each other after that. These happy memories keep me going through the dark times. Daniel goes within when he has a problem, and it's hard to reach him sometimes. The doodle is of a phoenix rising from the ashes. A symbol of hope. I smile. For all his complications, I've never had anyone love me with such intensity as Daniel.

Out here, thrust into desolation, it's the best place for our family. Isla, Teresa and Mossie need him too. It can't have been easy for them since he left. I stare at Daniel's creation, turning the paper napkin over in my hand. I dip my hand into his other jacket pocket until I am satisfied. I have the grace to feel guilty. What was I expecting? A note with 'I love Martina' written in pen? It was just a dream. Nothing to worry about. But I can't get the disturbed look on his face out of my mind. Had my lullaby triggered a memory of his childhood? I run a brush through my hair and tie it up in a ponytail before taking the stairs. The smell of baking bread wafts upwards from the kitchen. If we're going to settle here, I'll need to order some healthy alternatives from the mainland. I don't know how Teresa will feel about me cooking for my family but I'm not comfortable with her running around after me.

'Where's Kitty?' I say to Teresa, quietly resting yesterday's trays next to the sink. The travel cot is empty. Two loaves of freshly baked bread rest on the side and a pot is bubbling on the stove.

Teresa is staring out the window, so deep in thought that she doesn't register my words. The local radio channel is reading out the death notices. The windows are so overgrown with vines that the kitchen light is on.

'Teresa?' I say, lightly tapping her shoulder.

'Oh!' She stiffens. 'I was miles away. What's that now?'

'Kitty.' I point to the travel cot. 'She's gone.'

Teresa's face falls into her homely smile as she takes the pot off the stove. 'Isla's taken her out in the pushchair.' She examines my face. 'Don't look so worried, pet. She's a natural with babies. She's gone to meet Danny so he'll walk back with her.'

'I thought you were both taking her out this morning?'

'We did, but sure another little walk won't do her any harm.'

'What way has she headed?' I try to appear relaxed, but my heart is hammering as I imagine Isla walking along the unprotected cliff edge.

'Towards Smugglers' Cove. She'll be on her way back now.'

I deliver a tight nod but my insecurities continue to nibble. Daniel told me all about the seventeenth-century pirates when we were on the ferry. Animated, he relayed stories of the Englishmen, Irishmen, Flemish and renegade Dutchmen and explained how their lucrative hauls were stashed in secret caves dotted all over the Cork coast. At the time it fascinated me, but now my thoughts are with my child. The old man's warning still rings in my ears. I can't shake off the feeling that my daughter isn't safe.

'She should have waited,' I said, a little tersely. 'I would have gone with her.'

I regret the time spent unpacking and tidying up our room. This is what kills me. Before Kitty, I was always in control. I begin to pace, then realise what I'm doing as Teresa casts a watchful eye.

'How about we wash up these dishes? And if she's not back by then, sure we'll both go on the hunt.' She guides me to the porcelain Belfast sink and turns on the warm-water tap, giving it a generous dash of Fairy Liquid. 'You wash, I'll dry,' she says, no doubt hoping that handfuls of soapy dishes will stop me from running out the kitchen door.

I cast a regretful eye over the empty travel cot before setting to work. The sooner the dishes are washed, the quicker we can go.

'You mustn't think of Isla as having Down's.' Teresa takes the first plate from my hand. 'She's Isla. The woman who loves to swim in the sea, who prefers books to television, and who is a friend to everyone, including folk who are mean to her.'

I shake my head vigorously. 'No, it's not that I don't trust her . . .' I pause, trying to form the right words. 'I'm the same with everyone when it comes to Kitty.'

'I know.' Teresa smiles, setting the dry dish aside. 'But why do you think that is?'

The question surprises me. I presumed that Daniel had filled her in. 'You know what happened, don't you? A little girl died because of me.' A lump rises to my throat.

'But that's in the past, which exists only in your head.' The lilt of her Irish accent steadies me, like a lighthouse on a dark night. Soft and comforting, her voice is guiding me home. 'Life is short, and it's here to be lived. But you don't have to do it alone.'

'I know.' I nod. Teresa is right about Isla. Kitty is safe in her company and the fresh air will do her good. I scrub another plate, keen to change the subject. I don't want to talk about the past anymore. 'Who's Martina?' The words leave my lips the second the question rose in my mind.

'What's that now?' Teresa says, drying the patterned porcelain plate.

I look her in the eye, wondering if she's having trouble with my accent or is just buying time. 'Daniel talked in his sleep last night. He called out for Martina.'

'Sure that could be anyone. This house was always full of women when he was a lad. Martina's a common name.'

But her face has clouded over.

'There must be records of the women who stayed here. Where are they kept?' The doctor in me needs to see how they were treated, despite them being long gone. Something about the situation didn't sit right with me. The more I see of Árd Na Mara, the more I wonder how a professional establishment could be run from here. How did Mary and Gabriel manage with children under the same roof? Was it even declared? Daniel was always tight-lipped when I asked him to explain, telling me it was all in the past.

'The records went with the officials when the girls were relocated,' Teresa eventually says. 'Otherwise any Tom, Dick or Harry could see them.'

'But that old fellah on the ferry . . . what's his name . . .' I search my mind for an answer. 'Sean. He gave me a warning. Something about babies in Árd Na Mara.' I press on with my questioning. 'What's he talking about?'

'Pfft, pay him no heed.' Teresa waves my concerns away, her tone growing stern. 'There were a few babies born out of wedlock, that's what's annoyed him. But it was all dealt with by government officials. As if he's a pillar of virtue . . .' Her words descend into annoyed mumbles, and I decide to leave it there. But I'm far from satisfied by her answer. I'm about to ask more when I hear the sound of the heavy front door opening and closing. It's Isla. The wheels of the pushchair squeak down the hall. My spirits lift as she enters the kitchen.

'Did you have a nice walk?'

As I pull the rain cover back, I try to act casual, but I'm not fooling anyone. I can barely see Kitty beneath the layers of blankets. I was wrong to worry. Isla has taken good care of her.

'Loved it.' Isla smiles, her eyes twinkling as she sweeps her auburn hair from her face. 'Danny's a slowcoach, though. He stopped to take pictures.'

'Is he now?' I'm disappointed but not surprised that he couldn't spare the time to push his daughter back in the pram. 'Well, thanks for taking such good care of Kitty.' I don't want to sound condescending. Neither did I want to appear ungrateful. Isla smiles in acknowledgement, and I catch sight of something glittering on her collarbone as she takes off her duffel coat. It looks like a silver mermaid. 'I like your necklace.'

'Thanks,' Isla says, hanging her coat on the back of the kitchen door. 'It's a selkie.'

I wonder if it's handmade. There can't be many of them around.

Teresa goes outside to get turf. A thought occurs as I spy Isla's bag on the bottom shelf of the pram. Kitty would be alright for a minute. I pursue Isla as she goes upstairs. 'You forgot your bag.'

She stops halfway up.

'I hope Daniel didn't wake you last night,' I continue with a smile. 'He was talking in his sleep. Asking for someone called Martina.' I laugh, not wanting to make a big deal of it. Then I ask the question that's playing on my mind. 'Does the name ring a bell?'

I'm not prepared for her response as she violently shakes her head.

'No. No. No!' she shouts, grabbing her bag from my outstretched hand. Her footsteps are heavy as she runs across the landing to her room and slams the door.

I stand staring after her, aghast. The last thing I wanted was to upset my sister-in-law. I take a step to follow, but my daughter's cries draw me back. I will apologise later. And then I will get to the bottom of who Martina is.

CHAPTER 14

MARY

Then

I lay in bed, staring at the ceiling, needing to savour every moment of the day ahead. It was my wedding day, barely dawn, and already nerves had taken hold. There weren't many marriages in our small island church and all eyes would be on me. I just hoped that Father Hennessy would conduct the service sober. His fondness for whiskey was known to all. My gaze flitted to my wedding dress hanging on the back of my bedroom door. Mam wanted me to wear hers, but I couldn't fit my size fourteen body into her tiny little dress. To be honest, I was relieved. I didn't have the heart to tell her that the yellowed lace gown she'd dragged down from the loft wasn't for me. I scooted back on my elbows and took the satin material in. The dress was a Bo Peep style, rising above my ankles with full lace petticoats beneath and a pretty bow at the back. Was I doing the right thing? Not for me, but for Gabriel. I didn't feel good enough for him. Our romance had been the talk of the island. *Solid, dependable Mary, breaking it off with poor young Kieran Sullivan, for a French man no less! And him an artist, would you believe it? Seven years older than her too. Some say he hasn't a penny to his name . . . but a handsome face like that is bound to get him far . . .* I'd heard the gossip. Had it not been about me, I would have relished it too. The biggest casualty in all this was Kieran, who was inconsolable when I broke it off with him. I was mortified as he got down on his knees, his face wet with tears as he begged me to stay. But he recovered quickly enough, thanks to my best friend, Orla, who immediately took his side.

Gabriel quickly won over my parents and he was invaluable when it came to turning Árd Na Mara around. In under two years we were at full capacity, and had received funding from the government to develop the basement rooms.

As soon as we were man and wife, Árd Na Mara would be signed over to us and Gabriel would move in. Until then, he took up residence in a local B&B. We couldn't have people gossiping that we were living in sin. Even in the eighties, such things were frowned upon. I knew that Gabriel had history. He was seven years older than me and a terrible flirt. With his looks, he didn't have to try very hard. Tiny warning bells rang at the back of my mind. Would I be able to satisfy him? I'd never been with a man before and it played on my mind. But in times of worry, I'd distract myself with thoughts of Árd Na Mara. I'd always known the place would be left to me, but I didn't think I'd be taking the helm so soon. It wasn't that long ago that I was wandering the cliffs wondering what I should do; now everything was falling into place. '*Petit à petit, l'oiseau fait son nid.*' Little by little, the bird makes its nest, as Gabriel would say. I'd been learning French, although it didn't sound as pretty when it rolled off my tongue.

One day I asked Gabriel why he was marrying me, because I couldn't see it, not then and not now. He said '*Désire ce que tu as et tu auras ce que tu désires.*' He spoke perfectly good English but often reverted to his first language when I asked troublesome questions because it eased the passage of his words. By the time I'd written it down and translated it, he was long gone. 'Want what you have and you'll have what you want,' was the translation, and each word stung. But I had a choice. Let my beautiful Frenchman go, or marry him, and spend the rest of my life in gratitude that he chose me. I chose marriage.

I rose from my bed and pulled on my dressing gown. There were chores to be completed, wedding day or not.

We had fifteen patients in Árd Na Mara. Ten in the main area and five in the basement. I tried to make each room homely, but it was difficult with the lower-level rooms because of health and safety rules. The house was alive with the usual sounds of a full Irish breakfast underway. Mammy was a great cook, although she was slowing down, but she always made sure our residents were well fed. There was Fiona, who was just eighteen, then the newest resident, Maura, who was twice her age. Emily and Áine also lived on the upper floor, while Niamh, Olive and Wendy were three of our newest basement residents. Each had their own story, one as tragic as another, and none had a person in the world who cared.

I wasn't blind to their history, and professionals came to help. The women were allowed out of their rooms into the rear exercise yard every day. High wire fences may have kept them in, but it did not protect them from the unrelenting wind and rain. As a result, many chose to stay in their rooms when it came to their allocated outdoor time. Well-behaved women were allowed to spend time in our living room, which held a big chunky TV and a huge selection of books. We also scheduled regular classes, anything from basket weaving to painting, which Gabriel was happy to facilitate. In my opinion, the women would have been better off learning life skills, but we didn't have the staff or facilities to teach them cookery and DIY. Once a week, a psychiatrist from the mainland saw each one in turn. We strived to maintain Árd Na Mara as a place of peace and calm. Many of the women had come from chaotic backgrounds. I told them that staying here was a privilege, but equally, I saw their point of view. The island could be beautiful, but it was a prison too. Support was always available. A doctor attended once a month to issue fresh prescriptions, and there was a nurse on the island available in between.

I walked across the landing, admiring the holly gracing the stairs. The residents weren't yet awake. Some were prescribed sleeping tablets, while others were on cocktails of drugs. I walked downstairs, where RTÉ Radio 1 was playing in the kitchen. Soon Mammy would dish out breakfast and wake everyone up. I took the stairs to the basement rooms on my way to check on the residents. The lights were dim in the corridor, and I rested my hand on the switch to turn them on to full strength. I paused as a man's voice rose from one of the rooms. I would recognise the tone of that French accent anywhere. Gabriel wasn't supposed to be there. It was bad luck to see the bride on the morning of the wedding. I don't know what stopped me from switching on the corridor light, but I stood, unmoving in the dark, as I listened to Nora chuckle in her room. Nora was thirty-five, one of our newer residents. She was violent when she'd arrived, which was why she was in a basement room.

'We'll have you out of here in no time,' Gabriel said. ''Ow you say . . . by 'ook or by crook.'

He was met by a gale of giggles as he laid it on thick.

'Not if your new wife has anything to say about it,' Nora replied when she finally caught her breath. 'Why are you marrying her, anyway?'

'I need someone to save me from the naughty girls.'

Another gale of giggles left Nora's lips.

I clamped my hand over my mouth, my stomach churning. I didn't want to hear any more. I knew what Gabriel would say – that he was only easing her in, and it was important to gain her trust, especially when she was non-compliant. That we were here to make the women better, and all of that was true. But it was about more than Gabriel's flirting. His loyalty should have been with me. Orla always said that we didn't make a good fit. But I didn't want to leave the island, and I knew I'd never meet anyone like him again. *Want what you have, and you'll have what you want.* Those words would haunt me for ever. I should have let him go.

CHAPTER 15

CLAIRE

My afternoon has been spent with Kitty, carrying her from room to room as I make plans to renovate. Her hair has grown and soft curls are beginning to form. I'm beyond grateful that she's healthy. Being a doctor, I analyse every little sniffle and grunt. But now that Daniel is home, I've asked him for my mobile phone.

My pulse picks up an extra beat at the thought of ringing my sister, but I can't put this off any longer. Witnessing her grief is hard when there is an ocean between us. I won't allow her to be cut out of my life, no matter how uncomfortable things get. What is done cannot be undone, and we both must live with it. She has never blamed me to the level that I find myself accountable. My stomach clenches as I wait for her to pick up.

'Claire. Hi.' The familiar sound of her voice on the other end is a balm to my heart. I can hear a low hum of chatter in the background, and the sounds of coffee being made.

'Hi, how are you?' I ask hesitantly.

'I'm OK,' she replies. There's an awkwardness in her tone that makes me want to reach out and hold her tight. But I can only offer words of comfort.

'It's good to hear your voice,' I say, after an uneasy pause.

She briefly cuts away from our conversation to order a latte and as I listen to the baristas at work, I feel like I'm calling from a distant world.

'I'm glad you rang,' she says, the sounds of city life not loud enough to drown out our words. I wish I was with her, having this conversation in person. It's so quiet here in comparison. 'How's island life?' Susan's voice breaks into my thoughts.

'It's beautiful here,' I reply, the corner of my mouth lifting into a small smile. 'The place is a bit rough around the edges, but we'll soon put that right.' I tell her about my plans for renovation and how nice Isla and the others have been. I hear the clink of her coffee cup as she rests it on its saucer.

We fall into an awkward silence as neither of us knows what to say next. I break the tension by remarking on her location. 'Sounds like you're out and about. Am I interrupting anything?'

'No, just meeting a friend for coffee. I'm early.'

I can't help but feel guilty at the underlying sadness in her voice. I imagine her going about her day, piecing her life back together, then hearing from me and being reminded of all that she has lost. She has always been so strong, so unbreakable.

'I'm sorry,' I say, the words tumbling out of my mouth before I can stop them. 'I'm sorry for everything.'

There's a heavy pause on the other end of the line, and I brace myself for her response. Eventually she speaks in a soft voice. 'It's not your fault. If anything, it hurts me to see you torturing yourself like this. Nobody could have predicted what happened, do you hear me? It wasn't your fault.'

It's a relief to hear her repeat the words, although I still can't shake off the guilt. 'I miss you,' I say, my voice barely above a whisper.

'I know,' she replies, 'I miss you too. Be kind to yourself, Claire. Take time to heal. Come back to me when you're better.'

It feels like goodbye. I hear a cheery hello as her friend arrives, so we finish our conversation.

◆ ◆ ◆

Teresa seems to sense my sadness, as, when I go downstairs, she gently steers me outside, insisting it's my turn for fresh air while there's still light in the sky. She seems in tune with the outdoors, and I imagine Daniel and his siblings being pushed outside to play when they were young.

'Can we visit the local church?' I say, recalling a pretty picture I saw of it online. 'I'd like to look around the graveyard.' I'm a bit of a taphophile, but it's not an interest everyone understands. While some people are unnerved by graveyards, I like to wander around the tombstones, imagining the lives of the people who once lived as I read each epitaph.

'Not today,' Teresa counters. 'I'm taking you for a bite to eat.'

I know better than to argue. We walk along the island path, umbrellas up. The ground is damp from the rain but today I'm prepared, in my boots and coat. Teresa seems determined to prise me from my daughter, stretching our time apart. She isn't just a housekeeper. She's a qualified midwife who used to oversee the maternity unit in Cork University Hospital before she came to live here. Daniel is at home looking after Kitty and I enjoy the rugged scenery as I acclimatise to the outdoors. I'm in awe of the mountains in the distance, and the bearded grazing goats on the windswept hills. Then there are the ruins of the historic island guardhouses and the ancient standing stones. There's so much history here, and I look forward to exploring it all.

'Have you never been tempted to move to the mainland?' I ask as I walk between tufts of dewy grass. I want to get to know Teresa. The same can be said for Isla, who seems guarded each time we talk.

'I've had my fill of the mainland,' Teresa replies. 'Mossie and I are content to see the rest of our days out here.' She gives me a curious look. 'But I can't see you settling. You'll stay for a few months, but either you or Danny will be keen to move on again.'

She has a point. We've kept our London flat. The plan has never been to settle down here for good.

'Is it cliquey here?' I ask, watching my step over uneven ground.

'It's insular,' Teresa says diplomatically. 'There's a strong sense of community. But it's not worth the effort of you trying to fit in. Sure I've been here over twenty-five years and they still call me a blow-in.'

Not worth the effort? What does she mean by that? I've never had to worry about fitting in before. It's not as if I'm trying to join a cult. But then I've always lived in cities. Perhaps it's just the way small communities are made.

'Well, we've no firm plans to leave just yet. Daniel is enjoying catching up with you all again.'

I hope he will find fresh inspiration here. How can he not? I admire the heather and moss-covered rocks; the clouds rolling overhead, and the myriad of wildlife which I am unaccustomed to. Last night I heard screaming, and Daniel assured me it was a troop of local foxes out to play. Later in the night, I was woken by what I imagine was a badger's screech. That was in between the sounds of the owl hooting outside our window. It certainly beats the noise of beeping horns and ambulance sirens. Even the air smells better here. The rain dapples my black umbrella, and for the first time in a long time I feel content. I follow Teresa as she descends the cliff via a narrow path which leads to a bay.

'Are you OK to walk?' I offer my arm. 'I noticed you have a bit of a limp.'

'I'm grand,' she says proudly.

But I'm not ready to give up on her yet. 'It's OK to slow down, you know. Make the men do their share.'

'Whist now,' she says with a chuckle. 'I'm not ready for the boneyard yet, and the last thing I want is Mossie under my feet.'

I get the feeling that Teresa enjoys being the matriarch of the family as she waves away my concerns.

'This is our local hub – and Mossie's second home,' Teresa jokes as she points to the grey stone building, which has a car park to the side. It seems redundant, given many of the inhabitants don't own cars. The island roads aren't the safest, given the mountain goats which roam freely, and there's no shortage of pot holes. Visitors tend to leave their cars safely on the mainland. I glance at the building ahead, and its surrounding picket fence. Picnic benches are planted out the front on a grey-slabbed patio. A short walk from a small sandy bay, it's not the prettiest of buildings, but on an island as remote as this, I imagine it's a godsend. There are two front doors which separate the building. A swinging sign titled 'The Smugglers' Inn' hangs over the left, while the door on the right displays the Irish post office logo. With its array of goods on show, the building serves as a shop, post office and pub. I glance at the slate board menu on the wall. It's basic, but the food sounds wholesome and is reasonably priced at just three euros for a slice of cake and a cup of tea.

Teresa watches me read the board. 'Some of the locals bake and sell their apple tarts here. Cheaper to make them yourself, but handy if you're stuck.'

'So it's a bit of a one-stop shop.'

'Well, given the size of the island, it's all we have. You don't want to fall out with Orla or her family, that's for sure.' Teresa chuckles, pushing the door to the left. 'Come, I'll treat you to tea and cake.'

I shake off my umbrella and wipe my feet on the mat. Heads turn as I enter, and I gratefully absorb the heat from the large open fire. There are half a dozen people inside the bar area. Some are clearly related, with their fiery red hair and freckled skin. They hold my gaze for longer than is comfortable as I follow Teresa inside. It's a homely place despite my unease. I inhale the lingering aroma of burning peat and freshly cooked food. A few tables and chairs are positioned around the room, with well-worn armchairs around the fire. A long teak bar bends to the right, with a generous selection of beverages on show.

I'm about to talk to the barman when Teresa speaks.

'This is Claire,' she says, a little too loudly. 'Our Danny's wife. She's *English*. They're staying in Árd Na Mara while they renovate the place. Now you all know Danny, so make her feel welcome.'

I'm usually confident in public places, but I don't appreciate being put on display. She spoke about me being English as if I had landed from another planet. In my world, people go about their business and barely know your name, but today, each person nods in turn. I've been to Ireland before. Granted, it was on the mainland, but nobody minded where I was from. A smiling woman joins the young man behind the bar. Judging by her weathered skin, she's around Teresa's age. Her wavy brunette hair is beautifully thick and rests on her broad shoulders. She's dressed casually in a baggy grey jumper and blue jeans.

'Welcome to the island,' she says warmly. 'I'm Orla. My daughter, Aoife, is friends with your Isla. She sorts out the online stuff for Árd Na Mara too.'

'Nice to meet you.' I shift my stance as she looks me up and down.

She points to a stocky man in the doorway who watches us with curiosity. 'That's my son, Paul. He works in the post office.' He gives me a small, awkward wave before turning to leave. 'And this is my eldest boy, Emmett,' she continues, referring to the man next to her. 'He's our in-house chef.'

The attractive red-haired man delivers a small nod of acknowledgement. Orla continues with a lengthy introduction as she recounts each of her grandchildren's names. Now all eyes are on me, and I wonder if I'm meant to reciprocate. There's no way I will remember everybody's name.

'I haven't met Aoife yet,' I say eventually, 'but I hear she's quite the computer whizz.'

Aoife is currently off travelling, having been released from Árd Na Mara while renovations are underway.

'Indeed, she is,' Orla says proudly. 'My other children live on the mainland. Only four of them here with me now.'

Only? I think, and wonder how many she has. A tall, red-haired man sidles up behind her and she introduces him as her husband, Kieran. He is the image of his sons, apart from his wild, curly hair, and beard which is peppered with grey.

'Who can blame them?' he joins in. 'There are no jobs on the island. There aren't enough people coming in to keep it afloat.' He heaves a weary sigh. 'It's a shame, sure enough.'

'I'm sure once Árd Na Mara is renovated it will bring in some tourism.' It's the most reassuring thing I can think to say.

'Hopefully it will.' Orla inclines her head a little as her husband begins to clear tables. 'And what is it exactly that you're planning?'

'Sure it's early days, we don't know ourselves yet,' Teresa interrupts, saving me from further interrogation. She points to a padded armchair as she returns her attention to me. 'Take the load off your feet while I order us a bite to eat.'

I'm grateful for her intervention. I take the armchair next to the fire while Teresa speaks to Orla at the bar. I wriggle my toes as warmth infiltrates my skin. My boots are damp from the sodden earth, but I've enjoyed the fresh air. I wonder how many members of Daniel's family sat at this very fire. What conversations were held? What secrets were shared? Something clicks inside my brain, and I realise I've heard Orla's name before.

Teresa is deep in conversation as a craggy-faced man walks in. Our eyes lock and I realise that he's the one who warned me on the ferry. I try to recall his words but they're lost to me now. His bushy white brows meet in the middle of a scowl, and I wonder if I'm sitting in his chair. He rubs his hands together, the tips of his fingers unprotected from the cold due to his fingerless gloves. He splays his hands over the fire as he stands next to me.

'So, you're still here,' he whispers, staring into the flames. 'Where is the child?'

'Back at Árd Na Mara,' I say, as my day takes another odd turn. 'Why?' I shouldn't engage but I'm curious.

'More fool you,' he replies. 'Árd Na Mara is a place of death, and Selkie Island is a friend to no one.' He looks over his shoulder, raises a finger to his lips in a shush, and turns away.

I watch, dumbfounded, as he approaches the far side of the bar. Part of me wants to follow him and ask what the hell he's talking about. But now Teresa is here with a tray containing a pot of tea and two bowls of steaming apple tart and custard. She delivers a suspicious gaze to the man at the end of the bar.

'What's Sean been saying?' Her movements are stiff, her expression guarded. I don't want to cause problems on my first visit to the bar.

'Nothing much,' I say. 'He saw me on the ferry, so he was asking where my baby was.'

'Hmm,' she grumbles, giving the pot of tea a stir. 'The less said about him, the better. That old fecker has had it in for us for as long as I remember.'

It's obvious that she's getting annoyed and I spoon sugar into my cup. 'I've heard Orla's name before,' I say, changing the subject. 'Wasn't she friends with Daniel's mother?'

Teresa relaxes into her seat and holds her cup on her palm. 'Orla and Mary were best friends . . . joined at the hip, they were. Mary was destined to marry Kieran, the man you were talking to.

But she left him in favour of Gabriel. She kept the island in gossip for months. Six months later, Kieran proposed to Orla. Nobody knew they were an item, so it came as a surprise.'

I savour my apple tart, engrossed in her story. It's the right mix of bitter and sweet, with a hint of cinnamon.

Speaking in a low voice, Teresa glances at the bar before returning her attention to me. 'It was too quick for Mary's liking, but she couldn't have it both ways. According to Gabriel, Mary's friendship with Orla was turned on its head.'

I want to say things worked out for the best, but I'm not sure that's true for Mary and Gabriel. Daniel had an unconventional upbringing and doesn't enjoy discussing his childhood. From what he's said about his father, he fancied himself as a bit of a playboy and was hardly ever around.

'What happened next?' I say, between mouthfuls. But Sean is glaring at us both.

'Best not to dwell on the past.' Teresa is edgy as she checks her watch. 'Eat up. We should head back soon.'

It's a signal to end the conversation. The flames hiss as rain comes down the chimney. Orla is whispering to her husband, their gaze firmly on me. They're not the only ones. Sean cradles his Guinness from the end of the bar and the intensity of his gaze gives me the creeps. Suddenly, this place doesn't feel quite so welcoming anymore. I push back my empty bowl. I need to speak to Daniel. It's time I learned the truth.

CHAPTER 16

DANIEL

Our tall mahogany grandfather clock has been here as long as the house itself. I can't believe it's still going, standing witness in the hall. Perhaps it will outlive us all. One of my earliest clear memories is of my mother showing me the key to its stiff glass door. It seemed like a special moment as she explained how the clock had been in our family for generations. It felt good to be the centre of her attention. If it wasn't Isla distracting her, it was the demands of the many women she catered for. But as she showed me how to wind the clock, the outside world melted away. I watched as she inserted the crank while holding the clock steady with her left hand. She explained how the right weight kept time, driving the hands and pendulum, while the left weight made the gong sound on the hour. Then we counted as she wound thirteen revolutions. I remember the sad smile that rested on her face as she explained that life was like a clock.

'Life is all about balance,' she said. 'Good and bad, love and hate.'

I didn't understand her then, but I do now. Mum's tireless work with troubled young women was a way of counteracting the horrors taking place under this roof.

The clock chimes a gong, and I almost jump out of my skin as Claire touches my arm. I didn't hear her come in.

'Sorry.' I swallow a breath. 'I was a million miles away.'

'So I see.'

Claire's words are flat as she stands, her features tight. Her blonde hair is rain-damp, her cheeks flushed pink. I knew it was a bad idea, Teresa taking her to the Smugglers' Inn. She assured me she'd be alright, that it was better to accompany her rather than have her go there alone. It's not as if we could keep her under lock and key for the next six months. But now I'm reading her face for clues as she stands before me, tight-lipped. I'm about to ask her what she thinks of the pub when she speaks.

'Why isn't the baby monitor turned on?' She raises a hand and I see that she's been holding it all along.

'She's fine,' I say, knowing there's more to this than Kitty's welfare. 'Isla's played with her all afternoon. She's just put her down for a nap.'

'I know. I've checked. But the monitor stays on.'

'Why don't I make us a cup of tea?'

I've only been home a day and already I'm slipping into my Irish ways. But Claire won't budge. I want to tell her about the clock, or discuss my new painting, anything to stop the questions forming in her mouth. Because I know what she's going to ask me, and I'm not ready for it yet.

'What went on here, Daniel? What are you hiding?'

Then she tells me about her encounter with Sean and I must come up with something to satisfy her. Why can't the old codger keep his opinions to himself? Claire may discount one warning, but two cannot be ignored.

'And it's not just you,' Claire adds. 'Isla's upset about something too.'

It pains me to see the worry in her eyes when she's been brought here to rest. I miss my old Claire – the confident, career-driven woman with a penchant for designer labels who lived for her work. Once, Claire would let nothing get her down. Everything was different in those carefree days. I'll do anything to get her back.

'You don't want to mind old Sean,' I say, doing my best to reassure her. 'He's one of the original island residents. His people were the first to settle here. He's always hated Árd Na Mara and everything it stands for.'

'And what does it stand for?' she asks. 'Because it's about time I knew.'

'You already know. A place of rest. Of healing. Of second chances.'

'Then what did he mean when he said our baby isn't safe?'

I clench my back molars. I can almost hear my mother's voice telling me to balance the bad with the good.

'A couple of our patients were pregnant when they got here. Mam had a bed for anyone who needed it. But Da . . .' I run a hand through my hair as painful memories rise. 'He found it hard to balance the books. An old place like this costs a fortune to run, and the government didn't pay much.' I babble on about the cost of heating and staff, and the inconvenience of bringing supplies over from the mainland. But Claire won't be satisfied until she gets to the crux of the truth. I rub my beard. I hope she won't think too badly of my family. 'He took backhanders.'

'From who?' Claire says, her eyes bright with the need to know. My wife is still in recovery. I give her a sanitised version of the truth. 'According to Mossie, he was in league with some powerful men who used Árd Na Mara to make their problems go away.'

'What are we talking about? Gangsters? The criminal underworld?'

'Politicians. Although some would say there's little difference.' I force a smile as I take her hand. Her skin is deathly cold. 'Abortion was against the law here . . .' I pause, taking in the look of horror on Claire's face.

'You're not saying that your father performed abortions?'

'God, no, not in a million years. My parents were staunch Catholics, they wouldn't dream of—'

'Alright, I believe you,' she interrupts, impatient now. 'Then what did Sean mean?'

'I don't know,' I say quietly. 'It didn't happen very often. One woman jumped out of the top-floor window when she was full term. Another escaped one night and went tumbling down the side of the cliff. They're buried in the graveyard up the road.'

'That's awful.'

Claire's brow knots as she takes it in. Given her profession, she's encountered many tragedies involving a mother and her child.

The water pipes shudder, then make a choking, rattling sound that reverberates in the walls. The house is rarely silent. At night the timbers groan, as if the old place is taking a long sigh before settling down to sleep. It's easy to get lost in the past when living in a house that knows nothing of the present. Staying in Árd Na Mara makes me rethink my firm belief that ghosts aren't real. In fact, sometimes I walk through these corridors and feel like I'm being watched. But I can't tell my wife about Martina – the strongest presence of all.

'That woman who jumped out of her bedroom window,' I continue. 'It was long before I was born. What was her name again?' I cast my eyes to the ceiling. 'She was pregnant when she came here, rumour had it by some high-powered member of the Dáil. He was married. He couldn't afford for it to get out.'

'Hence why she ended up here.' Claire rests one clenched fist on her hip. 'In the middle of nowhere.' She's annoyed on behalf of these women. Claire is an empath, and injustices hit her hard.

I try to lighten the mood. 'People used to joke that we were getting like Spike Island, but it was pretty luxurious compared to that.' I tell her about the island prison, which was once called 'Ireland's Alcatraz'. The biggest prison in the British empire, it closed in 2004. But my brief history lesson didn't satisfy Claire. I wish she would leave to attend to Kitty, but she is still standing in the hall as the pipes continue to rattle and spurt. I pause to clear my throat. 'It wasn't all bad. Árd Na Mara had success stories too. Lots of young women were rehabilitated here, and Mam went out of her way to make time for them all.' I look to my wife in earnest because I don't want to talk about it anymore. 'Let's forget about it, eh? Look to the future.' But despite my platitudes, Martina will haunt me for the rest of my days.

'OK,' Claire says, her disappointment evident as she sighs. 'As long as it's safe for Kitty. That old guy in the pub freaked me out a bit.'

'Kitty's safe,' I lie. 'You both are.'

I've never been so grateful to see Isla as she walks in the front door. She's carrying two bags of groceries, and I offer to give her a hand. Claire leaves to take the monitor back upstairs. She gives me one last lingering glance before she goes.

I take the bags from my sister and follow her into the kitchen. I want to ask her what she said to Claire, but I don't want it to sound like an accusation. I know how hard this has been for Isla, having to lie. She's been carrying our secret for years. It doesn't just involve our family, but a few other islanders too. The ripple effect would be devastating if this gets out. But I can't stay away for ever. If Claire accepts the truth, we can live here in comfort and support Isla with the business during the busy summer months. If they managed to get bookings with the place in this state, they're going to be a lot busier once we do it all up.

'Everything alright?' I say, staring into Isla's sea-blue eyes.

Today she's wearing the silver earrings to go with her selkie necklace. She's always been fascinated with the legend of the selkies, and I wonder if it's there as a comfort to keep our mother's memory alive. It was Ma who had the jewellery specially made for Isla, Ma who told her the same selkie bedtime stories night after night. Sometimes I wonder if my sister would like to melt away in the water and become part of the fairy tale. She takes the eggs from the bag, carefully checking that they're not cracked.

'Yeah. All good,' she says eventually, slowly sealing the packet closed.

The hoover is droning upstairs, as Teresa cleans the rooms. I don't know where Mossie is, but it's not unusual for him to take himself off for hours at a time. I focus on my sister, who is carefully unpacking each item.

'You don't have to do this, you know. I mean . . . if it's too hard, having us here . . . we can go.'

But my sister steps towards me and wraps her arms around my torso in a hug. She closes her eyes and pushes her face into my sweater.

'Don't go,' she says softly, squeezing me tight.

How can I leave her like this? I stroke her long auburn hair and tell her everything is going to be alright. There's no denying it now – my place is here. I felt it this morning as I was lost in my painting, and I feel it again now. The sense of belonging is overpowering. My thoughts are clear. I know what I must do. Sacrifices will have to be made, but my allegiance is with my sister. We cannot leave Selkie Island. Claire will come around to my way of thinking. It's only a matter of time.

CHAPTER 17

THE ISLANDER

I stare at the fire, watching the flames bob and dance in the hearth as the wind drives its way down the chimney. The island is alive with chatter since Claire made a public appearance. We've had visitors before. In the summer the photographers and painters populate the cliffs, hills and beaches. Some venture out to the caves, although the smugglers' coves are dangerous places when the tide comes in. Selkie Island is no stranger to death, and the outsiders would be mindful to remember that. But no, they arrive with their picnic baskets and cameras, gushing about how beautiful it is on Instagram, while stubbing cigarettes out in damp sand and leaving a trail of litter behind. It makes me angry to think of it, but these hypocrites are nothing compared to the people who come here raking up the past. There's an undercurrent of nervousness now Claire is here.

People are hoping that she'll take pity on us should she stumble upon the truth. But how could a city woman who's travelled across the globe have any idea of our island ways? We've never needed police involvement. We have our own way of dealing with things.

She'll never be one of us, no matter how much she tries. The islanders need not worry – I'll take care of it. It's not the first time that I've shut someone up. I didn't have to get my hands dirty. When storms close in and the weather is rough, the island takes care of itself. The tide comes in fast in the small inland coves and it's easy to get trapped, particularly after dark. Then there's the unprotected cliffs and the jagged rocks below. The freezing-cold seawater which can bring on hypothermia. The lighthouse has lots of steep steps should anyone venture inside. Such thoughts bring me comfort as I suck on the coin in my mouth. I roll it over on my tongue. I can't say I'm enjoying the bitter taste, but my compulsion forces me on. I swallow the penny and it rattles down my throat like a warning bell. It's up to me to protect the island. But at what cost?

CHAPTER 18

CLAIRE

Tonight it's just the three of us. Teresa, Mossie and Isla have taken themselves off to the mainland to watch a theatre show. It's typical of Daniel to buy the tickets as a thank you for everything they have done. Thanks to the hotel room he booked, they don't have to worry about getting the last ferry back tonight. I was touched by my husband's thoughtfulness, but was disappointed that he disappeared after dinner, leaving me to spend my evening alone. I'm an art widow and sadly can't compete with his latest work.

I walk into the kitchen, holding Kitty against my shoulder, my hand gently patting her back as I try to get her wind up. Daniel has emerged from the basement and is drinking a glass of tap water. He's been in one of the rooms down there for over an hour, and there's a dab of blue paint on the back of his hand.

The house is chilly tonight, so I've dressed Kitty in double layers. I've booked some tradesmen to arrive during the week to give us a quote for a new central heating system. The walls will need to be treated for damp and we've been told we'll need a whole new roof. When Daniel said the place was a money pit, he wasn't exaggerating.

'How's it going?' I say, watching my husband intently.

'Good,' he says, rinsing his glass and turning it upside down on the draining board.

I don't ask him if he'd like to take our daughter or give her a kiss before bed. It pains me to admit it, but Daniel hasn't taken to fatherhood as well as I'd hoped. It's my own fault. I smothered Kitty with so much love that he's never had a look-in.

'There we go, good girl,' I say, as she emits a barely audible burp.

Daniel returns my smile, but his thoughts seem far away. His mind is on his painting. He's chosen to work in a basement room where he won't be disturbed. I know better than to ask to join him. A baby's presence doesn't exactly aid concentration.

'Can I come and see you after I've got Kitty down?' I ask, as he turns to leave.

He stops, his back to us both. I kiss Kitty on the cheek, deflecting the sudden coldness coming off my husband in waves.

'Why?' He turns around at last.

'I've not seen all the basement rooms yet. Why are they locked?'

'You know why,' he says. 'Because it's not safe.'

'It's safe enough for you to spend all evening down there.' I'm not sure if I believe his story of a recently burst pipe. 'The floors must be dried out by now,' I continue, as silence is returned. 'How am I going to plan the renovation if I can't access the rooms?'

Daniel's voice carries an edge. 'We're not renovating the basement just yet. We agreed.'

'Maybe.' I switch Kitty from my left shoulder to my right. 'But I'd still like to have a look.'

'And you will, in time. But Rome wasn't built in a day.'

Then he's gone, back to his painting, and I tell myself that he's distant because he's lost in his creative world. His best work is ominous and haunting, and his ability to lose himself in the darkness is what makes him a success.

I think about it when I'm lying in the free-standing tub. I deserve a little pampering, now Kitty is asleep. I feel like I'm losing Daniel . . . but to what? My thoughts turn dark when I think of the babies born beneath this roof. Were they really handed over for adoption? I gaze around the high, cracked ceilings and shiver in the water as I imagine ghostly figures lurking in the shadows, forever searching. Did the air echo with their sobs? How did it affect Daniel, growing up to the backdrop of mothers crying out for their little ones? Babies should be born in hospitals, not some run-down institution with crumbling walls and a sagging roof. How many women gave birth here? It feels like a veil has been lifted, and I'm seeing Árd Na Mara for what it really is.

My gaze falls on the old-fashioned wall tiles, stained with years of grime. I take in the crack in the mirror and the tarnished brass bath fittings. How did I consider time alone in this haunting old bathroom a treat? The light flickers above me and the water makes a gasping, choking sound as I pull the plug. I tell myself there's air in the pipes, but I can't get out of the bath quickly enough. I pat myself dry before slipping on my silk nightdress and dressing gown and taking the vast stairs.

I put myself in the shoes of the women who came here. Their fear and confusion still hangs in the air, even after all these years. Tonight, Árd Na Mara feels dark, cold and lonely – and carries a personality of its own. I can't imagine Daniel and his siblings growing up here. In all of my time as a medical practitioner, I've never heard of a situation like this. Once again, I find myself asking the same questions. Was it ethical to raise a family in the same home as disturbed young women? Was the situation monitored? Where are the medical records? The paperwork? Because I'm not sure I believe Teresa's story of everything being passed on. From the little information I've gathered, Daniel, Louis and Isla were left to their own devices a lot of the time. How has it affected them, and why is Daniel so cagey about the basement rooms? It's not as if Isla will talk to me, and Louis, his brother, is nowhere to be seen.

Perhaps I've been going about this the wrong way. Instead of pressuring Daniel for answers, I should handle him with kid gloves, just as I did in my practice when dealing with traumatised children. Because one thing is clear. Daniel has retreated into himself since arriving on the island. I shiver as I enter the kitchen. It's getting dark already and I've let the range go out. I root in the cupboard beneath the sink for firelighters, grumbling beneath my breath as my satin robe falls open.

My thoughts come to a halt as I stand. I'm face to face with an intruder peering through our kitchen window. I gasp as a sense of primal anger overrides fear. I'm not having this. I don't scream, neither do I rush to get Daniel. I tighten my dressing gown, find the closest thing to a weapon and venture into the night.

CHAPTER 19

MARY

Then

After the excitement of my wedding, there was little to look forward to. I was surrounded by people, but often overcome by loneliness too. I missed my parents and my days felt hollow and empty after they passed away. When I thought of the future, I saw years of back-breaking work stretching ahead of me. I had no life outside Árd Na Mara, apart from the occasional treat when Gabriel took me out. Forging friendships with our residents was against the rules. But sometimes listening to them made me appreciate how much better my life was.

Áine was just twenty-four, a whip of a girl with shiny copper-brown hair. I entered her room and took in the details of her face: her large eyes, her slight nose, the petal-like softness of her lips and her small, pointed chin. It was hard to believe she was capable of inflicting harm on anyone, much less setting fire to a convent as the nuns slept in their beds. I didn't ask about the motivations behind her crime because she came here with a clean slate, but there was a story to be told. I could see it behind her eyes. Today Áine appeared thoughtful as she stood next to the window. As a rule, they were expected to back away to the far side of the room when we entered to do anything. I hummed as she watched me arrange some wildflowers in a plastic vase. I loved the pretty purple sea asters, which I paired with some wild clary and some fluffy-headed purple sheep's-bit. I had an affinity for lavender and purples, although I had to be careful, as some plants such as bog rosemary were poisonous, and I wouldn't put it past some of the women to ingest them. I dotted the display with some cute buttercups. Their cheerful blooms and sweet scent never failed to make me smile. All the while I could see Áine watching me from the corner of my eye.

'Are you sure you're eating enough?' I said, scanning her slender form. 'You look like you've lost weight.'

'You sound like my mam.' Áine gave me a simple smile but appeared distracted as she picked at her nails. 'I like you, Mary,' she said eventually, resting one hand on the windowsill.

'Thanks.' I stood back to admire my handiwork. The room was decorated in dark colours and the freshly harvested island flowers brightened it up.

'Can I ask you something?' she said. She was buttering me up. First a compliment then a request. I'd seen it all before.

'There's nothing more I can give you. Our budget is stretched thin.' I picked up the loose leaves to throw in the kitchen bin.

'No, it's not about that.' She took a step forward and I took one back.

'Wait,' she said, biting her bottom lip. 'It's your husband.'

That stopped me in my tracks. 'What about him?'

'I . . . I don't like it when he comes into my room at night.'

I frowned. 'When he's doing his rounds? It's a security check, that's all. But he doesn't go into the rooms.'

'But lately he does. Usually when I'm sleeping. I don't like it. Please. Ask him to stop.'

My heart seemed to stop beating as I realised what she was saying. Questions flooded my mind. How long had this been going on? Had any of the other women been affected? How could I protect them?

I took a deep breath and tried to remain composed. 'Áine, you have my word that I will speak with Gabriel and make sure it doesn't happen again. Is that alright with you?'

Áine nodded slowly and went to her bed, her face unreadable. She sat down and took a deep breath. When she finally spoke, her voice was barely above a whisper. 'I don't know why he does it. It makes me uncomfortable.'

I felt my mouth go dry. This had never come up before. I cleared my throat.

'He won't do it again,' I said in a firm voice, struggling to keep the emotion from my tone. Many of these unfortunate girls had ended up here because of past abuse. There was a possibility that this was a false allegation but there was something in Áine's eyes that made me afraid. What if Gabriel had been there for more than a security check?

I thanked Áine for trusting me enough to open up and assured her that everything would be taken care of. After a few more words of comfort, I made my departure. As I left the room, my mind was fixed. This could not happen again.

Later that day I approached Gabriel to discuss Áine's claims. His face was a picture of surprise, but he didn't deny it. He stood before the medicine cupboard with a clipboard, counting the prescription drugs.

'I just wanted to keep an eye on her . . . make sure she didn't do anything rash,' he murmured, his voice soft and even. 'Áine has been feeling a little . . . depressed.'

I thanked him for his honesty and uttered a gentle warning. 'You need to protect yourself, Gabriel. If there's any more reports we'll have to have surveillance cameras installed.'

My suggestion did the trick. I was furious that it had happened, but I knew how to handle my husband. Putting him on the defensive would not work. I monitored the women closely and Gabriel was a lot more careful after that. But at night, I lay in bed next to my sleeping husband, wondering what else he was hiding from me. How long had he been doing this? And then a thought struck me that made my blood run cold. What if Áine wasn't the only one? My heart raced at the thought of my husband watching the residents as they slept. We couldn't afford the surveillance cameras that I threatened him with. Gabriel may have a weakness for a pretty face, but he wouldn't stalk the women under my nose. Would he?

CHAPTER 20

CLAIRE

I creep through the undergrowth, my fingers tight around the spanner that Mossie left on top of his toolbox next to the back door. I can accept feeling like an outsider, even being talked about, but I'm sure as hell not going to put up with some peeping Tom. I'm furious at the intrusion. Who does this pervert think he is?

But I haven't thought this through as I run out into the back garden. The house is widely bordered by rusted wrought-iron railings; the land dotted with thick shrubs and trees. But the front of the house is a short run away from the eroding cliff edge. Darkness has smothered the island, and I can barely see my hands. It lasts only seconds before the lighthouse beams its giant torch into the night. I blink against the sudden light, then catch sight of a broad, shaggy-haired man. He's tall and muscular enough to overpower me, even with a tool in my hand. A twig snaps underfoot, alerting him to my presence long before I've worked out what I'm going to do.

The man freezes as he's caught in the searing light, his head swivelling around as he sees me standing just feet away. It's too late for me to back out now.

'Hey, you!' I shout, raising my spanner aloft. 'What do you think you're doing?' My heart may be hammering but I'm angry with the trespasser.

'Jaysus, hold on there a minute.'

His Cork accent is strong as he raises hands in the air. His face carries a comical expression which suggests he's of little threat. There's something else . . . His dark eyes, his wild black hair. I've seen him somewhere before. He is better dressed than me for the weather, in his thick coat and jeans.

'Put that thing down, will ya?' he exclaims against the gathering winds. They howl through the outhouses in a myriad of ghostly screams. 'I'm not here to cause trouble,' the man continues, but he's trespassing on our land.

'Make a habit of peeping into strangers' windows at night, do you?' I retort, still wielding the spanner. The air is icy against my skin, and the soles of my feet are wet as my flimsy Joules slippers become soaked through. They're not made for the outdoors, let alone the damp, muddy field that this house is built upon.

The stranger's head swivels to the kitchen window and then back to me. 'You don't think . . .' He chuckles under his breath. 'You do, don't you? You think I'm some kind of voyeur?'

My expression remains grim as I meet him head on. 'Then what do you want? Because my husband's inside and . . .'

He shakes his head as he laughs. 'The rumours are true. I heard you were a feisty one.'

'Feisty?' I grind my back molars. It seems if you're a woman with an opinion you're known as 'feisty' in this neck of the woods. The cheek of it. Such small-minded thinking angers me even more. 'You're the one hiding in the bushes! What does that make you?'

I peer at his shadowed features, wishing I had my mobile phone. But then, who would I call? Even if I could get a signal, there's no police on the island. They would have to come from the mainland. There's another flash of white as the lighthouse makes another round. I can hear the sea pounding against the cliff and I don't feel safe here.

'What are you making that face for?' He's still smiling as he stands before me, wearing a stupid grin.

'I'm making a mental image for when I call the Gardaí. You can run if you want, but unless you're a good swimmer, you won't get far. Besides, everyone knows who everyone is around here.'

'Everyone except you, it seems,' he retorts, extending his hand. 'I'm Louis. Your brother-in-law.'

I lower the spanner, my mouth dropping open. That's why he looks familiar. I've seen him in old family photos. He has Daniel's eyes, the same strong jawline, but there are differences too. He is younger, but not by many years, and outdoor life has weathered his skin.

'I . . . I don't understand,' I say, feeling suddenly awkward. 'What are you doing here?'

'Well, I wasn't perving at you, if that's what you think . . .' He shuffles, plunging his hands deep into his coat pockets as the wind blusters around us. 'I heard Danny was back. I wanted to see it for myself.'

'And you couldn't knock on the door like a normal person?' I fold my arms across my chest as the cold air cuts through me.

'Knock?' Louis makes me tense as his laugh carries a bitter edge. 'That's my house. I grew up here. Why the feck should I have to knock on my own front door?'

I frown. There is clearly a lot going on here that I know little about. My loyalty towards my husband tells me I'm better off saying nothing until he's filled me in.

'Come in then,' I reply, knowing that, in Ireland, tea is the answer to everything. 'I'll put the kettle on. Daniel's in the basement, painting.'

85

Louis snorts at the mention of his name. 'Daniel? So he's changed his name as well as his identity. He may think he's a city boy, but here, he'll always be Danny. And I'll be on my way.'

'But—'

'Tell him I called. We need to talk. But not here.'

I want to tell him about his niece, and to ask if he's kept in touch with Isla. But he's stomping up the muddy path, leaving me in a state of bewilderment. The nearby lighthouse illuminates his broad frame as he walks away.

'Where are you going?' I call after him. 'Are you staying on the island?' But the wind steals my words. If he needs to talk to Daniel, then why was he skulking around outside?

I'm utterly frozen. The wind feels like sheets of ice and the tips of my toes are numb. I run back into the house, throw the spanner into the toolbox, and leave my slippers next to the washing machine. At least Kitty's still asleep. I relight the fire, gathering my thoughts before approaching my husband with the news. It was stupid, rushing out there in nothing but my nightwear, but I'm not putting up with such bizarre behaviour. At least it gives me an excuse to disturb Daniel.

The basement is at the end of a flight of steps which is hidden behind a door at the end of the hall. But first, I lift the lid from the range and poke some life into the fire, throwing in some firelighters for good measure. I can't let the house get any colder than it is. I jump at the sight of Daniel standing in the doorway.

'I thought I heard voices outside,' he says, his face creased in confusion as he looks around.

'I had a visitor,' I say, squirting Fairy Liquid on my palm to wash away the stink of firelighters. 'I caught him outside in the bushes. Thought he was a peeping Tom.'

Daniel steps towards me. I have his full attention now. 'Who?'

'Your brother. He's lucky I didn't cave his head in with a spanner.'

He relaxes, his face breaking into a sly smile. 'That wouldn't have done him any harm.'

'He said you need to talk.'

'Did he now?' He begins to tend to the range, giving it a rattle even though I've already brought it back to life. I know what he's up to. His diversion tactics won't wash with me.

'Just what happened between you two?'

I am met with a sigh. 'It's so long ago that I can barely remember.'

'Then surely it's time you made up? Louis said he wants to talk. He's made the first move. It's your turn now.'

'My turn for what?'

Daniel fills the kettle at the tap. I hate how he always refuses to meet my eye when he's uncomfortable. I'm cold, my feet are dirty, and the romantic night I'd planned with my husband is a million miles away.

'Stop avoiding the subject, Daniel. We're inviting Louis for dinner, where we can sit down and have a civilised conversation. I'm not taking no for an answer.'

I feel the fire in my belly reignite. Daniel is smiling. It seems he feels it too.

'Alright, I know when I'm beaten. Invite him if you like. Teresa has his number. It doesn't mean he'll come.' He disappears into the living room and returns with a blanket, wrapping it around my shoulders. 'You should buy some warmer clothes. I don't want you getting frostbite.'

He kisses me on the forehead before returning his attention to the range, mumbling something about keeping his girls warm. He doesn't notice when I leave to go upstairs. I may as well give in and buy some warm plaid pyjamas. But it's not as if I can pop to the shops or order next-day delivery. I peep in on Kitty, feeling guilty for allowing the temperature to dip. I've no idea how Daniel's mother managed to run this big old house and its occupants, along with caring for a family of her own. A gust of wind whistles through a loose pane and as the house settles around me I swear I can hear it breathe.

I stare into the shadowy corners of the room, unable to shake off the sense that I'm not alone. Perhaps it's me. I've been uncomfortable since we got here. It's not just that I feel out of place, it's the sense of foreboding that has accompanied me since I stepped off the ferry. I've watched Daniel take a breath to speak to me so many times, only to bite back his words. I never insist that he continue, because I'm scared that he'll turn the conversation on to me. He's not the only one running from his past. I don't want to talk about what happened. What I did. The guilt of my professional failures pushed me over the edge. But there's a little voice still inside me, waiting for its turn. Daniel's not the only one with demons to face.

CHAPTER 21

DANIEL

I stand in the basement room, my stomach tied in knots. I came down here to gather up my things, but I need a minute to catch my breath. At first glance, this room would seem innocuous enough. There's a bed, a basic wardrobe and a dressing table. Good lighting makes up for the lack of windows, which is why I chose to paint here after the sun dipped in the sky. Look closer and you'll see that the furniture is bolted down. The drawers can't be removed from their runners. The mirrors are made from safety glass. There are other bedrooms on this level. They once had straps and shackles – for the women's own good, of course. Claire isn't ready to see them yet.

Claire is keen to begin renovating, but I've put her off for now. I need some time to acclimatise myself with being back here again. I thought that by spending time in this room it would help reconcile me to the past. But now Louis has emerged and everything's happening too fast. I can't believe that Claire chased him down the garden path, spanner in hand. While I welcome the return of my spirited wife, I dread to think how this could have ended had

Louis let himself in. What was my brother thinking, turning up here unannounced?

I gather up my paintbrushes, bristling at the thought of his unwelcome visit. Claire comes from a happy family. She doesn't understand. I can barely remember the last time Louis and I spoke. I only hope that when he comes to dinner that he holds his tongue. I turn back to my painting. My brother's presence will shape the remainder of the image, bringing thunder to the background, and, with it, an impending sense of threat. I have a complicated relationship with this island. Louis will upset the balance I've worked hard to maintain.

Is it the house? Does he want to lay claim? Why now, after all these years? Another more worrying thought occupies my mind. What if he's here for revenge?

I can almost feel the ghost of my mother whispering in my ear. *Make it up with your brother. Do this one thing for me, Danny.*

I try to imagine a life with Louis in it again. Can I trust him enough to let him in? With a heavy heart, I lock myself in the room. I don't have long. Claire will be waiting for me upstairs. I feel a pang of regret. I should have told her how beautiful she looked tonight, but instead I remarked upon her getting cold. I need to make more of an effort, so she doesn't feel neglected, but it's easy to get overwhelmed with everything going on. I slide my hand beneath the dresser table and pluck the key from its hiding place. I've stowed away Claire's mobile in the drawer for now. Apart from that call to her sister, she's not in any hurry to use it. The Wi-Fi isn't great out here, and we both agreed that it would be hard for her to heal while checking calls and emails from work. They're aware that she's on a long sabbatical, but some of her old colleagues can't help but get in touch. Claire is an excellent doctor, and her absence is deeply felt.

I quickly open the dresser drawer, take out the landli... that I've hidden, and plug it into the connection that my ... had installed. Nobody knew it was here until after he passed away. Nobody except Isla, who told me about the phone calls that Da allowed the women to make under the right circumstances. He may not have hurt the women in our care, but neither did he give away favours for free. I think about the secret calls he must have made in a time before mobile phones were widespread. He wasn't happy unless he was plotting, and Mam turned a blind eye to it all. I dial my brother's mobile number, hoping it hasn't changed. Isla gave it to me months ago, in the hope that we'd get in touch.

'Hullo?' he says, a hint of suspicion in his voice.

'It's me, Danny.' I want to keep this short. 'We need to talk.'

CHAPTER 22

THE ISLANDER

I've come to accept the monotony that comes with stalking. On the island, it means cold feet and even colder toes. But tonight I haven't watched Claire for long. I didn't realise that she had so much fight in her. It's forced me to act with caution and take a step back while I reassess my plans. I don't want to have my head caved in.

I'm not a killer. Well, technically I am, but I get no thrill from it. I don't sit in my room at night, rubbing my hands in glee. I don't have a shrine on the wall dedicated to my next victim, nor do I store body parts in my fridge. These killers are the sensationalists, the stories that books and movies are made for, but in real life, it doesn't work that way. Sometimes I lie in bed at night wondering how many people have killed and merged back into everyday life with ease. I mean, if plain old me can do it, then anyone can. I think the figures would be frightening. There must be a lot of accidental deaths too. How many involuntary killers walk the streets, burdened by a secret they can never share? I think about how many people go missing every year and how many unmarked graves must occupy our lands. The island may be small, but it has more than its fair share. We are surrounded on all sides by the biggest graveyard of them all. It's wet, murky depths hide its secrets well. It destroys forensic evidence, is difficult to search, and will never tell. While the sea may be my ally, I am well aware of its strength.

Each day I keep my head down. I care for my loved ones, I do my jobs, watch TV, read books. I'll have a natter with my neighbours should I see them around. People think well of me, as far as I know. Outwardly, I'm like everyone else. But my thoughts . . . now they are my own. I am both a plotter and a protector. Everything I do is a selfless act. There's nothing in it for me, apart from the satisfaction of things remaining the way they should. My first kill was accidental. My second was forced. After that . . . well, I'm in too deep to back out now. But it has always been for the community.

You may call me an optimist, expecting things to remain the same on this island, but I have sat in our small church and held a private conversation with God. It was one-sided, granted, but his presence was strong. When I explained my reasoning, I knew that he approved. I am the shepherd of this island. Every parishioner is part of my flock. When I visit the mainland, I see how consumerism has affected the outside world. It makes me shrink back in horror and I don't stay there for long. In my mind, it has always been *them* and *us*. We have remained unchanged for decades. Everything I do is to protect the welfare of those who belong here.

It's not my fault that interfering outsiders turn up, asking questions about the past. Then you have the tourists, with their annoying mobile phone ringtones and inability to use a bin. I despise them with a passion, and it was a great relief when bookings at Árd Na Mara started tailing off. But now the Englishwoman is here, with her big fancy plans to renovate and encourage even more people to come. I imagine the place flooded with journalists, all staying on the island after they discover the truth. Or God forbid, one of those true-crime enthusiasts goes viral on social media. I've heard what that can do to a place and the thought of it makes my toes curl. So now I'm back at my drawer, looking for something, anything, to help me calm down. My secret obsession steadies my nerves and calms the buzzing in my head. My gaze settles on my chosen object. The small blue Bic lighter belonged to the last person who died before my eyes. I wouldn't exactly say I killed him. He lost his balance, that's all. If he was stupid enough to walk the cliffs with whiskey warming his belly, then it's hardly my fault. People who drink before nightfall deserve everything they get. Ditto for those who ask too many questions during their stay.

Mr Cornelius Murphy was a retired journalist, and a little too keen to be involved in island life. I was just being kind, offering to show him around. I happened to have my camera with me and he seemed happy to have his photo taken on the cliff edge. He didn't have to keep stepping back or indeed listen to my suggestions at all. Then he was gone, with nothing but a blue Bic lighter left behind. I did my best to look shocked in case anyone was watching, but my only witnesses were the curlews circling the darkening sky. So I picked up the lighter and here we are. Sure it's gas, when you think about it. Makes me chuckle even now. It nestles in my hand, a symbol of my loyalty to the island that I love. Nobody missed Cornelius enough to accept the verdict of accidental death as anything but the truth.

I rub my thumb over the hard plastic as I consider my next move. In the back of my mind there is a warning whisper. *It's risky — there's lighter fluid still inside.* But then I think of the Englishwoman and the position she has put me in. I slip the lighter into my mouth. The taste is electrifying. My tongue surveys its rough and smooth edges as I close my eyes. One gigantic swallow and it's gone.

CHAPTER 23

MARY

Then

My friendship with Orla came to an end the day I chose Gabriel. She was always a little in love with Kieran, so you'd think she'd be pleased that I'd paved the way. But no, she came to me the day after I ended things, her face reddened with anger as she lectured me about how Kieran was falling apart.

'How could you do that to him? And him about to buy a ring!' She'd spoken in a fierce tone that I'd never heard before. 'You may not care about being the talk of the island, but Kieran is humiliated!'

Again and again, she'd questioned my choice, ranting that yes, Gabriel was a 'heartthrob', but any fool could see that he was a sly beggar, out for what he could get. I knew what she was hinting at. She didn't need to spell it out because I'd thought it myself many times. Why else would someone like Gabriel want to be with a plain Jane like me? But my love for him bordered on obsession. He lived in my thoughts during the day and crept into my dreams as I slept. To let him go would be like cutting off my own air supply. But how could

I explain this to my sensible, down-to-earth friend? I admit, there was hurt on my side. Then I felt more than a tinge of jealousy when Kieran settled down with Orla so soon. I also had concerns about my husband's wandering eye. I ensured that I was the last person to check the women's rooms at night, although many of the women in our care seemed happy to speak to Gabriel each day. I shouldn't have had to do it. We were virtually newly-weds, and I was having to watch him like a hawk. Sometimes, when things got tough, I wondered what my life would have been like had I not bumped into Gabriel that day.

Orla fell pregnant not long after her nuptials. I couldn't avoid her for ever as I needed to use the shop. Instead of silently paying for my purchases, I offered my best wishes.

'Congratulations,' I said, forcing a smile. 'I heard the happy news.'

My ex-friend was three months pregnant. A blessing which had evaded me so far. I handed over my basket of shopping. Árd Na Mara was full to capacity, and we had run out of bread. Food was cheaper on the mainland, but Gabriel had been off on another one of his trips and I barely managed to keep the place running in his absence. The morning had been a busy one, and having risen at six, I had barely paused for a break. At least Teresa was a good cook, and we managed to get our residents fed in record time. Then they were allowed out of their rooms for supervised exercise in the outside yard while Teresa and I stripped and changed the beds. I didn't venture down to the basement rooms. Mossie and Teresa took care of the women there, issuing medication and bringing back up their breakfast trays. It felt like such a cruelty, not allowing the women to smell the sea air, or hear the backdrop of the waves. The lower-level rooms weren't meant to be occupied long term, but Gabriel had insisted on keeping the house full to capacity whatever the cost. If I couldn't bear the basement rooms for one minute, what was it like for the women who spent weeks or months down there? It proved to be a constant torment and kept me awake at night. It didn't matter how much the government paid us if Gabriel spent it at casinos during his jaunts away. I'd foolishly thought that as an artist he'd be content absorbing himself in the beauty of the island. But not Gabriel, my forever restless man. His gallivanting had a knock-on effect as I struggled to keep Árd Na Mara afloat. I couldn't blame the women for complaining about the cheap cuts of gristly meat that made up our stews, and it was lucky if the laundry got washed once a week. Employing cleaners was a luxury that we could no longer afford.

The reality of being married to my handsome Frenchman was not the fairy tale I'd imagined. I had never worked so hard for so long. It didn't help that one of the women had arrived pregnant. An arsonist named Catherine, she was the mistress of a top politician. No wonder she'd been forced to join us, given how outspoken she was about him, and the things they got up to together, which would make your hair curl. Had the papers got hold of it, there would have been holy hell.

'Thanks.' Orla smiled, her face flushed with happiness, as if she'd been bursting to share the news. 'Kieran's thrilled. He wants a football team.'

I swallowed down my resentment as she totted up my purchases on the old-fashioned till. She must have conceived on her honeymoon night, given the timings. I'd been trying for two years and faced nothing but disappointment each month. Hearing of her news felt like a kick in the teeth. Orla lived in a beautiful four-bedroom home just a stone's throw from the pub that Kieran had built from scratch. Their kitchen counter had been imported from Italy, and they even had a jacuzzi bath. I struggled to contain my bitterness. Her corridors would be filled with the sounds of children playing, whereas ours rang with the sounds of sharp-tongued women demanding attention at all hours of the day and night. Orla's home was an example of the life I could have had. My infatuation with my husband was a weakness that I paid for dearly. I handed over the cash, forcing myself to smile.

'Mary . . .' Orla touched my hand as my eyes grew moist with regret. 'Are you OK?' It was an uncharacteristic show of affection.

I heaved a deep sigh and blinked away my tears. 'I'm fine, it's just hay fever.'

Since living with my husband, I'd learned how to lie. Like lying to my parents each time Gabriel went to the mainland on one of his gambling trips. Like the lies about why we hadn't started a family yet. I loved my husband dearly. He was my whole world. But it wasn't reciprocated. Our marriage was built on shaky foundations. He never really loved me, only what I could provide for him. I thanked Orla and left, using the walk to Árd Na Mara to process my thoughts.

Our honeymoon had been a disaster. I'd been nervous during my first visit to France. Everything seemed so alien, and it didn't help that I couldn't speak the language. The people I encountered seemed rude in comparison to what I was used to in Ireland. Gabriel's parents took an instant dislike to me. They were still angry that Gabriel hadn't told them about our wedding. And here I'd been, thinking they hadn't bothered to show up. He'd confessed on the flight over. I remember clutching my bag of boiled sweets, nervous as it was my first time on an aeroplane. But Gabriel's bombshell turned my excitement into dread.

'I didn't want them making a scene,' he'd said, saying his parents had wanted him to settle down in France.

Their townhouse was tiny, and we stayed there a week before going home. I hadn't been able to stand the hostility a moment longer. Their arguments had always been in French, but I could tell by their glances in my direction that they concerned me. I was trying to learn the language and managed to translate a few words. Things came to a head when Gabriel told his family I was a wealthy woman. His mother spat a reply that he should have married for love. That stung, and I fled from the room. Gabriel's mother came to find me and curled an arm around my shoulder as she apologised.

'I am sorry,' she said in English. 'We are upset about the wedding. Gabriel never told us about you.'

My eyes had widened at this disclosure. Gabriel hadn't just withheld details of our nuptials, they didn't even know I *existed* until we turned up out of the blue. No wonder they were cross. I would have been too.

'It's done now.' The woman patted my hand. 'We will be friends.'

But we never were. They never visited the island, and I hadn't seen them since. At least once a month Gabriel made a trip away, spending our hard-earned cash on some kind of 'investment' that we never saw a return on. It was all about money for Gabriel, and he enjoyed the thrill of the chase. I worked my fingers to the bone while he squandered every free bit of cash we made. I gave up complaining because it always ended in a row. He said that the island was boring, that he needed time away every month. That I could choose: either live on the island and let him spread his wings, or he'd move to France – with or without me.

So I let him go and didn't ask any questions. It was my own fault for marrying him. Who had I been kidding? I should have stayed with my own sort. I remember the day he returned after being gone for two long weeks. I'd struggled in his absence. My parents needed full-time care by then and our residents had been locked in their rooms for longer than was good for them. I'd enlisted help from the mainland, but they walked out after the first week, saying the pay didn't cover the level of work needed to run the place properly.

I'd been so cross when Gabriel returned that I'd walked out and left him to it. I wanted to be the one to disappear for weeks on end and enjoy the money I worked so hard to earn. But of course, I didn't get much further than leaning against the lighthouse wall.

'*Reviens, mon amour!*' he called in an accent I was unable to resist. 'I have a surprise for you!' But Gabriel was never one to give chase.

Soon I returned to the kitchen, kicking off my boots. Gabriel flashed a smile that set off a hundred fireworks inside me. This was why I stayed with him. The term 'putty in his hands' was invented for people like me. Then he held my face and kissed me, long and lingering, which sealed the deal. My cheeks flaming, I turned to the people sitting at my kitchen table, drinking a cup of tea. The woman rose instantly, and by the way the man followed her lead, I guessed he was her husband.

'I've got you the help you need,' Gabriel said, obviously pleased with himself. 'Mary, meet Teresa and Mossie Nikolic, our new live-in help.'

Teresa did all the talking. She was a motherly figure, although not much older than me. She explained that she was from Cork, a qualified midwife, no less. Her husband's grandparents were Macedonian, hence the unusual name. They both seemed keen to roll their sleeves up, but I was wary of staff walking out on me again.

'Change isn't good for the girls,' I said, taking my husband to one side. Their welfare was always at the forefront of my mind. 'There's no point in them getting started if they're going to take off like the others. Why would a qualified midwife work for such a low wage?'

But Gabriel gave me a knowing smile. 'You say Árd Na Mara is a place for second chances, yes?'

I nodded. It had to be. I couldn't put in the hours otherwise.

But as Gabriel glanced in our visitors' direction, I realised he wasn't talking about the inmates. That's when I understood. They were running away from something. I never asked at the time because I was so grateful for the help. Like many things in life, I was willing to turn a blind eye.

CHAPTER 24

CLAIRE

I sit at the dining table surrounded by Daniel's family. The air is rich with the smell of freshly cooked food. It's good to take the weight off my feet. The last few days have passed in a whirlwind. I've managed to get some quotes for a new heating system and tradesmen are due to arrive in two weeks. This morning I took delivery of a new leather suite for the living room. It's a vast improvement on what was there before. We've already set to work painting the walls, but when it comes to clearing the outside windows, the vines are difficult to shift. I miss next-day Amazon Prime deliveries and the accessibility of local home décor stores and showrooms. Living here brings its own set of challenges, but it is a breathtakingly beautiful island.

I'm getting a routine in place, and while Mossie spends his free time in the local pub, Teresa is finally accepting my help with household chores. Even Isla is opening up to me. She helped me cook dinner tonight so we could give Teresa an evening off. It's a simple but delicious paella, made from seafood caught fresh from the bay. Isla knows the fishermen well and always gets the best price. Louis has been invited to dinner in the hope of building bridges, but as the brothers finish their food, there is tension in the air.

So this is why Teresa and Mossie went to the pub for dinner. Had they guessed that things would go badly? As much as they've done for Daniel and his siblings, they were never replacement parents, but caretakers of the children orphaned by the sea.

Louis arrived with the smell of alcohol on his breath, stumbling as he removed his muddy boots inside the front door. No wonder Daniel didn't want him to meet Kitty yet. Our daughter is asleep upstairs. I kept her awake for most of the afternoon so our evening will be undisturbed. Now Daniel sits at the head of the table, with Isla to his left and me to his right. Louis sits at the other end, and I sense a power struggle taking place. The air is thick with unsaid words. We get through dinner with small talk. Louis is vague about where he's living, but I gather that it's a short-term rental on the island. I'd always been led to believe that he lived on the mainland. Isla has never mentioned him, and from the way they're acting tonight, they don't appear close. I'm glad that she has Daniel, who constantly watches her movements to ensure she's OK. Our meal is coming to an end, and I wonder what happened between the brothers to tear their family apart. Louis thanks us for the meal and it feels like he wants to leave. But it's too soon. I won't let him go.

'Can I get you a drink?' I say, as Isla begins to clear the plates. It seems he's not the only person keen for our evening to end.

'I'd say he's had enough already,' Daniel mumbles sourly. I had hoped the smell of whiskey on Louis's breath was from a sip of Dutch courage, but he's barely touched his food and has drunk a lot of red wine.

'Coffee, then,' I say. 'Why don't we go into the living room? It's nice and warm . . .' I stand, raising my arm to lead the way. I'm about to ask Isla to join us when Louis interrupts.

'I know where the sitting room is,' he snaps. 'I grew up here.'

I give Daniel a pleading look, a silent request for patience. Already an argument is brewing between them.

'We've got great plans for the place,' I say, trying to change the subject. As we rise from the table, I talk about my ideas for interior design.

'That's all well and grand.' Louis casts an eye around the kitchen. 'But you didn't ask me here to talk about wallpaper or paint.'

'We didn't,' Daniel says, an edge to his voice. I try to read my husband's expression, seeing something more. Concern? Maybe. He and his brother are circling each other like wolves. Just what is up with them? Isla goes back and forth from the table to the sink as she hurriedly clears up. I want to help, but Daniel has tensed beside me. I hope he doesn't do anything stupid.

'So when are we selling up?' Louis's words hang in the air.

I exchange a glance with Daniel, who places a protective arm around Isla as her movements come to a halt.

'We're not selling. We're staying put.'

My eyebrows shoot up. This is news to me. The plan had been to renovate the place, then go back to London when it's on its feet. I tell myself that he's bluffing. He doesn't want to sell Isla's home, that's all. It's a display, strength in numbers, isn't it?

Louis's frown deepens. 'Oh, I see. Of course. Because it's all about what *you* want, isn't it? Just as it's always been – not a thought or care for the rest of us.'

My husband's response is instant. 'I'm not saying you can't have your share. We'll get an independent valuation and buy you out.' Daniel stands before the range, staring at his brother in disbelief. 'I thought you'd be pleased.'

'Pleased?' Louis approaches him. 'Like I was pleased when you left here with something of mine?'

103

Spittle flies from his lips as he is overcome with emotion. This has been building up from the moment he got here. Isla stares at the floor, her discomfort evident. I should put a stop to this, but I'm desperate to know the truth. I feel like I'm watching a car crash, yet I can't tear my eyes away.

'I presumed you were gearing up to sell the house,' Louis continues. 'That you were leaving here for good. How am I supposed to cope, looking at your face every day?'

'I don't understand,' I interrupt, trying to defend my husband. 'You've complained about Daniel leaving you, yet now you're saying you can't wait to see us go.'

'No, *you* don't understand.' Louis swivels towards me, his breath hot on my face. 'Because he's too ashamed to tell you the truth.'

Daniel cuts between us, grabbing his brother by the neck of his jumper. 'She's been through enough. Leave her out of this!'

'And what about me?' Louis pushes him back. 'You plagiarised my work!'

'Daniel?' I say, as Louis trembles in fury. I wasn't expecting this.

'*The Drowning Man* was mine!' Louis shouts. 'I painted it. It wasn't for sale!'

I look from Louis to Daniel, struggling to take this in. 'No . . . you're wrong. *The Drowning Man* is Daniel's.' Yet his accusation, it all makes sense. *The Drowning Man* was the foundation of Daniel's career, but it lacks the eloquence of his subsequent paintings. I take a sharp breath as I challenge my husband. Has he lied to me for all these years? 'Is this true? You . . .' I clear my throat. 'You plagiarised Louis's work?'

'It's not what you think.' Daniel reaches out to touch my arm. Instinctively I pull away. It's not what he's done, it's the sheer size of the lie that hurts. I knew he was hiding something, but I never imagined he was capable of such deceit. To his own flesh and blood too. Isla does not look surprised. How much does she know?

'Oh no, it's much worse than that.' Louis picks up the reins of our conversation. '*The Drowning Man* was private for a reason. We lost our parents not long after that.'

I'm blindsided by his words. So Louis painted his father drowning *before* it happened? How is that possible?

He steps forward and prods Daniel in the chest. 'Every day you're on this island is a mockery to their memory. You sold our family out the second you put a price on that painting.' His face is flushed, his eyes narrow, but Daniel's shoulders are back. He refuses to budge. I can see this coming to blows.

'If you weren't so pig-headed, you'd let me explain!' Daniel's voice rises, his fists clenched.

'It's too late for all that shite.' Louis prods him for the second time, goading him into a reaction. 'I want you and your family gone from this island.'

'Stop it! Stop it! Stop it!' Isla shouts, coming between them. 'Danny. Stays. Here.'

'Isla,' I say, hating to see her upset, but she turns and runs from the room.

'Catch yourselves on, the pair of you.' I scowl at Louis and Daniel. 'I'll go after Isla. I want this sorted when I get back.' It's an expression I've heard Daniel use, and I hope it puts an end to their ridiculous squabbling.

I see Isla in the hallway as she takes the stairs to her room. If there's one thing I've learned about her, it's that she hates confrontation. 'Sweetheart, are you alright?' I say softly. 'It's just a silly argument. They'll sort it out soon.'

But Isla is crying. 'Danny . . . has . . . to stay . . .' she says, between hiccups, as she takes the stairs to her room.

'Isla,' I say. 'Please don't hide away. You can talk to me.' Because there's more to this than a stolen painting. I've never seen Isla look so scared. 'What is it, Isla? I'm good at keeping secrets,' I say, in a low voice so as not to wake up Kitty. 'Trust me.' She pauses on the step and I can see she's mulling it over. 'I'm a doctor,' I continue. 'So I'm good at making things better. And I've seen all sorts, so nothing shocks me anymore. Whatever it is, I'm sure I can help.'

I follow her gaze as she looks to Kitty's room. 'The baby . . . You can't keep the baby here . . .' she sniffles loudly as she wipes her tears.

I can't hear crying. What does she mean? But then a door closes downstairs.

'Isla?' Daniel calls.

I exhale a frustrated sigh as Isla stomps heavy-footed to her room and closes the door. As Daniel climbs the stairs, I gently knock on her door, but all I hear is the click of her lock on the other side.

What baby was she talking about, my Kitty or one from long ago? Grim-faced, I turn towards my husband. I'm pissed off at him in more ways than I can think of.

'Louis has left,' he says, before I get a chance to speak. 'And we should talk.'

CHAPTER 25

DANIEL

I shouldn't have lost control. But the last thing I expected was for Louis to ask when we were selling up. Just like my father, he is the life and soul of any party, and popular with men and women alike. He's always the first to buy a drink, and the last to leave the table when a game of poker is in play. Therefore, I know what this is about. He's down on his luck again. No doubt he's lost his flat and is in debt up to his ears. He's barely exchanged two words with Isla, then he has the cheek to accuse me of only thinking of myself.

He'd promised not to mention the painting when I called with the dinner invite. But alcohol tempered his movements – that and hearing what Claire has planned for the place. I'd intended to speak privately and come to a financial agreement to suit us all. But now he's left me feeling like a piece of shit. I need to sort this out with my wife.

I catch her conversation with Isla as she mentions something about a baby. It's a sore subject and I know my sister is going to crack. I slam the door to alert her, then walk a few steps before I call her name. All I hear is the sound of her running to her room, as she usually does when she's upset. It's her safe space, her haven from the world, and I don't want Claire to see what's inside. Isla isn't like the rest of us, and I'm not talking about her Down's Syndrome. She's always been just Isla to me. She has had a lot to cope with, given she was there the night our parents died. I've told her a million times that it wasn't her fault, but it will always be a smudge on the horizon, blotting out even the sunniest of days.

But now I must face my wife and try to explain my deceit. This is the tip of the iceberg. If she's this upset over the painting, what will happen when she learns of the rest?

She follows me into the living room. It's a large space with an old-fashioned television that's rarely turned on. The Chesterfield sofas and plump cushions make it a comfortable spot. Some of my father's old wildlife paintings are hanging on the wall. I stoke the fire back into life as Claire takes a seat.

'This place hasn't changed much over the years,' I say. 'At least we have better furniture, a dishwasher and TV . . .' Sitting here, with the fire crackling, it's easy to be smothered by the past. My glance falls on an old painting of the island's three-metre-tall standing stone. It is thousands of years old, and a sister to the standing stone on Bere Island. Claire catches my eye. She's waiting. But I'm not ready yet, and I give her an awkward smile. 'The legend goes that a giant on the mainland threw stones at the Old Hag of Bera, but they missed and landed on the islands instead.' I pause, my head filled with the past. 'Isla used to love that story. Mam didn't need books when the island was so full of folklore.' I point to another painting: an icy scene of harsh stony hills and abandoned roofless cottages lined with snow. 'Winters . . . they were brutal back then. We all had our jobs to do. Isla's place was in the kitchen. Louis brought in turf from outside and swept and mopped the floors. I was woken at five thirty every morning to help Mam with the patients before taking the ferry to the mainland school. We had to walk the mile from the house to the dock, then be blasted by the cold air as the sea bobbed the ferry up and down.' I pause at the memories that shaped me as a man. 'The skin on the back of my hands was so chapped from the cold weather that it used to bleed. In the summer, I had blisters from turning turf and bringing it home. There were no days off. I worked long hours from an early age. We all did.'

'It sounds more like a workhouse than an institution.' Claire relaxes on the sofa, the anger leaving her eyes. 'It can't have been properly regulated. Where's the paperwork? The files? You should have been protected from it.'

I nod. Any paperwork was destroyed years ago. It's too late for regulation now. 'For as long as I remember, this place felt as much of a prison to me as to the women under our roof. I never felt like I belonged.' I take a seat next to Claire and she places her hand over mine. I've never told her this before. Now I've started, it's hard to stop. 'Sometimes, the women would tell me stories. A few were well travelled. I'd dream of visiting the places they described.' I recall how I'd sat on the landing as we spoke through the door. Some were just lonely, others took a shine to me. Sometimes I'd sit on the cold wooden floor until my bottom was numb. 'Anyway,' I say, moving the story on. 'After I left school, I went to London and hooked up with Sarah, who I met at night classes. She had an apartment in Wembley and was doing an internship at an art gallery in the city. She really inspired me, you know?' I tell Claire how Sarah had been a blessing, with her kind heart, colourful clothes and frizzy hair. 'When the lease ended on my flat, she insisted that I move in with her. I was ill at the time – more than I realised. She wanted to take care of me.' I recall those days when I was potless and struggling to stay afloat. They seem so far away now. I turn to my wife, who is studying my face. 'I was halfway through moving in my stuff when I collapsed. I didn't realise that I had pneumonia. Next thing I knew, I was waking up in hospital.'

I'm grateful that Claire remains silent, as I want to get this part of the story out of the way. 'Sarah brought me home from the hospital. She said she had a surprise for me. She'd found my painting when she was unpacking my things.' I rub my hands together, uncomfortable in my skin. 'She brought it to the gallery. The manager loved it so much, she put it on display.'

'*The Drowning Man?*' Claire says, returning me to the present.

'Aye.' I sigh. 'Sarah presumed I'd painted it after my father's death and that's why I'd hidden it away. But it wasn't my painting to sell. I wanted to tell her, but it was too late. There were so many collectors interested in it, they auctioned it off. That's when I painted another picture with a similar theme.'

'*The Burning Man*,' Claire confirms.

The burning man was half human, half monster. Instead of being consumed by the fire, he was strengthened by it. It made him more. 'It received critical acclaim. But *The Drowning Man* will always be known as the one that launched my career.'

'Why didn't you set them straight then? Why take the credit for Louis's work?'

'Because as far as he was concerned, the picture didn't exist.' I tell her about the first anniversary of my parents' death, when we struggled to keep it together as a family. The memory of Louis's drunken outburst is clear in my mind. I recall the icy coastal wind that caused my eyes to stream, the clear full moon and the booming thunder of the waves crashing against the rocks that night. 'Louis got it into his head that his painting was a premonition. He blamed himself for not warning Mam and Da. I told him that was crazy, that it was a coincidence he painted it, but it didn't stop him from lobbing it over the cliff edge.'

Claire listens, spellbound. It doesn't end there. I take a deep breath, weary from our evening. I only hope that she understands.

'Luckily, it didn't go far. I climbed down to save it after he left. I don't know what compelled me to keep it. When it sold, I thought it would go to a collector and never see the light of day.'

I can almost see my wife's thoughts turning over. 'The drowning man . . . how did he know?'

I shrugged. 'Da was always taking *Éireann Rose* to the mainland, but it was rare for Mam and Isla to be with him. Louis said he dreamed it. Who knows, maybe it *was* a premonition.'

The memory of that painting is imprinted on the back of my mind. *Éireann Rose*, our small wooden boat, being upended in the sea, with Isla and Mam clinging on for life. Half of the painting is above water, but the other half revealed what lay beneath. My father's haunted face as he stared from its depths, his white teeth sharp, his feet webbed. Did the drowning man metamorphosise and live on? It was the question on every art lover's lips. But what of my father? Sometimes, in the middle of the night, the question plays on my mind. He was unrecognisable when his body was found, battered from the rocks.

I dismiss the thought and exhale a deep sigh, drained of emotion as I go back to that time. Had Louis included the drowned babies in the painting, I would have destroyed it myself. I mention none of this to Claire. Nobody can know of the monstrosities that occurred that night.

I rise, telling Claire that I'll knock on Isla's door. I'm grateful for her understanding. She of all people knows that everyone makes mistakes.

But when I reach Isla's bedroom, I realise her door is open. She's not there, and according to Claire, nor is she downstairs. Isla has gone.

CHAPTER 26

CLAIRE

Anxiety returns like a hateful acquaintance as I stand in Isla's bedroom, surrounded by her things. Daniel's voice echoes downstairs as he calls for his sister. Mossie and Teresa are back from the pub and searching too. There's an urgency to their movements that is worrying. But I'm in awe of the sight before me, and a bit uneasy. Every inch of Isla's room is dedicated to the legend of the selkie. Daniel doesn't know I'm here; he's too busy worrying about Isla to notice he's left the door open. My gaze wanders over her unmade bed and on to the piles of clothes on the floor. On the dresser is an array of big and small seal ornaments, and there are posters of the sea on the walls. The air is thick with the aroma of damp and salt. It's as if she's captured the essence of the sea and brought it indoors. A black wetsuit dangles from a hanger and towels form a puddle on the floor. But it's the drawings that have stopped me in my tracks. The walls are covered with sketches of half-seal, half-humans – their big, dark eyes all on me. The images of the babies in their arms give me the chills. Blonde babies, Black babies, babies with ginger hair. Twin babies, naked babies, babies swaddled in blankets and all of them at sea. While Isla doesn't have the same flair for art as her siblings, the meanings shine through. She doesn't just love the legend she grew up with, she's obsessed by it. I'm about to open her dresser drawer when I hear Daniel's footsteps approach.

'You shouldn't be here,' he says, stony-faced. 'Isla doesn't like anyone touching her things.'

'But, Daniel, it can't be good for her, living like this.' I turn to the pictures. 'What does this mean? Have you ever asked . . . ?'

But Daniel interrupts me as he guides me out of the room. 'This is the very reason she wouldn't want you in here. This is Isla's private space. A place where she can be herself, without judgement from the outside world. She must have been upset to leave her room unlocked.'

'But the babies . . . what do they mean?'

Daniel exhales a harsh sigh. 'There were lots of babies born in Árd Na Mara. The women who came here were troubled. Some of them were pregnant when they arrived.'

'What happened to the babies?' I stand, rooted to the floor as he tries to guide me out of her room.

Daniel evades eye contact as he delivers a shrug. 'There were stillbirths, which isn't surprising, given their mothers were on drugs. Others were adopted.' He tugs on my arm. 'C'mon. I don't have time to talk about this now.'

I protest as I catch a glimpse of a drawing of a baby being swept out to sea. Its face is small and haunting, but the pink woollen hat with the star design is one that I recognise. 'Is that Kitty?'

'What?' Daniel sighs, impatient to get moving as he closes and locks the door.

'The baby in the drawing above her bed. It's wearing Kitty's hat.'

But Daniel's not interested as he marches down the landing. 'One baby looks much like another in Isla's pictures. I wouldn't make too much out of it.'

I want to ask more, but Daniel has pocketed the key and is heading down the stairs. I'm his wife, not a stranger. Why is he being so defensive?

I pull myself together. He's worried about Isla, that's all. The most important thing now is to find out where she is. 'Have you spoken to Louis?' I slide my hand over the banisters to keep my balance as I follow him down. 'The more people out looking for her, the better.'

'I can't get through. There's no signal on his phone.' Daniel is distracted, or 'mithered', as Teresa would say.

'And she couldn't have gone for a swim?' I'm trying to be practical, but even I know that's unlikely at this hour of the night.

'Didn't you see? Her swimming gear is drying out in her room.'

That explains the smell. Perhaps Isla likes it that way.

'Stay here,' Daniel instructs, pulling on his coat. 'In case she gets back. She can't have got far.'

But the cliff edge is treacherous at night. Even someone who's grown up here could slip and fall if their path isn't well lit. I hope she had the sense to take a torch.

Daniel is gone just minutes when Teresa returns from searching the grounds outside, her cheeks ruddy from the cold and her limp even more pronounced. She shakes her head in disbelief. 'God Almighty, we go out for a few hours and all manner of hell breaks loose.'

It feels like a dig. I was the one who invited Louis for dinner, after all.

I grab my coat from the hook on the wall. 'Can you stay here and mind Kitty while I join in with the search?' She's acting strangely tonight, and it takes a couple of seconds for my words to kick in. She stares at me uncomprehendingly, as if she'd forgotten about the baby sleeping upstairs.

'But we all need to look for Isla,' she insists. 'She's not safe in the dark. She could slip and fall.'

'It's not safe for you either, Teresa,' I say firmly, surprised at her attitude. Surely she's not suggesting we leave the baby alone? 'I'll go. You stay and listen out for Kitty. With any luck, Isla will come home.'

'Of course,' she eventually says. 'I'll stay, if you think that's best.' But her words are cold and robotic. Has she ever cared about Kitty, or has it all been an act?

I zip up my coat and pull on my wellington boots, taking a torch from the cupboard in the hall.

She stands at the open front door, watching my every move.

'Mind yourself!' she calls after me. 'Keep away from the cliffs!'

I raise my hand in acknowledgement as I trudge down the path. She's stressed, that's all. Perhaps Isla is like a daughter to her, after all. Daniel and Mossie are searching the coastlines, so I put myself in Isla's shoes and try to imagine where she'd go. I head towards the lighthouse. She's always liked her privacy, and she wouldn't find anyone there – that's if she can get in.

The wind whips my hair against my face, and I almost take a tumble against the broken ground. I pause to catch my breath, keeping my focus on the lighthouse path. The building looms ahead, a stunning beacon of white. It's unlikely anyone is inside, given that it's automated, and, according to Daniel, the door is always locked. It fires a beam of light into the sea, and I am guided by the dry-stone wall that surrounds it. I've become unfit. I can't believe I'm out of breath.

'Isla,' I shout into the night, but no response is returned, nothing apart from the steady crash of frothy surf against rock. The moon is blotted by dark clouds. The tide is in and making itself known. I climb the steps to the building ahead. The lighthouse stands as a testament to the unpredictable nature of the sea and is a warning to all. I only hope that Isla is safe, and her brothers' arguing hasn't driven her away. But where could she go? Teresa and Mossie came straight from the pub, so she's not made her way there. Would one argument really cause Isla to run away? As sincere as Daniel was, I could hear it in the cadence of his voice – he's holding something back. I blink to clear my eyes as the lighthouse makes another dazzling round. I don't know why I haven't visited it yet. The tall white giant jutting out of the landscape is impressive, yet strangely intimidating, as I approach.

I press my hand on the metal door handle. I expect resistance, but my lips part in surprise when it gives way. I've never been inside a lighthouse before and I'm not sure what to expect. A gust of wind forces the door closed the second I step in. It's colder inside than out, with stark white walls and the ominous sound of the whistling wind. I frown as I take in a pair of boots next to the door. A man's donkey jacket hangs on a hook. There's a bag of shopping on the floor. I peek inside. It's not shopping, it's empty beer cans ready for the bin. Has someone been sleeping rough here?

'Isla?' I call out, less sure of myself now.

My voice echoes as I step through the corridor and open a second door. I wrinkle my nose at the stench of overcooked fish. There are doors to my right and left, but my attention is drawn to the huge black metal spiral staircase ahead. I don't have time to dwell, as I catch sight of a mass halfway down the stairs. My breath catches in my throat as I realise it's not some*thing* but some*one*. Now I'm running up the staircase, and all I can see is the blood dripping down.

'Oh my God,' I whisper in disbelief. It's Isla, lying bleeding on the stairs. 'Isla!' I call, my boots clattering harshly against the circular steps as I rush towards her. 'Speak to me!'

But all I can hear is the screech of the wind and the buzz and clicks of the lights above. My heart picks up an extra beat as I reach out to touch her face.

CHAPTER 27

DANIEL

Forty-eight hours have passed. Forty-eight hours of waiting, agonising and praying that my sister will be OK. The journey to the
hospital was terrifying as the air ambulance brought her in. Heads
bowed, the paramedics loaded my sister on to the helicopter while
I followed behind. It was a blessing they were able to fly in such
unpredictable weather and the short journey to the mainland will
stay forever in my thoughts. I'd clutched her cold hand, mumbling
every prayer I'd learned as a child as I begged God to spare her life.
But all the while a thought rebounded in the back of my mind: why
did we deserve God's mercy after everything we did?

Claire visits each day, but I've barely left Isla's side. My sister can't
bear hospitals. Hates anything that takes her away from the island, in
fact. I saw Claire's face as she took in Isla's room, and the crudely drawn
pictures on her walls: dark, watery entities with soulless eyes and gaping
mouths. She doesn't understand what Isla has come from. How could
she? Today it hit me hard. Claire, however well-intentioned, just isn't
one of us. I reinvented myself when I lived in London. The only part
of me that was remotely true emerged through my art. But even that

suffered. Now I'm back where I belong. It was almost too little too late. I cannot leave Isla again.

I've paced the hospital corridors until the back of my legs hurt. I don't know how Claire used to do it, spending her days in a place where emotions are running high. Each person who passes tells a story: the family with balloons to announce a new baby, their children's faces lit up with excitement as they prepare to meet their sibling for the first time. Then there are the families who cling to each other, their tear-streaked faces relaying that they've received the worst kind of news. The doctors with shadows beneath their eyes, and tired nurses coming off a backbreaking shift. I don't know how they do it, but I'm grateful for the care they've lavished on Isla. The deep, bloody gash that matted her hair was frightening. But it was the concussion that worried us the most, and the length of time she was unconscious as her brain swelled.

Everybody has asked after her, some of the islanders even turned up to see if she's OK. The first thing I did was to offer to give her a blood transfusion. I've never been tested, but I know Isla's blood is rare. It was tested when she was eight and had her appendix removed. Claire is in her element here. She may not understand us, but she's growing stronger by the day. She comes alive in hospitals. This is the place she's most at home. I've watched her speak with doctors and nurses about Isla's care. They have all been kind and respectful. Some are even a little in awe of her work. I rise from my chair in the corridor as Claire strides towards me. She's been chasing an update and her face is fixed in a resolute expression that I've seen before. It's the one she uses when giving people bad news. My legs wobble slightly, and I take a deep breath, telling myself to be strong. Isla was so poorly when she got here, her lips blue, her limbs floppy. She briefly came around, but not long enough to say what happened to her. I've tried to stay by her side, but now I've been told to wait in the corridor as she has a check-up. The operation to reduce the swelling on her brain was deemed a success, but the look on my wife's face tells me something is very wrong.

'Come with me,' she says, taking my hand and bringing me into a side room where we're offered some privacy. She's dressed in black slacks and a designer blouse, looking the ultimate professional. Claire is far from vain but believes in power dressing. Already, she knows her way around this place and is very much in control.

'What is it?' I say, my throat thickening. I force myself to swallow. I need to be strong.

'Relax, Isla's fine.' Her smile breaks through, and I exhale in relief.

'Oh good,' I say, taking a seat beside her. 'For a minute there, I thought—'

'There's something you need to know,' she interrupts.

Now I'm back to square one, waiting for the dreaded news. But if it's not Isla, what could it be?

'You won't be able to donate blood, at least not for Isla,' she begins, and while I'm disappointed, it's not a huge deal. But then the second part of the bombshell lands as Claire takes my hand once more.

'Because you're not blood related. They've tested your blood against Isla's and . . . I'm sorry to say this, Daniel, but she's not your biological sister.' Then she looks at me, and I know she's half-expecting me to say that I knew. But the truth was, I didn't, and I'm completely taken aback.

'No . . .' I say, gathering my composure. 'They're wrong. Just because we don't have the same blood type, it doesn't mean we're not related.'

'I spoke to Teresa,' Claire said gravely. 'She told me before I left the house.'

My world jolts as I take in the news. How can this be?

'Go home,' Claire advises. 'She'll fill in the gaps. She only broke the news to me because I mentioned the blood tests. She got it into her head that the doctors would find out.'

Claire talks about DNA testing and tells me not to worry, that Isla will always be my sister in the true sense of the word. But I'm barely taking it in. If Mam and Da weren't Isla's parents, then who were?

CHAPTER 28

Mary

Then

'I can't do it!' Catherine screamed. 'I can't! I won't!'

But given she was two weeks over her due date, the poor woman didn't have a lot of choice. I didn't know who the father of her child was, other than he was a married man too politically important for such a scandal to get out.

Catherine held on to the bedrail on all fours as she fought against nature. A storm was raging outside, and we were at its mercy. Thankfully Teresa was an experienced midwife. I had often wondered what made her leave her profession on the mainland to work here for minimum wage. She may have received bed and board, but her hours were long and she would not get rich from the money she made.

Tonight her face was flushed, a sheen of sweat coating her brow and staining the armpits of her blouse. Her sleeves rolled up to her elbows, she gripped Catherine by the hand.

'Now you listen to me,' she said firmly. 'This baby is coming whether you like it or not, so the best thing you can do is get it over with.'

I winced as Catherine emitted another ear-splitting howl. 'Isn't there anything you can give her for the pain?' I couldn't bear to witness it.

Teresa grimaced at the mention of using up our stock of medication. She sucked a breath between her teeth, and Catherine roared once more. 'Go get the gas and air if it's bothering you so much.'

'I won't be long,' I said to Catherine, who was lost in a world of pain.

I was not a runner, but I sped down the stairs to our medical room. It was locked for good reason. Our stock of drugs was not finite, and some of the women beneath our roof would have loved to get a hold of them. But every second of pain was one too many for the young woman in our care. Catherine was one of several in our home who had fallen in love with the wrong man. The father of her child didn't want to know. Apparently, he was close to the Taoiseach and had a family of his own. His rejection had hurt so much that Catherine had set fire to his family's home. Now she was the one paying the price as she screamed Árd Na Mara down.

She should have gone to the hospital, but the storm would not have ensured a safe crossing. Now her baby was coming so quickly the trip was impossible anyway. I grabbed the canister of gas and air, locking the door before galloping back up the stairs. The room was one of the best in the building, with windows, curtains, carpets and a comfortable bed. Teresa said it was the least we could do, given her distress. Sometimes she surprised me with her small acts of kindness. Now my parents had passed away, Árd Na Mara had been left to me, but I was in no doubt – Teresa was the matriarch of our home. Catherine's screams echoed through the corridors.

She sounded like a wounded animal in pain. Breathless, I thrust the canister of gas towards Teresa as I ran through the door.

'It's too late for that now!' she shouted.

Catherine was on her back, writhing in pain. She gripped the bedsheets, her eyes tightly closed. I wrung a cool wet cloth over the basin and dampened Catherine's face. I felt ill-equipped and wasn't surprised that the men were keeping their distance. But Teresa wasn't having any of my squeamishness.

'You're no good to her up the dry end!' she roared, calling me to assist.

My stomach churned as I saw the baby crowning. With two long pushes, the small, helpless creature was born, wet and naked to our world. Catherine slumped back against her pillows, exhausted.

'It's a little girl,' I announced, as tears blurred my vision.

She emitted a soft, gurgling cry, and I watched as Teresa showed me how to clear her airways. I felt new admiration for the woman as she diligently explained each step. After clamping the cord, Teresa handed me the scissors and showed me where to cut. Then she weighed the naked baby, declaring she was seven pounds three ounces. I held out a warm towel from the radiator and we wrapped her up. But as she opened her eyes, I could see she was different. I looked at Teresa, but she didn't appear surprised.

'She has Down's Syndrome,' she said matter-of-factly. 'She's a very special baby indeed.'

She *was* special. Her eyes were so blue it was like looking into the sea.

'You're beautiful,' I said softly, realising I was the first person in the world to speak to the little girl. 'Would you like to meet your mammy?'

But Catherine was shying away. 'I don't want to see her!' she sobbed, throwing her hand over her face.

Teresa shook her head, offering little sympathy. 'She half makes a meal of everything,' she whispered. 'Take the baby over to the window.' She tapped Catherine on the leg. 'We're not done here yet, miss. We need to deliver the afterbirth.'

I brought the baby over to the window. Her cries were soft, but sounded healthy to me. 'Shush now,' I murmured gently. 'Would you like to see the island?'

I stood at the rain-dappled pane, looking out at the sea beyond it. White foam crashed against the rocks and I felt happy to be alive. For so long, I'd wanted a baby of my own and holding the newborn in my arms made me ache even more. The island had been battered by the storm, but it had so many colours and moods and I loved them all. Teresa busied herself cleaning Catherine up and changing the bedding. The room seemed so quiet compared to minutes before. Catherine had finally stopped crying and Teresa provided pads to help her leaking breasts.

'She needs a feed.' Teresa beckoned at me, but I felt reluctant to part with the baby I had instantly fallen in love with. I was giving her to someone filled with bitterness and hostility.

'Catherine, look at her. She's beautiful,' I said. 'A little island baby.' But again Catherine covered her eyes. I sighed in frustration 'If you'd just look.'

But Catherine was enraged, her words as sharp as knives. 'I don't want to look at her. It's her fault I'm in this mess. He never would have left me if it wasn't for that . . . that thing! Get rid of her.'

I stared in disbelief, but my judgement came from a comfortable place. I was a married woman with the security of a regular income and a husband. Perhaps deep down Catherine had a sense that her baby would be different in some way. One thing was certain, the little island baby didn't feature in any of her plans. The tinkle of cups snapped me out of my thoughts as Mossie entered the room. The tray was laden with a pot of tea, cups and rounds of hot buttered toast. But I didn't want a drink. I wanted to care for the newborn in my arms. Catherine would not accept her, despite Teresa's insistence.

'Very well,' Teresa sighed, turning to me. 'There's a bottle of formula all made up in the fridge. Warm it and give that poor child a drink.'

After taking one last look at Catherine, I left the room. Mossie was already downstairs, and a bassinet had been placed near the range. It wouldn't be the first time a young mother had rejected her baby under our roof. The women we dealt with were troubled, and barely had the emotional capability to care for themselves. I turned to follow Mossie downstairs when I heard Teresa speak with harshness in her voice. She was talking to Catherine, and there was no comfort in her words. I leaned into the door to catch what she was saying.

'Sure enough, you'll have to serve your time, so you're right not to get attached to the wee one. But you need to get over yourself. Wailing like a banshee won't do you any good. That man is not going to come for you. Sure you almost killed his wife and son.'

'He might,' Catherine replied meekly. 'He doesn't care about them. Tell him I want to see him. He might change his mind.'

'You stupid girl,' Teresa spat. 'Who do you think put you here in the first place? That man of yours made sure he wouldn't have to see you again.'

'You're lying, I don't believe you!' Catherine cried. But Teresa's reply was razor sharp.

'I heard it with me own ears. He said you meant nothing, and that you weren't worth what he got out of you. So best you get on with your sentence because you've no future with him.'

I bit my bottom lip. Teresa was a straight talker and wanted Catherine to snap out of the denial that wasn't helping her. But she'd already been through so much. Had Teresa pushed her too

125

far? The baby grizzled in my arms to be fed. Poor mite; no name, no parents and no home. What would become of her? I carefully took the stairs, telling myself that once the newborn was comforted that I could try again with Catherine.

She took her bottle, eyes closed, cheeks pink and plump. She truly was an island rose.

'Isla,' I said aloud, as the little one turned her full blue eyes on me. Teresa watched me from the doorway.

'You're a natural,' she said warmly, so different from minutes before. I returned her smile, part of me not wanting to let my island baby go.

'Shouldn't someone be with Catherine? At least until she's transferred to a secure room.' I shifted in my chair as the infant continued to feed.

'She's fast asleep and the door's locked,' Teresa continued. 'Hopefully she'll wake up in a better mood.'

But a sick feeling enveloped me as I thought of her up there alone. The baby was in my arms, sucking the bottle of warm formula milk, but it did not stop me worrying about the woman who'd given birth moments before.

I was about to tell Mossie to check on her when something flew past the kitchen window from above. A flash of white. A glimpse of long auburn hair mid-flight. The blood drained from Teresa's face, and time stood still as the dull, heavy thump of a body hit the ground.

'Jesus, Mary and Joseph!' Teresa screamed. She knocked over a chair, a flurry of legs and arms as she rushed outside.

I couldn't move. I couldn't bear it. I wanted to take little Isla and protect her from the truth.

Teresa roared for Mossie to come outside. Tears pricked my eyes. The uncharacteristic panic in her voice told me that it was too late. Catherine was dead.

126

CHAPTER 29

CLAIRE

I stand at the coffee vending machine waiting for my brew. I have never liked vending-machine coffee, but today it tastes like home. While the last two weeks have been fraught with worry, my time here has brought pleasure too. I'd forgotten how much I've enjoyed the hustle and bustle of a busy hospital, and the satisfaction gained from being treated like an adult. I inhale the scent of antiseptic and watch with envy as doctors and nurses stride past. Their days are filled with purpose, whereas mine feel empty and sad. Recently, my life has merged into Kitty's, and I've lost a huge part of myself. To the doctors treating Isla, I'm not Kitty's mum, or the much gossiped about 'Englishwoman' from Árd Na Mara. I'm a respected professional.

People on the mainland seem more professional and forward-thinking, and during the course of Isla's treatment, I've enjoyed getting to know them. But each day I return to Árd Na Mara and, if I'm honest with myself, I don't feel safe there. My thoughts keep wandering to Kitty on that strange, isolated island. Teresa may be minding her, but I miss her every second I'm away.

Daniel has barely left Isla's side since she was admitted, only coming home for sleep and a shave. She gave us all a terrible fright. The moment I found her unconscious on those steps, I was horrified. I was so torn at the time, not wanting to leave Isla but needing to call for help. Then Louis turned up at the lighthouse, pale from shock as he used his phone.

I called the Gardaí from the hospital. For the first time since I visited the island, I realised how lost I was without my phone. I've been walking around in a daze since coming here. It's not like me at all. I make a mental note to ask Daniel where it is when he next comes home. I couldn't believe that he didn't want to call the Gardaí. But now they've spoken to Isla, they're satisfied that her tumble was an unfortunate accident. I don't know, though. Something doesn't feel right. I think of the jacket hanging on the back of the lighthouse door, and the bag of rubbish I saw inside. I mentioned it to one of the officers, but she said it was probably someone taking shelter from the storm. Could it have been the same person who pushed Isla down the steps? I can't help but feel that Isla is being threatened into keeping secrets and when she hides away from the outside world, it's the only time she feels safe. Is that why she's so grateful to have Daniel here – so he can keep her safe? But who would do such a thing, and why? She could have died. What sort of secret is worth murdering for?

I sip my coffee as I mull it over. I don't want to suspect Louis, but he appeared out of the blue. Surely he's not capable of that. I shake my head as my thoughts crowd in. I told Daniel that I was going back to Selkie Island, but I've got plenty of time before the ferry. I'll pay one last visit to Isla before I leave. I want to run an idea by Daniel before I go. We've always planned on renovating Isla's room, so it would be a nice welcome-home surprise if we have it finished for when she gets back.

I get to Isla's ward and deposit my empty coffee cup in a bin before entering her room. I pass the other patients, my steps slowing as I see a slim, red-haired woman standing at Isla's bed. She's holding a bunch of colourful flowers. They're various shades of blue, white and aqua and remind me of the sea. Her expression is bright and happy, and she's chatting animatedly to Daniel, with the energy of someone who has just arrived. She's very pretty and seems to regard him warmly as she laughs and touches his arm. I catch Daniel's eye and the look on his face stalls me. His smile evaporates, and the colour begins to drain from his cheeks. It's as if he's been caught doing something he shouldn't. As the woman turns to face me, my stomach twists. Is this Martina, who he was talking about in his sleep? Why does he look like guilt personified? His face snaps back into his usual expression so quickly that I wonder if I've imagined it.

'I thought you'd left,' he says, coming to my side.

'I have . . . I mean, I am.' I'm flustered now. 'I just wanted to check on Isla one last time.'

It's easier than saying I want to stretch out each precious moment in the hospital that I can. My mother was a surgeon, and when I was little she'd bring me to her office every now and again and show me around. I'm pleased that I can replace my recent horrific hospital memories with positive ones. I return my focus to the woman, who is watching me with curiosity. I'm about to ask who she is when she stretches out her hand.

'I'm Aoife. Isla's best friend and all-round dogsbody.' Her bangles jingle as she gives me a hearty handshake.

'Oh,' I say, returning her smile as it all clicks into place. I can see her mother in her now. Aoife's a slimline version of her. 'You're Orla's daughter. You've been sorting out all the online bookings for us.'

'And anything else Isla finds for me to do.' She looks at her affectionately. 'She's a right slave-driver, this one.' But the words are delivered with a wink, and Isla returns a cheery smile, ready to join in with the game.

'Someone has to crack the whip,' Isla says, reaching out for the flowers, which Aoife has laid on the bed. There's a box of chocolates too, and a balloon shaped like a dolphin. It seems Aoife knows Isla well. I catch Daniel checking his watch, but I want to know more.

'I thought you were away, backpacking.'

'I was. But then I heard about Isla and came straight here. She can't get rid of me that easily, you know.'

I'm glad Isla has a friend who obviously cares so much about her. 'Come for dinner when Isla is out of the hospital. I'd love to hear more about your travels.'

'Sounds great.' Aoife turns to Isla. 'That alright with you, boss?'

Isla grins. 'As long as you do the washing-up.'

'See?' Aoife turns back to me in mock disgust. 'Slave-driver.'

I'm enjoying the banter, but Daniel's checking his watch again and giving me the concerned eye. The thought of my little one delivers a rush of emotion. My place is with her.

'I'd better get back to Kitty,' I say. 'Teresa's on nappy duty. I'm sure she's had enough of it by now.'

'Nappy duty?' Aoife tilts her head to one side.

The room falls quiet and I'm conscious of Daniel's hand on my back as he tries to guide me out of the room. He's been doing a lot of that lately, and I'm getting fed up with it.

'Yes, our baby. Kitty.' I frown as Aoife looks at me quizzically. 'Didn't you know? We have a little girl.'

Aoife's mouth falls open, and it's a couple of seconds before she finds the words to speak. 'A baby? In Árd Na Mara? No . . . I . . . I didn't know.'

My heart quickens, because she's not the first person to have reservations about a baby staying in Árd Na Mara.

'Oh,' I say, gathering my thoughts. 'I'm surprised you're not aware, given that everyone knows everyone's business on the island.'

I don't mean to sound rude but she's scaring me. But then I see her backpack, which is resting nearby, and I realise that she came straight here.

Aoife turns to Isla, who is rocking ever so slightly in her bed, staring at her flowers intently.

My husband breaks the brittle atmosphere with a chuckle as he looks at Aoife. 'We've not seen you, have we? That's what happens when you go off grid. I'll tell you all about her.' Then he turns to me. 'Sweetheart, you're going to be late. It's not fair on Teresa . . .'

I check my watch and exhale a sigh. I can't afford to miss this ferry, not with everything going on. I need to get back to Kitty. This will be a conversation for later. I say my goodbyes to Isla and Aoife, who seems to have got over her surprise. Why hadn't Isla mentioned Kitty to her friend before? I know she's been travelling, but they must have kept in touch for Aoife to be able to rush back after Isla got hurt.

I wait for the ferry, unable to get Aoife's stunned reaction out of my mind. It's a grey day, and the drizzle is making my hair frizz. I think of Kitty and feel my new-found confidence fall away. What have I done, leaving my baby on the island? Playing at doctor, then returning to that creepy old house with its dark, empty rooms. I know nothing about Árd Na Mara, and even less about the island it was built on. I think about the people who live there, with their strange, uncertain smiles. My perception of Daniel's birthplace has changed, and I'm not sure that I want to stay there anymore. But then I think about Isla and how anxious she appeared as our conversation took an unsettling turn. I can't leave until I get to the bottom of things. Seagulls scream above my head, vocalising my discontent.

Why is it so strange to have a baby in Árd Na Mara? Just what went on there? Daniel's night terrors are so disturbing that they're beginning to frighten me. Last night he pounded on our bedroom window, eyes wild as he screamed something about getting to the boat on time. My heart was beating so hard as I guided him back to bed, and it took me forever to get back to sleep. Yet I know if I ask him about it, he'll say he doesn't remember a thing. Just what happened in Árd Na Mara to affect him like this? I mull over what I know.

Daniel's father, Gabriel, was ambitious but selfish, only out for what he could get. His mother Mary was well-meaning but a doormat who took on the brunt of the work. As for Árd Na Mara, it seemed to be a sinister dumping ground for the women society wanted to forget. How could all the paperwork mysteriously disappear? What happened when Gabriel and Mary died and Árd Na Mara closed its doors as an institution? Teresa always fobs me off with a vague response. What happened to the women who were released back into society? Have any of them returned? Yes, there were problems, but there must have been success stories too. Why do people speak of the place with such dread? Then there were the babies, and Isla's fascination with the legend of the selkies. Did Mary tell her the tale of the selkie to explain what happened to the babies after they were taken away? How many babies were born? Who were Isla's parents, for that matter? It pained Teresa to tell me that Isla wasn't blood related to Daniel but that was as much as she'd say. I've tried to delve deeper into Daniel's past, but he always finds a reason not to talk about it. I know that women died here. Had childbirth robbed them of their lives? It was a lot more dangerous back then. I stare out to sea, wondering what secrets it's hiding. I inhale a deep breath of salty air. If Daniel won't go into detail then I know someone who might.

CHAPTER 30

THE ISLANDER

I didn't want to hurt Isla, but when she started talking, I didn't know how to stop her. She is one of our own, an island girl through and through. But she shouldn't have spooked me. Thankfully, there's no real harm done. It was just a little push. I didn't intend to kill her, but neither could I risk her blurting everything out. She's been told to stay quiet. It's not as if she wasn't warned. We all have a role to play when it comes to keeping Selkie Island safe.

Now she's lying in hospital and I hope to God that she's learned to keep her mouth shut. I've tried to get her alone, but it's impossible with so many people around. Ahead of me, a member of staff mops up a spillage, and I dodge the hazard cones. I hide behind my flowers as I stride down the corridor, head down. I hate being on the mainland, but what choice do I have? At least the visitors have left her ward. There are four beds in this room, and I'm grateful that Isla is situated in the furthest corner. She's wearing headphones, so she doesn't see me until I'm almost upon her.

She jumps at the sight of me standing at the end of her bed. I emit a nervous laugh as she grips her waffle blanket. We've spoken countless times. I'm no stranger, that's for sure. But today I've come to issue a warning and she can see it written on my face. Isla communicates better without words. I draw the thin blue curtain around us, ensuring our privacy as visiting time winds down. From my knowledge of the hospital and how it works, we have another ten minutes or so.

'I was going to bring chocolates, but I bought flowers instead. We wouldn't want you to choke, now would we? Especially when you're so accident prone.' I draw back my lips in a smile. 'It was quite the near miss, you falling down the steps. You could have died.'

My message has hit home. She's staring at me, eyes wide, knuckles white as she holds on to that blanket for all she's worth. She looks like she's going to scream and I press a finger to my lips to shush her once more.

'It's OK,' I say, taking a seat next to her bed. 'There's nothing to be afraid of. It's just little old me.'

But it's not little old me, not when I'm on my own like this. I've warned her once before when we argued on the edge of the cliff. She knows what I'm capable of.

'Sorry you fell down the steps. Lethal, aren't they?' I choose my words carefully. 'You were acting the eejit, weren't you? Threatening to tell our secrets to all and sundry.' I take a carnation from the bunch and stroke the long stem. 'But sure everyone makes mistakes.' I stare at her, wondering if I'm getting through. I want her to say that she's sorry for what she made me do, but she's sitting there, hugging her knees, tears filling her eyes. I peep through the gap in the curtain surrounding the bed, before turning back to her. 'We had a deal, Isla. You've as much to lose as anyone. Do you know what they do to girls like you in prison?' She flinches as I rip the petals from the stem. 'To them, you're a prison officer. You locked up women for years.'

'No, no, no . . .' She's shaking her head now. 'I was their friend.'

'And even if they believed you,' I continue, ignoring her distress, 'you'll never see the sea again. Imagine that, being locked up in a strange place, with violent offenders. They carry knives in those places, you know. I've heard all the stories.' Big, fat tears trickle down her face as I take another flower from the bunch. 'Are you going to tell the Guards who pushed you, Isla? Because next time . . .' I rip the petals and scatter them on Isla's bedclothes as she quietly sobs.

'Stop!' she exclaims, pulling the bouquet back as I reach for a rose. 'I won't tell.'

I tilt my head to one side, amused to see her so upset about the destruction of some boring flowers. I've known this woman all her life, and she still manages to surprise me.

I take a tissue from my pocket and hand it to her. 'Good girl. Don't you worry about Claire. She'll be gone soon. Then things can go back to how they were.' I stand, gathering up the petals to throw into the bin. Her shoulders drop an inch with relief as she realises that I'm about to leave. The rattle of a nearby trolley makes me check myself. 'We're friends, aren't we?' I say, because I can't afford for her to act all jumpy with other people around. She responds with a nod of the head. 'Now give me a smile,' I say, before pulling the curtain back. She sniffles, forcing her lips into a grin.

Then I'm away, confident that she won't tell. But Isla's little accident is bound to raise questions in the Englishwoman's mind. I have more work to do. The island isn't safe yet.

CHAPTER 31

MARY

Then

Catherine's death changed everything. I will never forget the sickening sound of her body thudding against the hard, frosted ground. The moments following her fall felt surreal. 'What? No. Noooo!' I'd screamed, high-pitched and disbelieving as I tried to comprehend the horrors of what had just occurred. Teresa, slack-jawed with shock, knocked over a stool in her haste to get to the back door. The baby snuffled in my arms, oblivious to the drama, whereas every limb in my body began to shake. Sick to my stomach, I staggered out into the hallway, cradling the wee one close to my heaving chest. 'Gabriel!' I'd shouted, barely managing to call my husband's name. 'Come quick!' A damning slam of a door followed upstairs. Gabriel appeared, not from the basement, but on the landing, before taking the stairs two at a time. Coldness enveloped me. I'd barely seen him all day, so why was he coming from the direction of Catherine's room? I didn't need to tell him what had happened. As he rushed past, it seemed he already knew.

I couldn't face seeing Catherine, so I waited in the sitting room, my heart aching as I sobbed. What a shocking start in life for the baby in my arms.

'It's going to be alright, little one,' I uttered, my heart heavy. I was inconsolable as Teresa broke the news that Catherine had not survived the fall. Gabriel stood at the fireplace, chewing his thumbnail as he worked out what to do.

'I'll cover her with a blanket,' Teresa said, her face paper white.

Mossie was the last to arrive, the stench of whiskey on his breath and his eyes watery from the wind. Only then did it strike me just how alike Teresa and I were, both managing the homestead while our men thought of only themselves.

Then it was just Gabriel and me, the orchestrators of events which ended up with a motherless child. I shouldn't have let this happen. Catherine should never have been in that room when she was feeling so low. I knew what Gabriel was thinking as he stared at Isla, asleep in my arms. *Who is going to want her the way she is?* Well, I did, and I was willing to fight for her. But not until I had rid myself of the acidic words I needed to say.

'Was it you? Did you push Catherine out the window?'

What else would he be doing up there, just before she died?

Gabriel denied involvement, his face a storm of emotions. '*Comment peux-tu dire une chose pareille?*' he'd said, cross that I'd accuse him of such a thing.

'Then call the Gardaí,' I retorted. 'What are you waiting for?' I knew about more than he gave me credit for, including his secret basement phone.

'Get the fuck off my back!'

Gabriel's words reverberated with violence around the room. He rarely swore in my company, and it was enough to silence me. I swallowed back my tears as he strode out of the door.

'Hush now,' I whispered to Isla, who'd emitted a thin cry as she squirmed in my arms. 'Mammy's here.' The words felt like poetry on my lips. I knew then that I could never let her go.

Mossie was posted to the front of the house to ensure nobody stumbled upon the scene. Teresa was out the back, dressed in her coat and headscarf, standing guard over Catherine's body. I crept down to the basement, where Gabriel was on the phone. How many times had I stood in the dark, lonely corridor, listening to him flirt with the women under his care? But this time, his voice was solemn. When he said that everything was 'sorted', the pieces came together in a puzzle of deceit and lies. My stomach rolled as a wave of nausea overcame me. I couldn't listen to any more. Being part of what happened made me feel dirty and shameful. My parents would have been turning in their graves.

Gabriel met me in the kitchen, where I was walking up and down, cradling the baby I'd named Isla. 'I'm calling the Guards. But first, you have a choice to make.'

'Choice!' I said in a hushed whisper. 'What about Catherine's choice? Why did you put her in that upstairs room?' Because I knew my husband. He didn't need to physically force her out that window. Not when he could bend her to his will by words alone. This time he didn't deny involvement, but made me see what I could lose.

'What do you want me to say?' He gesticulated with his hands. 'That we are angels? Nobody under this roof is an angel, and that includes you.'

'What do you mean?'

I backed away from him. Because my handsome husband looked ugly at that moment, and it scared me to think what he was capable of.

'What do you think is going to happen to her?' He pointed to Isla, who was nestled in my arms. I loved her already, my little motherless child.

'Can't we adopt her?' It seemed like the natural conclusion. 'Please, Gabriel. I've wanted a baby for so long. This may be my only chance.' By then, we weren't even sleeping together very much.

'It's not that easy.' The whites of Gabriel's eyes flashed as he closed the gap between us. He was staring at the infant now, his face near mine. 'Her father is a powerful man. He will bury the truth – literally.'

'No!'

I couldn't bear to believe it. I knew from the start that Catherine was a special case, but I didn't fully understand the implications. I was so naïve back then, busy with cooking and cleaning and seeing no further than the end of my nose.

Gabriel explained that the islanders had been talking long before Catherine fell to her death. Lubricated by Guinness, Mossie had let Catherine's identity slip down the pub. Nobody could know about her pregnancy. The scandal had implications that would affect everyone.

'Isla's father is a married man,' Gabriel continued. 'A powerful one at that. It's safer for Isla if he thinks Catherine was pregnant when she died.'

I finally understood what Gabriel was so worried about. The father could not afford for his scandalous baby to live. And what sort of life would that mean for Isla if everything came out? My head was buzzing. Gabriel's voice softened as he told me not to worry. He placed an arm around my shoulder as his words flowed like honey, speaking in French as he advised me to take a few deep breaths.

'Just focus on the choice ahead,' he soothed, as Isla slept in my tired arms. When he was like this, gentle and caring, I remembered why I fell in love with him. He kissed the side of my forehead, wiping away my tears with his thumb. 'Either we give Isla to the authorities and confess, or Catherine's death will be recorded as suicide and we'll raise the little one as our own.'

My husband had friends in high places. He could make this all go away. I gazed down at Isla. I knew the answer, but it didn't take long for the harsh reality to creep in.

'Nobody will believe she's mine . . . will they?' It would mean lying that I'd been pregnant all along, but mentally I was doing the maths. I'd been working so hard for the last few months, only going to the shop and back. 'Orla . . .' I began, as I thought of my friend. But Gabriel silenced me.

'Don't worry about her. It's not as if you're close anymore.' He looked me up and down. 'Besides, you're never out of those baggy clothes. Look at your big, fat belly. Nobody could tell if you're pregnant or not.'

That was my husband. Kind one second and scathing the next.

'What about Mossie? You know what he's like when he's had a drink.'

Gabriel snorted. 'Don't you worry about him. I've got enough on that *bouffon*! Drunk or not, he won't breathe a word.'

He seemed so assured that I wondered what was going on beneath my nose? And who else was involved? But then Isla moved in my arms, her tongue poking out from between her rosebud lips. I melted at that moment. My thoughts switched to making it work. I *had* put on a lot of weight. Perhaps I could get away with it.

I blamed myself for Catherine's death when I should have blamed Gabriel. But I didn't want to see it back then. All I could think of was Isla and raising her as our own. There had been a few other babies born in Árd Na Mara, but I'd never felt like this before. I physically ached for a child of my own. I even thought better of my husband for suggesting it. But to him, she was a tool to blackmail me with later. I would have no choice but to go along with whatever he suggested when it came to running Árd Na Mara. Isla would come with her own set of challenges. She wasn't our flesh and blood. But I had wanted a baby for so long. I saw our future, and I turned to Gabriel to seal it.

'Do what you need to. As far as anyone needs to know, she's our baby now.'

I hid her away upstairs until Catherine's body was removed by the undertakers and everyone had left. She was buried in a forgotten part of the cemetery at the back of the local church. But she would not be alone for long. Soon, others would join her, and I'm ashamed to say that I kept silent about them all.

We christened the baby Isla, after the island, and it owned her as much as we did. Orla was supportive, but our friendship was never the same. Orla was no fool, but if she had her suspicions, she didn't say a word. By agreeing to be Isla's mother, I became bound into a deception so deep I would never find my way out. Little was I to know that Gabriel would use it against me at every turn. It was a small crumb of comfort that I had been there from the beginning, providing love when her poor mother's judgement was clouded by betrayal and pain. I should have been kinder to Catherine, and not left her alone. I should have stood up to Teresa when she tore a strip off her. I should have kept an eye on Gabriel. Those 'should have's' would haunt me for the rest of my days. But torturing myself wouldn't change things. I owed a debt to Isla's mother and vowed to give her daughter the best possible life.

CHAPTER 32

CLAIRE

There is a change in the air. It feels like everything has shifted. Isla's accident has been the focal point of conversation in the Smugglers' Inn. I've been down there a few times over the last couple of weeks, and it's always the same – heads swivel in my direction and the loud chatter drops to a low hum. Isla has been in hospital for over four weeks now. I've busied myself getting her bedroom ready for when she returns. She's going to love the sea theme that has brightened up the room.

But my good mood is marred by the fact everyone's talking about Louis and Daniel, and word of their argument has got out. I blame Mossie for that. People are always buying him drinks, and Guinness has a habit of loosening his tongue. Funny how he'll open up to anyone but me. I've tried to corner him a few times, but he always seems to have something urgent to do. Then I see him, skulking away to the cliff path which will lead him to the pub. But he keeps the house stocked with timber and turf, and helps Teresa when she asks, so there's not a lot that I can do. I've tried to speak to Aoife, but she disappears into the back room of the pub whenever I show up. I'm beginning to feel like a social pariah. The paint fumes in Isla's room have given me a headache, so I've taken myself out for a walk to clear my head. It's nicer now there's a stretch in the evenings, as I walk the cliff edge in the dusky evening light, but I'm no happier living here. I still find it hard to leave Kitty, even though she seems happy and content. There are days when I believe the island is a dangerous place. But while the past may be clouded in secrets, can it harm us now? But still . . . something is gnawing at the back of my mind. An unshakeable feeling that things aren't quite right.

I should go home now the sun is setting, but there's no point in speaking to Daniel. He'll only fob me off. Kitty is safe with Teresa, and Daniel's there if she needs anything. He wants me to gain back my independence, after all. There are workmen in our house; Daniel drafted in a team to get the boiler replaced quicker so they wouldn't have to come back. I've barely seen them and when I have, they've kept their heads down. So much for Irish people being friendly. I pause to admire the view, filling my lungs with revitalising sea air. I've come to know my way around this side of the island, but there's so much I have yet to explore – the graveyard, for one. I've asked Daniel to take me there countless times, but he's always managed to find a reason why we couldn't go. But now I don't need him, thanks to the map of the island that I found stuffed between two books in the living room.

I retrieve it from my pocket, all bent up – just how I'm feeling inside. My old life in London feels so long ago. On the island, it's as if time has stood still. I follow the map, grateful it's not raining, and smile as a rabbit crosses my path. Not a day goes by that I don't encounter wildlife of some sort, but when darkness closes in, the island can feel spookily isolated. Twenty minutes later, and I'm going around in circles. I pause as something rustles in the undergrowth ahead. I'm sure I've been here before. I take a small torch from my coat pocket and sweep it across the land to see a set of open rusted gates. I'm here.

The graveyard is encircled by a crumbling moss-covered stone wall. Leafless trees creak around me. Suddenly, I feel very alone. I press on, walking past row upon row, reading the same surnames and family lines. Some graves are so old that I can't make anything out. I touch the ribbon on a May bush, thoughtfully decorated over a child's grave. Painted eggshells shiver in the breeze. It's one of many Irish traditions that I have become acquainted with. I walk past the boundaries of the graveyard, casting my torch over small wooden crosses by graves that haven't been graced with proper headstones. That's when I find them. The graves of the young women who died far too soon. Catherine McGovern. Fiona Cassidy. Niamh O'Connor. Each of the dates coincides with when Árd Na Mara was run as an institution. There's no grave belonging to a Martina anywhere. All that's left to mark the women's passing is a small wooden cross and an even smaller engraving on each one. Apart from the date, that's it. No epitaph, no words of love. No flowers, nothing.

I want to pick some wildflowers and lay them as a mark of respect. But that's for another day. What about the babies of Árd Na Mara? I look for crosses to mark their graves but there's no marked resting place for those poor, lost little souls. The wind whistles around me. I'm about to turn away when I see the remains of a bunch of red roses beneath a crooked old apple tree. The cellophane they are wrapped in is sprinkled with rain, its bouquet long since withered away. No lilies, or chrysanthemums, but red roses. The type of flower you buy for a wife or lover. I bend to retrieve a note, reading it beneath torchlight.

To Martina. Much love.

The ink is too blurred from rain to make out the writing style. Has Daniel been here?

The hairs on the back of my neck prickle as I sense a presence. There is movement behind me. It's too big to be island wildlife. I don't need to turn around to know I'm being watched. My grip on my torch tightens as something scampers out behind me. My heart skips a beat as I spin around just as a goat trots out of the shadows with a defiant 'bah'. I exhale a laugh, slightly shaky now, as I tell myself it's time to get back. I turn for home and come face to face with the person who's been watching me all along.

It's Sean, the islander who has uttered two warnings so far. We eye each other warily. Has he been following me? He stands there, hands deep in the pockets of his old baggy trousers as he peers out at me from beneath his flat cap. His nose is red from the cold – or is it from drinking? He's chewing something as he watches, eyes narrowed. From what I've seen, he's fond of the pub. So what is he doing at the graveyard at this hour of the evening? I straighten my posture and turn to leave, watching him from my peripheral vision as I pass.

'You won't find answers there,' he says, and I stop in my tracks.

'Have you been following me?' I'm not going to let this strange little man intimidate me.

'Just watching. No law against it.'

'I think you'll find there is.' I glare at him. I've been searching for answers and now I'm face to face with the one person who may be able to give them. But can I trust him? What sort of person lurks about in the dark? But then the same thing could be said about me. I take a breath and compose myself. 'You said my baby wasn't safe at Árd Na Mara. What did you mean?'

He rolls his eyes towards me, a dark grin rising to his face. 'Is she still alive?'

'Of course she is,' I say, incredulous. 'And you should be careful what you say.'

He shrugs. 'I wasn't trying to frighten you. It was a warning, that's all. That place is cursed. Best you get yourself back to the city where you belong.'

He's taking too much pleasure from this. I wonder what I'm doing here, listening to this superstitious old man. He's clearly got mental health issues and I don't feel safe.

'Mark my words!' he calls after me as I leave. 'That babe of yours won't see the summer! They never do!'

His words are like arrows, and they've found their target. I round on him, hot anger welling inside me as painful memories are shaken loose.

'How dare you say such a wicked thing! Just stay away from me and my family, you hear? Or I'll have the police on you!'

'No Gardaí will set foot on this island,' he sneers, standing his ground.

I take a breath to calm down. I'm tired and cold and I just want to get home. But as I take the path back, I mull over his words. He's right. In all the time I've been here, I haven't once seen a police officer. Has it always been this way? I think about the night Isla got hurt. What if she'd been pushed? Would they have come from the mainland then? The women in those graves were so young when they died. And as for Martina . . . had she been buried in an unmarked grave? Was there a proper investigation launched into their deaths? It seems that Selkie Island has its own laws. Does that include the islanders too?

Instead of going home, I retrace my steps to the lighthouse. I've visited a few times since I found Isla, but the door has always been locked. I've never visited it since at night though, and I check over my shoulder, grateful I'm alone as I make my way down the weather-beaten path. Tonight the breeze has calmed, bluish moonlight guiding my way. Island weather can be violent, but I live for its softer days, when it's sweetly fragrant and lush.

I switch off my torch. I don't want anyone to know I'm here. Daniel has reverted into himself, spending his days out painting and his evenings in the basement room touching up his work. At least Isla's on the mend, and we can get back to the planned renovations, but I won't sleep until I know more. Someone was living in that lighthouse the night I found Isla. How else to explain the donkey jacket on the door and the bag filled with empty beer cans that I saw when I first went in? I haven't kicked

146

up a fuss because I don't want to spook whoever is there. By the time Daniel caught up with us that night, paramedics were preparing to take Isla away. If I hadn't found her, she could have died. I press against the door handle, feeling a jolt of surprise as it opens. Quietly, I enter.

CHAPTER 33

CLAIRE

The smell of bacon hangs heavy on the air, and I can hear the crack and spit of frying eggs. I head towards the door on my left, following the sounds. He's here – the person I suspected, living rough, just as I knew he would be. I'm faced with a tall, burly man.

'Feck's sake!' Louis shouts, turning to greet me, his spatula held tight in his hand. I'm not surprised to see him here. 'Are ya trying to give me a heart attack, is that what it is?' he says, turning off the small gas stove. Louis is wearing a woolly jumper with a hole in it, dirty jeans and thick grey socks. There's a can of beer on the side and an electric fire has injected some warmth into the poky room.

I smile at the irony of *me* frightening *him*, but I'm still on my guard. I need to get to the point. I've been gone some time and Teresa will be asking questions if I don't get back soon. 'How long have you been sleeping here?'

He turns back to his pan and slides some greasy-looking fried eggs, sausages and bacon on to a chipped plate.

'Longer than I want to,' he replies. 'I could hardly go home now, could I? Not with Little Lord Fauntleroy living there.'

Ignoring the barb, I perch on a wooden stool next to a small fold-up table. I loosen my scarf and unzip my coat a little. 'But Teresa said you haven't lived in Árd Na Mara for years. Where have you been before now?'

'Here and there,' he says sulkily, but I hold my gaze and he relents to my question.

'I was renting a place, but I had to let it go. Couldn't afford the rent.'

'How did you get in here?'

'Orla gave me the key. I'm here with her blessing.'

He rests his plate on the table and roots around in a drawer. Sounds echo loudly in this space and the cutlery clatters as he takes out a fork, then a sharp knife. As I glance at his knife, I'm uncomfortably aware that it's just the two of us here. The lighthouse is far from homely. It feels industrial and cold. The sound of clicks and whirrs fills the air as the giant beacon spans the island from above. But I'm not here for a guided tour. I must keep going. I don't want to believe that Louis would hurt Isla, but like the rest of his family, he's holding back. The table wobbles as he sits. He's a big man and his knees bump against its narrow legs. I want to ask him if he pushed Isla but as we sit in this isolated space, my courage deserts me. Instead, I skirt around the subject, shifting on my seat as the waves rhythmically crash and churn against the rocks outside.

'Why did Orla tell the Gardaí that this place has been lying empty the night Isla fell?' Teresa informed me she'd said it, probably in an effort to put a halt to my questions. But the comment has played on my mind ever since.

Louis's face contorts before resting in a frown. 'Because I asked her to. Since Mam died, Orla's been like family. You wouldn't understand that, coming from the city, but—'

I prickle as his comment touches a nerve. I'm fed up with being treated like an outsider.

'Don't give me that, Louis.' I shake my head in disgust. 'I'm not an alien from some distant planet. Why did you lie about staying here?'

'Because if a man doesn't have his pride, what does he have?' Louis's words are delivered with passion and I get a feeling they're ones his father had spoken while Louis was growing up. He pauses. Takes a breath. 'Orla and Kieran offered to put me up, but I told her this was just a stopgap until I sorted things out at home.' He starts tucking into his food, pausing mid-chew. 'What about you? What are you doing out here this hour of the night?'

'I'm trying to get to the bottom of things,' I reply. 'Isla's fine, in case you're interested.'

'You don't need to tell me,' Louis said, somewhat affronted. 'I've been in to see her. I know how she is.'

'Oh, I wasn't aware.'

Louis snorts before spearing his sausage with his fork. 'You're "not aware" of a lot of things.'

'Then how about you enlighten me?'

But he ignores my comment and eats like he's been starved for a week. The sound of his chewing is getting on my nerves.

'Why don't you come back with me to Árd Na Mara?' I say, trying a different approach. 'Your old room is empty. I'm sure Teresa would love to fuss over you again.'

Louis wipes his mouth with the back of his hand. 'What do you want from me, Claire? Do you think I put Isla in hospital? Because I wasn't here when she fell.'

'I'm not saying you've hurt her,' I say, with more conviction than I feel. 'But something *is* troubling her, and you know more than you're letting on.' I exhale in frustration as Louis continues to shovel food into his mouth. 'I just want to help.'

Louis chews steadily, his gaze in the middle distance.

'How long have you known,' I continue, 'that Isla isn't blood-related?'

At least Louis doesn't insult me by trying to act surprised. He sighs, his face shadowed with weariness as he drops his knife and fork.

'Da told me.' I stare at him in silence. I'm not moving until he gives me more. Reluctantly, he continues. 'Her mother was Catherine, a patient at the institute. She was done for arson and shipped to Árd Na Mara to serve her time. But she was pregnant when she got there, and everything was hushed up.'

I stare at Louis hopefully, waiting for long-buried answers to be revealed. 'I've been to the graveyard. Catherine . . . Fiona . . . Niamh . . . Why did all these young women die?'

'Catherine died at her own hands.' He takes another deep breath. 'The silly mare threw herself out of the upstairs bedroom window not long after Isla was born.'

I am shocked by his lack of compassion. 'Jesus, Louis, have a heart. The poor woman must have had mental health issues. What about the others? Are you telling me they were suicides too?'

I'm not surprised when he nods. 'Some from suicide. Some were sick when they came to us. Others died giving birth. But the institute was open for years. Hundreds of women went through those doors. There's bound to be a few losses along the way.'

'There must have been records,' I continue.

But Louis shrugs. 'It wasn't like it is now. We didn't use computers back then. We got rid of most of the paperwork after Mam and Da died.'

Got rid of? According to Teresa, it was handed over to officials. I see an image of him in my mind, flinging *The Drowning Man* painting over the cliff edge on the anniversary of his parents' death. Was that how he disposed of the paperwork too?

Louis cracks open a can of beer, mumbling something about the 'Spanish Inquisition'.

I press on. 'Does Isla know about her mother?' I say, because now I'm wondering why this has never come to light.

'Mam and Da are down as parents on her birth certificate, so I can't see how she'd know.' He gives me a cautionary glance. 'Don't tell Danny I told ya. Some things are best left in the past.'

At first glance it seems like an act of kindness that Gabriel and Mary passed Isla off as their own. I turn to Louis, unsure. 'Do you know who Isla's biological father is?'

'How would I?' Louis swigs from his can of beer. 'Sure I wasn't even born back then.'

I check my watch. It's well after nine. I have so many questions, but I've already been gone too long. 'Who's Martina?' I ask, zipping back up my coat as I stand to leave.

Louis's eyebrows shoot up at the mention of the name. 'Who told you about her?'

'I asked first.'

'That's no business of yours,' Louis says firmly, his irritation evident as he pushes back his seat. He's standing and I'm aware of how small the space is around us. 'I think it's time you left.'

'But . . .' I say, as Louis advances upon me. I have clearly struck a chord as his irritation has escalated to anger.

'Off you go,' he says, guiding me towards the door. But I dig my heels in. 'Come back with me. Wouldn't it be nice to present a united front for Isla when she comes home?'

'Tell that to your husband.' Louis opens the door to let me out.

'What do you mean?'

'He's made his position clear. He said I'm not allowed to set foot in me own home. So before you come knocking on my door, have a word with him.'

'But that was just a silly argument. He didn't mean what he said.'

'I spoke to him yesterday at the hospital. He seemed fairly calm to me.'

My mind is spinning. I know nothing of this conversation. 'I'll talk to him,' I say. 'But first, tell me. Just what's going on with your family, Louis? Because I know you're hiding something. You all are.'

Louis scowls in fury, his lips pressed tightly together, his muscles tense. 'You've no idea what you're getting yourself into. Do you even know who you're married to? You need to watch your back.' He slams the door behind me, and I'm out in the night air, the sound of the waves thundering in my ears as I try to make sense of it all.

CHAPTER 34

DANIEL

I stand beneath the harsh lights of the basement room, left breathless by my latest work of art. I take in the colouring, a natural chiaroscuro of depth and strength with its blues, greys and black. I barely remember painting it and I am transfixed. This image is so unlike the others, in which Martina is either facing away, or a blur in the distance. Today, she faces forward, standing at the window of the bedroom in Árd Na Mara, her palms pressed against the glass as she stares mournfully out to sea. Dormant memories are reawakening. I called out her name in my sleep again last night. I was sweating profusely, reliving the night my parents died. Martina played such a big role in my life during that traumatic time. Yet I can't tell Claire of our shameful family secret. What good would it do now? I think about the flowers I left on her unmarked grave and the note I could barely bring myself to write. I wanted to say so much more. For now, I express myself through my paintings, because 'sorry' will never be enough.

I stiffen, aware of someone standing behind me.

It's Teresa. Her eyes are not on me, but on the painting. Her thick fleece dressing gown covers her pyjamas and a hair net masks her hair. How long has she been standing there?

'You've captured her likeness well enough.'

Her features are stony, her voice flat. She doesn't need to ask who it is. We all remember Martina and the impact she had. I don't know how to respond, so we stand in silence, drinking in her image as it is brought to life on the canvas.

'I'll always remember her like this,' I eventually say. 'I can still hear her singing that lullaby every night. I don't believe in ghosts but . . .' I catch my breath as emotions close in. 'If there were such a thing, then this is where she'd be, standing at that window, waiting for her babies.' I rub my mouth, because the words are distasteful, but need to be said. 'How could they do it? You were there. Why did they do it? You've never said.'

Teresa sighs, looking old, as the ceiling lights illuminate each crease in her face. 'If you're looking to point the finger, then maybe you should start with me. I know you've thought it. I can see it on your face every time we meet. You've got questions, lots of them. But you're too scared to ask.' She's referring to Isla's parentage. I'm still coming to terms with the bombshell. I don't want to discuss it. Not yet.

'I'm not the only one with questions.' I return my gaze to the picture. 'What's Claire going to say when she sees this?'

'Aye, sure enough. And the agreement was that you'd tell her the truth as soon as she was strong enough to hear it. This is a family matter. Put an end to her questions before any outsiders get involved.'

'But this . . .' I gesture towards the picture. 'How can I explain what happened?'

'Tell her to start with me. I should have done more to stop them.'

155

'Then why didn't you?' I finally ask the question that's been in my mind from the day that I returned.

A shadow crosses Teresa's face and I regret uttering the words. She's been good to us. The last thing I want is to is cause her pain.

'When I first came to the island, I saw it as a refuge. Mossie and I . . . well, I don't want to get into that now, but we were in trouble and needed an escape. Your father gave us a way out.' She rubs her arms as the temperature in the basement drops. Despite our new heating system, there are still times when the rooms turn cold. 'At first, I was biding my time, counting the days until I could return to the mainland. But then I came to love the island,' Teresa continues. 'And the people who live here . . . for all of their faults. Do you want my advice, Danny?'

'Always,' I say simply, because I'm feeling adrift right now. The floors above our heads creak and moan as the house settles in for the night.

Teresa nods to herself, as she always does before imparting well-meaning advice. 'Claire comes from a normal family. All this upset . . . it's alien to her. You've got to present a united front.' She slips her hands into her dressing-gown pockets, just as my mother used to do all those years ago. 'Did you know your brother has been living rough?'

'No . . . I . . . I didn't.' I'm shocked to hear it, and a little ashamed. I should have been there to support him.

'It's time he came home,' Teresa continues. 'Get Louis back on side and we'll face this together. All of us.'

'But it's not that easy,' I say, recalling his outburst the last time we met. 'He hasn't forgiven me for *The Drowning Man*.'

'Then apologise. Get down on bended knee and beg if you must. Having you all together will settle Claire. She can't understand why you're all at odds with each other and, to be honest, after all this time, neither can I. Tell him everything . . . and I mean everything. Louis is a grand lad when he's sober. If he sees what you're facing, he'll support you. It will be good for Isla too.'

'You think that will help Claire . . . when the time comes?' I ask, unconvinced.

'Aye.' She delivers a small but reassuring smile. 'But tread lightly. People react in different ways.'

'Yes, but the baby . . .' I begin. I can't see any way out of this other than telling her the truth. 'How can I tell her to give up the one thing she loves most in the world?'

CHAPTER 35

MARY

Then

I stood, staring out of my bedroom window, waiting for the opportunity to get my husband alone. So many times, I wanted to have it out with him, but each time my worries silenced me. It was my own fault, because I'd grown too dependent on him. Since my parents died, I ran Árd Na Mara surrounded by people Gabriel had taken on. Their allegiance was with him. There was not one person who I could talk to who wouldn't report back to him. Each of them held their own secrets and Árd Na Mara was a sanctuary to them all. Police didn't visit the island. There was never any cause to. Selkie Island was the perfect hideaway.

It was not all bad. Once a week, Gabriel and I would visit the mainland and have a meal in his favourite French restaurant. On these days, I felt like a fish out of water next to my handsome, well-dressed husband. I wasn't blind to the attention that Gabriel received, but then they would look at me, their gaze curious as they tried to work out what he was doing with me. Then Gabriel would pick up on my insecurities, place his hand over mine, and tell me what a wonderful woman I was. When he shone his light on you, you felt like the most important person in the world. Even if I went out annoyed and resentful, I warmed to his company with each minute that passed. We'd discuss current affairs, and he'd tell me how much he missed painting and would one day take it up again. He'd talk about how we met, and I would reminisce about what the island was like back then.

Warmed by whiskey and a good meal, we'd take the boat back to the island. I would kiss each of my three children goodnight and count my blessings as I said my prayers before I went to sleep. The three of them were so different. Isla, my little island baby, with her sweet, loving nature and devotion for the sea. Then Danny, always chasing butterflies or holding a crayon in his hand. An artist, like his father, whose perception of the world was much bigger and brighter than mine. Then Louis, my dark-haired, brooding little boy. I saw so much of his father in him. He had not been expected, but he was truly a gift from God.

I missed my parents bitterly and wished they were here to see them. But after the pain of their illnesses, the end had been a blessed relief. Besides, they would be so ashamed to see what Árd Na Mara had become: a house of ruin, of corruption and greed. No amount of outings with Gabriel could make me at ease with that. But what power did I have to make it change? I'd signed so much of the business away to my husband. Without the extra money he made, the house would fall to ruin. But there were only so many errant mistresses to deal with.

Gabriel was constantly coming up with new ways to make Árd Na Mara pay. Up until now, I'd gone along with it. What would become of me if he left? I had three children to rear, but I could not keep my silence about my husband's infidelities. His trips away were one thing, but now it was going on under my roof. I clenched my fists as anger bloomed. There was no denying the truth. Once, women arrived at Árd Na Mara pregnant, but now and again women were falling pregnant while they were here. Everyone who worked here seemed happy to turn a blind eye, except for me. It was humiliating, and I was grateful that my children were too young to understand. I stiffened as the steady drum of his footsteps echoed up the stairs. He always waited until long after I had gone to bed, in the hope I'd be asleep. But I knew what he'd been up to as he delivered the women's meds, and I was in no doubt that the women he flirted with gladly gave themselves to him. Age had not marred his stunning good looks but enhanced them. Despite everything, I still loved him. I had to take my share of the blame.

I turned away from the window as the sound of approaching footsteps rose from the landing. He was always the last person to lock up. Sometimes his night-time security checks took up to an hour to complete. He opened the door, having the decency to look sheepish as I folded my arms. I knew I couldn't compete with some of the young women who he treated like playthings. In my floor-length nightdress, and curlers in my hair, I wasn't going to turn his head. But he owed me some common decency, given I was his wife. But whatever happened tonight, I knew I wouldn't be leaving. Gabriel controlled our income. Even if I wanted to, where would I go?

'I need to talk to you, Gabriel.' Already I could feel my pulse picking up. 'And I'm not putting this off,' I added, before he gave me his usual line of '*La nuit porte conseil*,' as he advised me to sleep on it. 'You can sit down and listen to what I have to say.'

Gabriel's eyebrows rose at this sudden showdown. I had always been the chatty sort, but since losing my parents, I avoided confrontation because I'd been through enough pain. I could talk forever about the weather and the island's fishermen and even what was on television that day. But when it came to confronting my husband, my mouth was barren. But not tonight. This had been building up for months.

Gabriel sat on the edge of the bed and pulled off his shoes. 'Do we 'ave to? I'm tired. It's been a long day.'

But I was too worked up to back down. '*You're* tired?' I stomped around to his side of the bed and waggled my finger in his face.

'Well, guess what? I'm tired too. Tired of you being unfaithful to me every night of the week. Tired of you breaking every marriage vow you made. And most of all, I'm tired of being treated like a doormat. I'm not taking this anymore. Either you change or leave for good.' A tearful heaviness settled over me as I allowed the words to sink in.

Gabriel's mouth twitched in a smile. 'What's brought this on?' he said, his eyes mocking as he looked me up and down. ''Ave you been on the gin? Or 'ave the English landed?'

I wanted to slap him. He was asking if I had my period, but his culture dictated that he used the tired euphemism referring to when the British Redcoats fought Napoleon's army in the Battle of Waterloo. I used to find his ways endearing, but now he was getting on my nerves. 'Really?' I said instead. 'How would you feel if I told you I was sleeping with other men? Even if you didn't care about me, wouldn't you prefer to be spared the humiliation? I know what you're doing with those women. They're no Virgin Marys. They didn't get themselves pregnant.' I tilted my head to one side as I tried to get through to him. 'It's bad enough, taking in other people's shameful secrets, but now *you've* decided to join in!' I cursed myself for crying, but my heart was filled with grief. Our marriage was dead.

'You're right, they didn't arrive with child.' Gabriel rose, his smile evaporating. 'But it isn't what you think.' My stomach churned as I awaited his admission. He didn't deny it. I took a deep breath, steadying myself against the bedpost.

My husband looked carefully around the room, as if hoping someone would walk in and save him. When he realised he was trapped, he drove a hand through his hair before standing to face me.

'You don't know how expensive it is to keep this place going. Food does not come cheap. Neither does the upkeep of this great big building. You always think the worst of me, Mary. But everything I do is for you and the children. What do you think my business trips are for?' He continued with a shake of his head. 'You see the hotel and bar receipts and think I'm having fun. I mix with influential people. You can't do that on a pittance.' He hesitated in that moment, and I noticed the tremble on his breath. Then he spoke about being in business and staying one step ahead. I was shaking from a mix of anger and humiliation. The air in the room was thick with unsaid words.

'I have acquaintances . . . rich people,' he continued. 'They wanted to help me out. They put me in touch with some of their friends, the Lynch family. More of a clan than a family . . .' He stared at his hands. 'They knew about the women who came to us with child.'

'The women? What do they want with them?' I guessed where this was heading, and I was filled with disgust.

'No, no, hear me out. It's not what you think,' Gabriel said, reading my face. 'They help infertile couples. Good, decent people who pay good money to take an unwanted baby and raise it as their own.' Gabriel didn't lower his voice as he spoke, most likely because I was the last to know. 'I waited and waited, but no more women came to us with child. I . . . I decided to make it happen. It meant nothing to me. You and the children are my world.'

'What?' I uttered, numb. 'No! Don't you dare try to justify what you've done.' I should have walked out of the door and slammed it behind me after hearing his feeble excuses, but I was rooted to the floor.

He rubbed his thumb against my cheek. 'Think of it as a kindness. We're changing lives. You, of all people, should understand.'

I'd always known that Gabriel would never be mine alone. His mainland affairs were part of a silent agreement. But I wasn't putting up with this.

'Don't talk shite! This cannot and will not happen here,' I said finally, a quiet fury in my voice. 'Not for money, not for anything.'

'OK, OK. Then I have no choice but to tell you the truth.' Gabriel turned to face me, and for the first time in my life, I saw fear behind his eyes. 'I've run up debts. Big debts. I didn't tell you because I was scared you'd leave me and I . . .'

'How much, Gabriel?' I said solemnly, my pulse picking up pace. I was shocked to see the impact of his confession as he crumpled before me. I'd never seen Gabriel cry, not even at my parents' funeral or when his beloved dog died six months before.

'Tens of thousands,' he sobbed. 'Remember when I came home last year after three weeks on the mainland? I was in the hospital. They put me there.'

'Who? Who put you there?' I demanded, spittle lacing my words.

'The Lynch family. They loaned me money. But when I couldn't pay it back, they said we could work something out. That's where the babies come in. It's the only way I can pay off my debts.'

'You should have said . . .' I began. I'd been so cross with him when he'd eventually returned. I'd noticed the bruises on his body, but he said he'd fallen down the hotel stairs after having too much to drink.

'You don't say no to these people, Mary. They're dangerous. And they won't just come for me if I don't pay them back.' He swallowed to clear his throat. 'I'm sorry, but it's out of my hands.'

'So they're using you to sell babies to pay off your debts?'

'They give me a finder's fee and keep the rest.' He sniffed, wiping his tears with the back of his hand. 'Everything's in motion. It's the only way to keep us safe.'

My anger was replaced by fear as I pulled my husband close. 'Shh,' I comforted. His ribs heaved against mine as he cried in my arms. 'It's alright,' I whispered. 'I'll stand by you. Everything's going to be alright.' But inside my stomach was churning. His actions made me sick. What choice did we have? I swallowed uneasily. The die was cast.

CHAPTER 36

DANIEL

I head out to the shed with Teresa. Claire is cleaning up after breakfast. I brace myself against the wind as I volunteer to help Teresa bring in turf so we can catch a moment alone.

We take the path to the turf shed and our wellington boots squelch in the mud. 'Everything OK?' I say as soon as we're out of earshot. I thought we'd cleared the air last night, but she's been shooting me worried looks all morning. Something's up.

'I don't know,' she sighs. The shed door flaps on its hinges and she turns to close it. The air screams as the wind whistles through every crack like a melancholic symphony. 'Mossie said Claire was in the pub last night asking questions.' Teresa turns to face me, her expression worrisome. 'Nobody's said anything, but Mossie got talking to Sean later on. He saw her down at the graveyard. All these questions about the babies . . . She's not going to let this lie.'

I thought my wife went for a long walk to rid herself of a headache last night. I didn't think she even knew where the graveyard was.

'The problem is,' Teresa continues, brushing a lock of errant grey hair off her face, 'Sean and Mossie's conversation might have been overheard. If word gets out that Claire is asking questions about the babies . . . well, we all have a lot to lose.'

I swallow, clearing the dryness in my throat. 'I told you. Claire can be trusted. I'm going to tell her soon.'

But Teresa doesn't look convinced. 'My sweet boy.' She reaches out and squeezes my arm. It's a rare display of affection, and I'm dismayed to see tears forming in her eyes. 'Nobody was happier than me when you finally settled down. But Claire's a city girl, a well-educated one at that. You don't know how she's going to react.'

'She's just curious, that's all. I'm sure she'll understand.'

'Don't take me up wrong. She's got a kind heart, but she has her own demons too. If she can't face them, then what chance have we got? Because there's more to this than Árd Na Mara. If this gets out . . .'

'It won't.' I reassure the woman who has always been there for me. 'I promise. We'll make a new life here. She'll soon be one of us.'

'I'm glad you see things that way. Family has always meant a lot to you.' She pauses, thoughtful, as the shed is rattled by another gust of wind.

'What is it?' I say, adept at reading her expressions. There's something else on her mind.

'Isla's blood . . .' she begins. 'It's so rare. When you volunteered to donate yours, I panicked. I didn't want you to find out like that.'

She's talking about my sister's parentage. I nod, filled with dread as I take in her sorrowful expression. It tells me that Isla's not the only cuckoo in the nest. 'What about me?'

'Mary always considered you and Isla as her own.' She glances down at her wellington boots, unable to meet my eye.

'What about my father? What about Isla's?' I've not reacted to the news because, like other bad experiences in my life, I've kept it firmly repressed.

'Isla's daddy was a politician. A well-known one, by all accounts. Catherine was his mistress. She tried to set fire to his family home. It's half the reason why she was sent here.'

I nod, aware of the name. 'Was she my mother too?' But that would mean that she got pregnant while she was here. At the back of my mind, there are dim memories of Gabriel slipping into some of the women's rooms.

But Teresa shakes her head. 'Gabriel was your father. His relationship with your mother was consensual, before you get any ideas in your head. He may have been a playboy, but he never, ever forced himself on anyone.' She looks at me sternly as she utters the words said by someone who genuinely cares. 'You remember that now, Danny, won't you? He wasn't all bad.'

I nod, reminding myself that Teresa knew him long before me. Perhaps it was guilt that led him to treating me less than favourably. I realise I'm touching the scar over my lip, and I quickly drop my hand. I'd always blamed it for our rift because it made me less than perfect, unlike Louis, who could do no wrong in his eyes.

'Would you like to know about your mam? Some women . . .' She sighs, trying to find the words. 'They're not cut out for motherhood. It doesn't mean they loved you any less.'

'I know,' I say quietly. I don't want her to feel bad. She's dedicated her life to holding everything together. I already owe her so much.

'Would you like me to tell you who she is? Not here of course.' She utters a laugh. 'Somewhere we can have a proper chat.'

I'm tempted, but only for a second. I've got too much going on right now to think about my biological mam. Because I wasn't born in a hospital. I emerged from a battleground. The women who were sent here were fraught with problems. 'Maybe some other time, after things have calmed down.'

'As long as you're sure,' she says, before turning to get some turf. I gently take the turf bin from her hand.

166

'You do too much. I'll bring this in. Go and put your feet up. I'll take Claire to the pub at lunch time and smooth things over. I'll ring Louis too. We'll sort the rest out after Isla comes home.'

'Aye, it would be nice to have you all here under one roof, sure enough.' I can tell by her sad smile that recent events have taken their toll.

I don't blame Teresa for worrying, but I have faith in my wife. I fill the bin with turf and carry it inside. It would feel strange to have Louis back here, but I can almost sense Árd Na Mara's approval. Sometimes when I paint in the basement rooms, the place feels more like a living entity than a house rooted to the ground. When I'm in my creative world, I'm lost in the memory of the women who occupied this space. This home had a law of its own, ruled and governed by my father on the upper floor.

Now I'm feeling more adrift than ever. I must stay focused on restoring Árd Na Mara and being here for my family. One day, this building will flourish, and peace on Selkie Island will be restored. Once the family are back together, Árd Na Mara will be bathed in an atmosphere of calm. We will restart the yoga retreats, and I can hold painting classes and writing retreats too. But none of this can take place without Louis being on board.

CHAPTER 37

CLAIRE

Afternoon sunlight beams through the open door as Louis enters the vast hall. He drops his battered holdall on the floor with a thud. Kitty is asleep upstairs and the smell of freshly baked soda bread wafts from the kitchen where Teresa is baking. Louis's visit is expected but given the last time we spoke, I still can't believe that he's here. The stench of cigarettes follows him, and as he takes off his donkey jacket, I can see that his jeans need a wash. He attempts a smile, but it's not reflected in his eyes as he hangs his coat on the hook on the wall.

'You're travelling light,' I comment, trying to brighten the mood.

'Living rough will do that,' he replies in a weary tone as he finger-combs his unruly hair.

'Oh, sorry, I didn't mean . . .' I say, relieved to see Daniel striding across the hall. He's looking every inch the artist in slim-fitting black jeans and a baggy white linen shirt. I don't know what he said to Louis, but I'm relieved they've come to a truce.

Louis's demeanour shifts as Daniel offers his hand in a gesture of peace. They shake hands firmly.

'Sorry for ruining dinner,' Louis says sheepishly.

'Sorry about the painting,' Daniel replies with a smile. Their words appear forced, and somewhat for my benefit, but it's progress just the same. How quickly things have changed in the space of a day. Daniel knows I've been upset by his family dynamics, and he wants to put things right.

'Water under the bridge,' Louis says as they continue chatting. 'You're a better damned artist than me anyway.' The ice between them seems to melt away. 'Where's the babby?' Louis turns to me. 'I'd like to meet my niece.' But there's an air of unease as Daniel stands stiffly next to me. Once again, I can't put my finger on it, but a tiny warning bell rings in my mind. Why is Daniel so tense when our daughter is around?

'Oh, she's upstairs, just got her down for a nap,' I say, glad that someone is taking an interest in Kitty. Even Teresa doesn't seem that bothered about her these days. She's happy to babysit, but her movements are perfunctory and there's little affection there. It's almost as if she's scared to get too close to her. I snap out of my thoughts, conscious that my imagination is running away with me. My time in the graveyard has invoked nightmares of me reading headstones with Kitty's name inscribed. Between that and Daniel's night terrors, it's no wonder I feel tired today.

'I should probably have a shower and a change of clothes first anyway,' Louis says apologetically. He kicks off his boots and wiggles his big toe as it pops out of his sock.

'Louis!' Teresa exclaims as she joins us. There are no hugs offered; she displays her affection through food. It's good to see her smiling. She's seemed troubled lately. Sometimes I catch her looking at me, as if I'm a problem she needs to work out. 'Some of your old clothes are in the wardrobe upstairs, all washed and pressed.' Teresa brushes her flour-dusted hands against her apron.

'Mossie!' she shouts at her husband, who makes an appearance from the kitchen. 'Take his bag upstairs.'

'There's no need,' Louis protests, as Mossie plods in. His eyes are bloodshot, and he slouches with the demeanour of someone who's had too many pints of Guinness the night before.

He gives Louis a watery smile. 'It's easier if you just give in.' It sounds like his life mantra as he takes Louis's bag. Every movement seems like an effort as he heads slowly up the stairs.

'Come.' Teresa gestures to Louis. 'There's food on the table and tea in the pot.' She looks at us both. 'Will I pour you a cup?'

'No, thanks.' Daniel shakes his head. 'We're heading out to the Smugglers' Inn for a bite to eat.'

I check my watch. We're going in under an hour, and I haven't put my face on yet. Teresa and Louis head into the kitchen, chatting amongst themselves in low voices. Daniel's already bounding upstairs and now I'm on my own in the hall, standing in a beam of light. I should be happy; Louis is here and making an effort to get along. He's a different person when he's sober, but what lies beneath? I haven't forgotten his comment about watching my back. I store it away for later. Isla deserves a warm welcome when she comes home.

CHAPTER 38

DANIEL

Silently, I approach Louis's room. I've ironed things out as best as I can. He was more understanding than I gave him credit for and although things have been difficult, I'm glad he's moved back home. When sober, he's prepared to listen to what I have to say. But there's a demon on his shoulder, a part of him that isn't ready to forgive, and that's the side of him that frightens me the most.

His door is off the latch, and I press it slightly open, pausing as I take in his form. He is fresh from the shower, a bath towel around his waist as he dries his hair. He doesn't see me as he gazes through the open curtains. How simple our relationship was when we were primary-school age. Louis soon became taller than me. He was much more athletic and a real hit with the girls. I've always looked up to him and treated him like a big brother, and he gladly took on the role, despite being the youngest in the family. During thunderstorms I'd climb into his bed, and we'd huddle together beneath thick blankets listening to the storm rage outside. In the summer we spent our free time exploring the island's rocky shores, collecting seashells and driftwood to build forts.

But all that changed as Louis grew older, and our interests divided us. We're not children anymore, and I can't bring myself to enter his room. I tear my eyes away from his muscular frame, backing away. He was always the sporty one, the person Da turned to when he needed a hand. They always seemed so close. I can't help but wonder about the painting of *The Drowning Man* and the way our parents died. *His parents*, I correct my thoughts. Because he's always known. Isla and I are nothing but outsiders to him. In his mind, he is the only rightful heir of Árd Na Mara. We are the cuckoos in the nest.

Claire greets me on the stairs, her smile fading as she takes in my face. 'Hey, everything alright?'

I recover quickly. 'Oh, I'm fine. Someone just walked over my grave.' I look at Kitty, who is in her arms. 'New outfit?' I say, taking in her pink frilly dress. Claire's been able to dress her a bit lighter now that the heating has been fixed and a new boiler is in place. I'm glad the workmen have left. They came from the far side of the island and were paid generously to keep their heads down and get on with their work.

'It's gorgeous, isn't it?' Claire's smile returns as she stares at the baby in her arms. 'She's so lovely when she's like this. Why don't we take her with us? The fresh air would do her good.'

I shake my head, trying to come up with a reasonable excuse. 'And have mad old Sean breathing whiskey fumes all over her? The pub's no place for a baby. We can bring her for a walk later on.'

I gently kiss the baby's forehead, and the gesture makes Claire happy. I know I've been distant, but I'm confident that soon our troubles will be over. I'm hoping she won't ask me to hold Kitty. I'm not ready for that today. I'm an 'emotionally absent father', according to the textbook she's bookmarked. Things will be so much better when it's just the two of us. I feel guilty for my thoughts and press a hand against Claire's back.

'I love you. I know things haven't been the same between us lately, but we'll get there, I promise, and it'll be even better than before.'

She walks to the kitchen to Teresa, her step a little lighter as happiness creeps in. Soon she will learn to fit in with our island ways. She doesn't need the baby to make her happy, she only needs us. With my family here to support her, Claire will get through what lies ahead.

CHAPTER 39

CLAIRE

It feels good to be out of the house with Daniel. At least he's trying to get us back on an even keel. I thought I'd be on my own for the evening watching RTÉ with Teresa and Louis in the living room, but he has reserved us a table for supper in the Smugglers' Inn. Now I'm sitting in a private corner while Daniel is being served by Orla at the bar. Kieran, Orla's husband, arrives with our cutlery, but there's no sign of Aoife tonight. I look around the room for Sean, but he's not made an appearance either. The air is rich with the smell of cooking and it makes my mouth water as I've not eaten much today. Stress had robbed my appetite, but tonight Daniel has promised to answer every question in my mind. I need to pin him down.

Kieran speaks, but his accent is so strong that I have to ask him to repeat what he said, and listen intently to his words.

'How are ya settling in?' he says again, delivering a warm smile.

I like Kieran. I've spoken to him a couple of times and he seems like a friendly, hard-working soul. His family brings food and supplies to our side of the island and we'd be lost without them.

'I'm fine, thanks.' I give him the generic reply. 'Where's Aoife? I've not seen much of her since she got back from her travels.'

'She's about,' he says, glancing over at the bar. 'How's Isla? Aoife said she's coming home tomorrow. We've missed seeing her about the place.'

Isla doesn't spend much time in the pub, but she swims in the nearby bay.

'She's good, thanks, although she'll be taking it easy for a while.' I pause, seeing that Daniel is in deep conversation with Orla. 'Kieran,' I say, as he goes to turn away, 'what's the craic with Sean? Every time I see him, he warns me off.'

'Does he now?' Kieran's eyebrows raise. 'He's a quare fellah alright. I'll be having a word with him. Can't have him causing ructions with my customers.'

'It's not just here,' I continue. 'I bumped into him when I was out for a walk, and he said something about my baby not seeing the summer out.' I've already told Daniel, but he told me to ignore him. 'What's his deal?'

'Ach, pay no notice. Sure he's wired to the moon. He used to turn up for Mass pished out of his skull.' An amused smile rises to his face. 'Wouldn't have been too bad if he wasn't the one giving the sermon.'

'Sorry, what?' I say, wondering if I've misheard. 'Did you say Sean was a priest?'

'Oh aye, didn't you know? Father Hennessy said Mass in the local Catholic church until old Father Flanagan stepped in a few years ago.' Orla calls Kieran from the bar and he excuses himself.

I smell the fresh woody tones of Daniel's Paco Rabanne after-shave and realise he's behind me. He places our drinks on the table, and I ease into our evening.

'Food won't be long,' he says, having ordered at the bar. 'I'd asked him to order me a traditional Irish dish.

'You looked deep in conversation,' I say, taking a sip of wine.

'With Orla? Oh, she was just asking after Isla.'

'So was Kieran,' I say, crossing my legs. I feel better about this place now I've been here a few times. But there are too many unanswered questions for me to fully relax.

'Who's Martina?' I say, willing to spoil the pleasant mood in order to get to the truth. He's promised me answers, and the question of Martina's existence plays the most on my thoughts.

Daniel rests his glass on the table as if he's been expecting the question all along. 'She was a patient at the institute. But I don't like talking about her. There are too many bad memories.' He looks at me uncertainly. 'I know this hasn't been easy on you. But there's no point in dwelling on the past.'

I clench my teeth, annoyed that he's going back on his promise. I glance over at the bar to see Orla watching us. Has she influenced his decision to clam up? I return my attention to Daniel. I'm not going to let this lie.

'But it's not the past, is it? She's part of the history of Árd Na Mara, not to mention the root cause of your night terrors.'

Daniel gives me a measured look as he sips his drink. 'She was a resident, just like all the women before her. I have recurring nightmares. You know that. My subconscious fixes on one thing and replays night after night. They'll stop when things settle down.'

'Fine,' I say, because his comment about his night terrors is true. 'I visited the graveyard. What happened to the women's babies? Because I didn't see any children's graves.'

'I don't know, Claire, maybe they were buried on the mainland. Then after Mam and Da died, everyone was re-homed.' His words are quiet now. Focused.

'But Isla wasn't,' I say softly. 'Don't you think you should check your own background?'

Daniel looks at me and I can see he's considered this too.

'You think I'm one of them, don't you? An unwanted child from a psychotic woman. What does that make me?'

'Don't be silly,' I say. I quieten as two plates are rested on our table.

'Enjoy your food,' Orla says, hovering over us both.

'It looks lovely,' I say, wanting to get back to our conversation.

It's a simple dish of boiled ham, mashed potatoes and cabbage – classic Irish fare. But she's standing there like she wants to say something. She pauses, opens her mouth. Thinks better of it, then smiles and leaves.

'Teresa's already confirmed it.' Daniel's voice interrupts my thoughts.

'Sorry, what?' I pick up my knife and fork.

'That I was adopted. She told me in the shed. She asked if I wanted to know who my real mother was and I said I'd wait.'

'Oh. I wondered why you were both gone so long. God . . .' I shake my head. 'Your family has so many secrets.' I want to expose them all, but Daniel is cutting forcefully into his food.

'This isn't the place to have this conversation,' he says, spearing a chunk of ham with his fork. 'I promise. Everything will be clear after Isla comes home.' He looks at me, his eyes bright with sincerity. 'I should have cleared the air sooner. Told you everything.'

'Yes. You should,' I agree. 'I'm not made of glass, Daniel. I'm stronger than you think.'

'I know you are,' he said. 'I saw how you took control in the hospital when Isla was brought in.' He pours some gravy on his mash as he chews. 'Mmm, this is good.'

I mirror his actions. The food smells delicious, and my stomach rumbles in response.

'Louis seems to be settling in,' he says, as I slice off some tender ham. It's salty but delicious and I sip my wine to clear my throat.

'I'm glad. We couldn't leave him sleeping rough when there's so much space at home. It's as much his place as ours.'

'Home?' Daniel smiles hopefully. 'That's the first time I've heard you refer to Árd Na Mara as home. Can you see yourself settling here?'

But that's not what I meant, and I don't want Daniel to get carried away.

'I mean, it could be more homely if you keep making an effort with Louis. Then Isla will have the support she needs when we move on.' Our London abode has been leased out short term and I am missing my old life.

He dips his head towards his plate, but not before I see the disappointment in his eyes. 'There's no rush to leave. Isla's been through an ordeal. Having us all together is the best thing for her.' He stops himself. 'And you, of course.'

He doesn't mention Kitty, the very heart of our family.

Baby steps, I remind myself. But I've sensed a change in Daniel. It's like he's two different people – the Daniel I knew in London, and Danny, my mysterious Selkie Island man. We eat the rest of our meal in small spaces of silence. There are a few people at the bar, and the open fire has warmed the room.

'I had a long chat with Louis,' he says, draining his glass of wine. 'You don't need to worry about him.'

'Good,' I say, because that's all I can ask for right now. 'And tomorrow you'll tell me about Martina? Because someone left flowers at the graveyard for her.'

Daniel snorts. 'Martina is a common name. You're reading a lot into an old bunch of roses, aren't you?' He pauses, his knife and fork hovering over his plate. Because he's realised his mistake.

'I never said they were roses,' I counter. 'Nor did I mention they were old. You left them there, didn't you? On that bumpy ground under the tree. Is that where she's buried?' I lean forward, trying to keep my voice low. We're attracting curious glances and I don't want to be overheard. 'Is that why you won't let me go into the basement? Is that where it happened? Was Martina killed there?' I know I'm becoming obsessive, but I can't help myself.

'Not here,' Daniel growls, checking over his shoulder. 'Tomorrow, I'll tell you everything. There won't be a question left in your mind.'

But while I'm desperate for answers, I'm also scared of getting them, as he looks at me with absent eyes.

I return my attention to my food as the fire crackles and spits nearby. There is a low murmur of chatter from the patrons perched at the bar and I'm beginning to feel like I'm on display. My appetite has left me. I should be pleased to hear Daniel's going to tell all. This is what I've pushed for, after all. So why am I overcome by feelings of dread?

CHAPTER 40

THE ISLANDER

The sun has descended, and the stars are shining brightly in the vast night sky. The moon looms above, a crescent over this midnight seascape. Standing on the rocky cliff edge, I inhale a breath of crisp cold air, soothed by the slow rise and fall of the tide. On nights like these, I want to wade into the sea and surrender to its sharp needles of pain. I suck air between my teeth as my abdomen clenches. My mouth feels dry and empty, my stomach heavy from the treasures unable to make their way out. My habit is escalating and will one day be the death of me. Nobody knows about my worrying cramps, or the foreign objects that cause them. Perhaps I'm in denial of my ritual of self-harm. It's not as if I want to hurt myself. Stopping just isn't an option. But it worries me that they're staying put.

My thoughts return to the island as the cramping sensations pass. I take strange comfort in the darkness. There are no intrusive street lights here, no car headlights, no flashing sirens to spoil the view. Just the steady strobe of the guardian lighthouse, which comes awake as we ready ourselves for sleep. In the distance, the lights of the mainland twinkle, but they are not enticing to me.

It's all coming together now, building in a pressure cooker of events. As if Árd Na Mara could go back to what it once was. I was there for all of it, and the shame makes me sick to my stomach. Even in exile, with not an ounce of remorse or dignity, those brassy women were selling their babies to strangers. It's hardly any wonder that the house was plagued with misfortune, as the curse of Selkie Island became a reality.

Now it's like nothing happened at all. Don't they remember the shame? The finger-pointing and rumours that took years to extinguish? Old widow Hagerty was the worst of them. She even went to the mainland once a week to spread the story around. That's until she tripped and fell into the basement of her home. People had a lot of accidents on Selkie Island that year. People learned to shut up.

There is no room for babies in Árd Na Mara. The sound of children's laughter will never echo in that house of ill repute. I'm not the only islander who thinks the same way. I thought a warning would work, but more needs to be done. There's only one way to rid the island of the Englishwoman, and that's by ridding her of the one thing she cares about the most.

I stand at the cliff edge, close my eyes and surrender to the whisperings of the sea. I know what I have to do, and I gladly accept the task. The Englishwoman will regret the day that she ever set foot here.

CHAPTER 41

CLAIRE

'My bonnie lies over the ocean . . .' The tune dies on my lips as Kitty falls into daytime slumber. Day or night, these words come to me when I stand at her bedroom window. It feels more like the song is flowing through me than me actively singing it myself. I don't dare utter it aloud when Daniel is around. It sparks a memory from his childhood that he is struggling to reveal.

My husband has always been intense. It's what drew me to him. I'd never met anyone who cared so passionately about things. His art, his home and, of course, me. If only he felt the same way about our child. But there is hope on the horizon. He checked on Kitty last night. I hadn't heard her crying, but when I found his side of the bed empty, I got up to look for him. I discovered him in her nursery, silently standing over her cot as she slept. I crept back to bed, not wanting to disturb him. It was a small thing but spoke volumes to me.

Each time he acknowledges our daughter is a real step forward for him. He's trying. We'll get there. Today is a new day. I sense change is on its way. So why has a feeling of dread been following me around all morning?

This house is a graveyard of memories where every corner holds a relic of the past: the well-thumbed library books that creak when you part the leather spines. The ancient radio that still manages to work. The battered oversized washing machine that once took full loads. I cast an eye over the dent on the floorboards where a heavy object was no doubt once dropped and smashed. My gaze moves upwards to the looming ceiling and the decorative covings more suited to another time. The floorboards creak as I walk on to the landing, my gaze falling on the dusty framed photographs lining the walls. The island hasn't changed much over the years. I recognise the cliffs near the Smugglers' Inn where beautiful coastal views give way to the solitude of the sea. I admire the images of the old ruins, and the seagulls caught in time as they wheel over the crumbling watchtowers.

My focus switches to the old family photographs, where an unsmiling Mary stands next to their children outside the island church. Mary's expression seems so fixed, apart from in one photo where she's picking wildflowers and caught unaware. I want to trace a finger over her face and ask what life was like here. There is a rare clear photograph of Gabriel up close and I'm taken aback by his looks. He was the type of man who could turn heads without trying. He and Mary do not seem to make a natural couple. I know they weren't happy, as Daniel has told me as much.

The hairs prickle on the back of my neck as a chill sweeps over me. Perhaps when the house is fully modernised, I won't feel so uneasy. The place hasn't been the same without Isla, and I'm looking forward to having her home. I switch my attention to the window as a car door slams. Louis and Daniel have left to pick her up from the hospital, while Teresa has gone for a walk. I haven't seen Mossie around, but no doubt he's in the pub. It feels like he's gone into retirement since we arrived. I'm glad. After years of running this place, he deserves a break.

It occurs to me that for the first time since I got here, I have Árd Na Mara to myself. There's a room I'd like to visit, one shrouded in secrecy. Satisfied that Kitty is settled, I take the stairs and head into the kitchen, unhooking the keys in the pantry before going to the basement. The baby monitor is turned on and I'll hear Kitty if she cries. So why am I tiptoeing around the house? I feel like I'm being watched by a pair of disapproving eyes. But I'm contributing towards the renovations – I've every right to explore.

I open the door that leads to the basement and take the steps down. I try to imagine what it must have been like for the women who were forced here against their will. There are no windows in this space and my heart beats a little faster as a feeling of claustrophobia sets in. The steps lead to a long, dimly lit corridor with lights on the wall. A rusted radiator hangs on its hinges, and there are cracked white tiles on the floor. Perhaps they were deemed easier to clean than the wooden floors above. The air is filled with the stench of damp and mould. How can Daniel spend hours of his time down here? To my left is a series of metal doors, much like cells. A couple of rusted metal chairs are lined up against the wall in the hallway to the right. I need to hurry up. Teresa could return at any minute. This still feels more like her house than mine.

I slide a thick metal key into the lock of the first door, and it turns straight away. I push the door open and enter an empty room. There's no evidence of any flooding, as Daniel claimed, although the place needs airing out. I'm filled with disappointment. What did I expect? It has all the character of a musty old shoebox. The walls are thick and my blood runs cold as I notice small scratches gouged into the cold stone. I take in every aspect of the depressing space, from the cracked and uneven floor to the light bulb which hangs in a metal cage from the cobwebbed ceiling. I feel like crying for its previous occupants, because I wouldn't keep a dog in this place. I flick the grubby switch on the wall, but it doesn't work.

In the corner of the room is a metal toilet, like you'd find in a police custody cell. I've never been in trouble with the law, but when I was training to be a doctor, we visited a police station to see the different environments in which people with mental health issues could be detained. Only now do I notice the metal hatch and peephole in the door. This was not a place of healing. This was a prison cell. No wonder Daniel didn't want me coming down here.

My eyes are drawn to an envelope, its contents spilled out on the floor as if whoever hastily cleared out this room dropped it on their way out. I imagine Teresa rushing around before we came here, clearing out this place. I bend at the knees, pausing as I squat to pick them up. The images remind me of mugshots, each one a photo of a previous inmate taken in this very space. I turn each sad photo in turn, whispering their names as I read. Fiona, Maura, Emily, Niamh – each face haunts me as they stare from the pictures, their hollow faces filled with despair. I pause at the image of a beautiful young woman who wears a hint of a smile. She is different from the others and before I turn the photograph, I know. It's Martina. The name written on the back in blue pen confirms what I felt in my gut. She's utterly bewitching. No wonder Daniel still thinks about her. But where is she now? Unanswered questions invade my brain.

I go from one identical room to the other, finally coming to the last. It is double the size of the others and must be the room in which Daniel has been working. It takes me three attempts before I find the right key. The air feels thick and stale. Perspiration dampens my armpits as I rattle the key in the lock. My pulse accelerates. Daniel has been lying to me about the flooding. What else has he lied about?

I open the door and take in the room, which is set apart from the others. There are spotlights in each corner of the ceiling, and I blink as they flood it with light. The walls are painted buttercup yellow and there is a thin blue carpet on the floor. I wonder why this living space appears more like a bedroom than a prison cell. Daniel's easel takes centre stage. Tentatively, I approach the painting he's been working on, my sense of trepidation growing as I turn to face it. I inhale a sudden gasp, my hand rising to my face as I absorb the scene as Árd Na Mara takes centre stage. I stare at the image of the woman standing in the window, her palm pressed against the glass as she stares out to sea. I compare her to that of the photo still in my hand. It's Martina. She's strange and beautiful, and her image has been captured with love.

My chest burns with conflicting emotions of jealousy and sadness. Daniel has never painted me like this. Sighing, I glance around the room. There's a double bed in the corner with a dresser across from it, but everything is bolted down. I open the double drawers to find an old-fashioned landline phone.

How odd, I think, *they've kept it for all these years*. There's a socket in the corner of the room. It seems calls were made from here too.

I continue with my snooping. I cannot stop now. But my attention is drawn to something glinting behind the metal bed frame. I'm frowning because I can't believe what I'm seeing. No. It can't be.

I approach, not wanting to believe what's clearly in front of me. Embedded in the wall are two thick chains with metal shackles attached. I'd wondered why this room wasn't fitted with safety features. Were its patients kept bound? The chair in the corner, was that for a watcher? The very thought makes my flesh crawl. I don't want to climb over the bed, which consists of a damp double mattress, but I'm compelled to do it to examine the marks on the wall. I trace my fingers over them, pressing my fingertips into the five narrow grooves of what can only come from nails.

'What sort of place was this?' I whisper in a low voice.

And what were in the other cells before they were cleared out? Torture devices? Cameras? My thoughts run riot as I try to fathom the dark secrets in the bowels of this house.

The slam of the door makes me shriek. My heart falters as I realise that I've left the keys on the other side. A shadow passes over the safety glass, but I can't make out who it is. All I know is that I'm trapped. There's someone else in the house. Then another terrifying thought enters my mind. What about Kitty?

I jump off the bed, disbelieving, as I reach the door. This can't be happening. I tug on the handle, but the door is firmly locked.

'Let me out!' I shriek, peering through the grubby safety glass. But all I can see is the rusted empty chair pushed up against the wall. 'Let me out!' I scream again, hammering with my fists.

Then the lights in the room go out and I'm left fumbling in the dark. In the distance, another door slams. Who is out there? I stumble around in the dark, heart racing as I realise that whoever it is, I'm at their mercy. Is someone watching me? Are there cameras in this place? I bump against the furniture, unable to see my hand.

'Please,' I whisper in the darkness. 'Please don't hurt my baby!'

The air chills around me and I'm overcome with a sense of knowing. I'm not the first woman to utter those words from this desolate space.

CHAPTER 42

DANIEL

'Just for the record, I think you're fecking crazy.'

The sentiment comes from Louis. The sea breeze ruffles his hair as he leans over the water taxi, staring into the sea. We're its only passengers, and it was worth the cost to hire it. My stomach churns as I drink from my bottle of water. At least the seasickness tablets have helped. I don't want anyone else hearing this conversation. I shudder to think what people from the mainland would think. Louis is aware of my plans. He had to agree with them in order to move back in.

'Crazy or not, it's happening.' I take another slow breath. The sea is choppy today, and I keep my gaze fixed on the mainland as it comes into view. 'What choice do I have?'

'She won't understand,' Louis cautions. 'No chance. You're going about this all wrong.'

'Have you any better ideas?'

But Louis shakes his head. 'What if she goes public? You can kiss goodbye to your island retreat. This doesn't just affect you, either. Think of Isla . . . of the rest of us.'

He has valid points which I'm finding unnerving, but it's too late to back out now. 'She's not some stranger off the street. She's my wife. She deserves to know the truth.'

'She won't stay. Mark my words.'

'Why didn't you tell me?' I say, changing the subject. 'About Da. How long have you known?'

Louis brushes his wavy fringe off his face. 'I don't know . . . Do you really want to go raking all this stuff up again?'

'Wouldn't you, if you were in my shoes?' A fisherman's boat chugs past us, and a flock of seagulls spins and dives as their shrieks fill the air.

'Aye, I suppose I would.' Louis gives a resigned nod of the head. 'I found out when he took me to France to see Grand-mère. They were speaking in French, but I knew enough to get the gist of it. I confronted him about it later that night, and he said he was glad I knew.'

I frown as I recall the French trip. Mam wouldn't go, and I sulked all week because I was forced to stay home and help her. She'd said that she needed me, but looking back now, I think she was trying to soften the blow, because Da didn't want to bring either me or Isla along. He made little effort to hide the fact that Louis was his favourite child.

'It must have been nice,' I said wistfully. 'That Da was so proud of you. I never got that from him.'

Louis gives a one-shouldered shrug. 'You had Mam and Isla. We all had our little cliques.' The boat begins to slow as it approaches the dock.

'We should all pull together now,' I say, before our conversation ends. 'For Isla's sake.'

'It's always been about Isla, hasn't it? Sure the girl runs rings around us.' Louis straightens, preparing to disembark.

It's true. Had Isla not survived her fall in the lighthouse, Árd Na Mara would have been put up for sale. We'd each be given our share of the estate as stated in Mary and Gabriel's wills. It's doubtful Louis or I would have met again. I want to ask him more, but my stomach turns as the boat bobs up and down. At least it's pulling up alongside the dock. I'm just glad that we're on speaking terms again. I'm going to need the support of my family when all is said and done.

◆ ◆ ◆

Isla is overjoyed to see us. She hasn't said it but I know every day in the hospital has felt like a prison sentence for her. She basks in the sea air as we make the return crossing, turning her face to the drizzle and savouring every moment. We're standing near the engine, but the noise and fumes don't seem to bother her as she takes in her surroundings as if she's never seen them before.

'Do you want to sit down?' I say, signalling towards Louis, who has taken shelter from the rain in the small cabin.

'I'm OK,' she says, smiling at the gulls as they dive-bomb the water in our wake.

I take in her features, and she seems no worse for her experience, just glad to be home. She's wearing a bobble hat over the scar on the back of her head, but otherwise she looks the same. Like Claire, I've questioned her about the accident, but she wants to put the whole thing to bed.

'No swimming for a while,' I say, raising my voice against the sound of the engine.

Isla gives me a knowing look, as if to say it will take more than a head injury to keep her out of the water. She stares at the waves so intently that I don't want to leave her alone in case she gets it into her head to swim the rest of the way home. Her smile grows even wider when I see what surfaces from the foam.

It's Dolly, the local dolphin, and she's swimming next to our boat. I steady myself as we're bobbed about, my knuckles white as they grip the side. But Isla is keeping perfect balance, her smile endless as she watches Dolly duck in and out of the water. She is putting on quite a display. It's all lost on Louis, who is checking his watch. It seems I'm not the only one uncomfortable on the water today. A sense of finality washes over me. Soon Claire will know everything. I only hope she can deal with what's to come.

It's not long before Árd Na Mara comes into view. Isla looks from me to Louis, the smile fading from her face.

'No more fighting?' she says, gripping my hand. I'm touched by her gesture, and I deliver a reassuring smile.

'No more fighting,' I repeat. 'Soon, everything will be sorted out.'

'Good,' Isla replies. 'I want things how they used to be.' She spares a glance at Louis and gives him a smile as he approaches us both. 'All of us, back together again. Claire too.' Isla pauses, looks at me uncertainly. 'But not Kitty?'

'No, not Kitty.' I confirm what I told her at the hospital. 'Because that's not how things should be.'

She seems satisfied with this and her smile returns. I glance over Isla's shoulder at Louis. Judging from his stony expression, he's thinking the same thing. Claire will have to make sacrifices if she wants to be one of us.

CHAPTER 43

DANIEL

We are met at the door by Teresa, who gives Isla a warm hug.

'It's wonderful, just wonderful,' she says, her eyes swimming with emotion as Isla comes home. I look beyond her, but there's nobody there.

'Where's Claire? I thought she would have been here for this.'

Teresa looks at me, confused. 'She's not with you? I'm only just in the door myself. I was out looking for Mossie. I thought Claire headed on to meet you at the dock.'

But I shake my head, a sense of foreboding growing as I follow Isla inside.

Already, Isla is itching to go to her room, but she gracefully accepts the welcome party of balloons and cake.

I turn to my sister. 'Claire gave your room a little tidy . . .' I pause as her face falls. 'It's nothing to worry about. She just wanted to help.'

'But the pictures . . .' she says, pink blooms rising to her freckled cheeks.

I raise a hand to reassure her. 'They're fine. Everything's fine. I told you it would be, now didn't I? She just gave it a little hoover and aired it out.'

Claire made a real effort to keep the place to Isla's liking, while adding little touches like fairy lights and sea-themed bunting to brighten the space. She also cleared the window to allow more light to come in, and added a washing basket, new towels, and a few other nice bits. Isla's face relaxes as I explain. The kettle whistles on the range, signalling that it's time for tea.

'I'll go get her,' I say, knowing she's probably fussing over Kitty. 'She can't have heard us come in.'

'She's not upstairs.' Teresa shoots me a look as she re-joins us in the kitchen. 'But the basement key isn't on its hook. Maybe you should start there.'

My happy moment fades. So Claire has gone to check out the basement, despite me telling her that it isn't safe. We've cleared out all the rooms bar one, which I paint in. The old furniture is still there – my way of preserving the past. I'm not the only one. But it's time to move into the present and create a new future for us all. I didn't expect Teresa to leave the house after we went. I returned, vowing to tell Claire everything, but it seems that she's gone hunting for clues. I take a breath and prepare myself. This won't be easy.

'I'll go and look,' I say to Teresa, forcing a smile on my face. 'Don't eat all the cake!' I wink at Isla, determined to keep things light.

We've invited Aoife over, but she said she won't come until things are put right. Soon, I've told her. And it frightens me a little because of how much things are going to change.

It's only when I take the basement steps that I hear shouting from below.

'Hello? Is anyone there?' It's Claire, and she sounds distressed. 'I'm locked in! Let me out!'

'Claire? Are you OK?' I switch on the corridor light and check each of the rooms.

'Daniel!' she calls, her voice filled with relief. 'The door, it's locked. Kitty! Someone check on Kitty!'

But I'm not worried about Kitty. I'm worried about my wife and the fact she's in this last basement room. I think about the shackles on the wall and the scratches ingrained in the plaster. She will have seen it all. Claire is a health professional, and it's been a struggle for her to reconcile herself with what went on in Árd Na Mara, the place people chose to forget.

I peep through the safety glass and see only darkness. Her voice is hoarse from screaming, and I'm flooded with childhood memories as she screamed for her baby while I stood at the door.

Just how long has Claire been down here? And how did she get locked in? I turn the key, which is on my side of the door. She almost falls into my arms as she stumbles, desperate to get out. She's back to square one, fretting over her baby, and unable to think straight. 'Where's Kitty?' she babbles, clutching my arm. 'Have you checked on her? Is she safe?'

'Claire.' I grab her by both arms. 'Calm down. Take a breath. How did you get locked in?'

She gulps down a breath, her eyes wild, her face sweaty. 'Somebody locked me in. I saw them through the glass. They turned off the lights.'

'I believe you,' I said, annoyed, because this wasn't how it was meant to be. 'Everything's going to be OK.'

'Is Kitty with Isla?'

I can't lie. 'We've literally just walked in the door.'

Claire draws away from me, incredulous. 'So you've not seen her yet? Jesus, Daniel, what the hell is wrong with you? Why don't you care?'

She pushes me aside, bolting down the corridor. My jaw sets firm. Isla doesn't need this drama. None of us do. I should have dealt with this sooner. I only have myself to blame. The sooner we get back to being a couple, the better. Claire will cope without Kitty in time.

Slowly, I emerge from the basement. Teresa and Louis are in the hall.

'She's gone tearing up the stairs like her arse is on fire,' Louis says, with little sympathy.

'She thinks something's happened to Kitty,' I sigh. 'I can't go on like this.'

'You promised Isla you'd sort this out,' Teresa says, in a low voice.

'I will,' I say, following her back to the kitchen where my sister is waiting. 'It's not easy. Just . . . give me a little more time.'

But Isla's face reflects her disappointment. She's been listening all along.

'Hey, don't worry.' I force a smile. 'I'll speak to Claire. Everything will be alright. Now why don't you have some cake and I'll go get her?'

I squeeze her shoulder in reassurance as Louis sits at the table, an amused smile on his face. He reminds me of our father during times like these, and that's not a good thing.

I ponder my decision as I climb the wide stairwell. The day has turned overcast, and the house is shadowed in gloom. Was this what it was like for Mam? Agonising over her decisions, balancing wrong and right?

I find Claire pacing our bedroom floor, Kitty in her arms. Her face turns to stone as she regards me once more.

'What is wrong with you?' she hisses. 'Anything could have happened to her and you don't even care!'

'I care about *you*,' I say truthfully. 'More than anything in the world. And I don't want anything to come between us.'

She slaps my hand away as I reach out to touch her. She is trembling with fury, her breath coming in stops and starts. I've never seen her this furious before.

'Is that what you think of our baby?' she whispers angrily. 'I know you don't care about her, but that is an evil thing to say.' Her face reddens as she rounds on me, clutching Kitty to her chest. 'Just because *you* had a weird upbringing doesn't mean that all babies are bad. I know that horrible things went on here, things you haven't even told me about. You . . . You're not well. You need to get help.'

The irony of that last sentence almost makes me roll my eyes.

'OK,' I quickly reply, ready to agree to anything if she calms down. 'Claire, listen to me. Teresa was only gone a few minutes, and she checked on Kitty the moment she came in. I should have said straight away, I'm sorry. But you were in such a state . . .'

Claire's frown deepens. I'm lying and I feel cruel making her doubt herself. 'So you . . . you knew she was alright when you found me? Why didn't you say?'

'I did,' I lie.

She stops pacing, takes a breath, and the tone of her voice drops a notch. 'I see. I thought . . . I thought someone had hurt her.'

'There was nobody else in the house. The door slammed behind you, but the key wasn't turned in the lock.'

Another lie. I don't know who locked her in, but I wouldn't put it past Teresa to teach her a lesson for snooping around. I would be eternally grateful to Teresa for everything she and Mossie have done, but there's another side to her that reveals itself to very few.

'But I saw someone . . . and the lights . . .' Now Claire's doubting herself as she comes back to reality.

'The lights are always flickering on and off,' I say. 'No matter. We'll look into it. I'm just glad you're both OK.'

She eyes me dubiously, because she knows I couldn't care less about the baby in her arms. My attention is drawn to a voice in the hall. It's Isla, calling for us to get some cake. It's been a long day and I imagine she wants to check out her room.

'Come and have some cake with Isla. She's been looking forward to seeing you. She's been through a lot.'

'We've all been through a lot.' Claire flatly echoes my words. 'I'll be down in a minute.'

But the look she gives me is sharp and unforgiving. And I don't know if we can ever come back from this.

CHAPTER 44

CLAIRE

I did my best to be there for Isla, putting my feelings aside to help her settle back in. I even went back to her room with her to ensure she was happy with the changes I'd made. She loved the new paintings of the sea that we bought on the mainland, and the extra touches like the twinkly lights and blue bunting overhead. Despite the size of her room, it only took me a few hours to complete. There's a lot more space in her bedroom now that it's clean, and it smells a lot better than it did before. I didn't disturb her drawers, just tidied up what was on the floor. I was able to fit a comfy love chair in the corner near the window for her to read the books I bought. It takes a lot of effort to get furniture over from the mainland, but it was worth it to see the smile on her face. I'm glad she likes it, and I hug her tightly before leaving her to enjoy her room. I'm tired and it feels like a never-ending day. The last few hours have moved so slowly, and I've declined supper in favour of an early night to catch up on some much-needed sleep.

The glow I felt from spending time with Isla dissipates as I go to bed. At least Kitty is settled, although she's been so quiet lately that I'm worried about her. She barely cries anymore, and I have to wake her for a feed. Something's wrong. She doesn't feel the same and I can't help but wonder if the family dynamics are having an effect. I correct myself, because I should know better. There's nothing physically wrong with my child. It's me that's uneasy, and who would blame me after being locked in that basement room earlier today? Did the door really slam shut all by itself? I'm sure I saw a shadow behind the glass, but Daniel has made me doubt myself. I was positive Kitty would be gone when I finally made it to her room, despite Daniel's assurances telling me everything was OK.

I sit on my bed, grateful to be alone as I try to work out what has been a most bizarre day. Isla is where she should be, happily tucked up in her room. Louis is downstairs in the kitchen, chatting to Teresa as they wait for Mossie to come home. He's pulled all-nighters before, according to Teresa. He's got a few friends on the island and he sometimes goes back to theirs for some homemade poitín. Mossie doesn't use mobile phones, although he sometimes calls Teresa from the pub when he's going to be late. He hasn't done that tonight. I didn't even know Teresa had a mobile phone until she mentioned it today. It's a brick of a thing, mind, with no internet access. It surprises me that I haven't missed my phone more. I meant to ask Daniel to return it but I'm too wrapped up in Árd Na Mara to think outside my bubble these days.

My eyes flick to the ceiling as a strange jittering noise vibrates from above. The wind is dashing against the roof tiles and through the rafters in the loft. Every night that I spend here makes me dislike Árd Na Mara even more. Even Louis has been acting distant around me tonight, declining the offer to give his niece a cuddle when it was presented to him. Even Isla barely spoke two words to her tonight. I didn't expect thanks for persuading Daniel to give him a second chance but it feels as if the family are closing ranks on

Kitty and me. I don't know what I've done to deserve such bizarre behaviour, but it makes me uneasy in my skin.

I'm not alone for long, as Daniel enters the room. I glance at him with the eyes of a stranger. I cannot work him out.

'Sorry,' he says, his gaze apologetic. 'Is she alright?'

I don't know if he means Isla or Kitty, so I deliver a nod of the head. I don't want to speak because if we do, I'll get upset. Being locked in the basement has left me feeling vulnerable and scared. I won't pressure him for answers tonight.

I undress silently with my back to him. I'm not even sure if I want to lie in this bed. I'm considering grabbing a pillow and sleeping on the rocking chair in Kitty's room when he speaks.

'It wasn't just Mam and Da who died that night.'

I stiffen, wondering if I've heard him right. I turn to face him and the hardness I'm feeling melts away. His face is pallid, awash with grief.

'Who else died?' I simply say. Then I'm sliding into bed beside him, because maybe . . . just maybe . . . he's about to tell me the truth.

CHAPTER 45

THE ISLANDER

I should be used to island weather, but on nights like these the wind and rain seep into my very bones. My stomach is erupting with pain, but I've caught up with Mossie, because I need to speak to him somewhere we won't be disturbed. In all the times we've spoken, we've rarely been alone. I guide him along the cliff path in the guise of getting his sorry drunken arse safely home. He's been gone far too long, and whines about how much trouble he's in.

Mossie is an incurable gossip, and, up until now, I've encouraged it, as long as he shared his news with nobody else but me. It's our unspoken agreement. A confessional of sorts. I listen to his shameful chatter and he gets things off his chest. He knows it won't go any further. I deliver an understanding response and Mossie is unburdened for the day. But now it seems that our mutually beneficial relationship has come to an end. That's fine by me. I don't need him anymore. As we walk down the cliff path, the lighthouse makes another round.

'What's wrong, Mossie?' I watch my step on the muddy path, blinking against the wind and rain. 'You don't seem yourself tonight.' He is uneasy in my company. It's as if he can read my thoughts.

'I want to draw a line under everything.' Mossie gives me a quick sideways glance. 'We have history, all of us, and I know you don't like change. But Isla needs a fresh start. If Claire wants to renovate Árd Na Mara, I won't stand in her way.'

'We have to do what's best for the island,' I say firmly, as the wind blows my hood off my face. 'Isn't that why you've been confiding in me all these years?' I slip my hand into my coat pocket and finger the goodies within. The urge to pop one into my mouth is strong.

'Look,' Mossie says. 'I know you hate Árd Na Mara, but things are different now. The old place is going to bring in money. You don't need to worry anymore.'

I growl a response as we continue to walk. 'You have a short memory. I remember the day when you told me the place was nothing more than a whorehouse and didn't deserve to stand. You can make them sell up, Mossie! Isla will be quite happy living on the mainland.' I slip something into my mouth. It's sharp, but I store it in my cheek pocket.

'How dare you!' Mossie stops to wave a bony finger in my face. 'Isla is more of a part of this island than any of us. She's been swimming in these waters before she could walk. It's all she's ever known, and nobody, not me or you, is taking that away from her!' It's quite a speech, considering how much he's had to drink.

'This isn't just about Isla, or what you want.' I push him backwards with a stern reminder. 'You don't know who you're dealing with. There are powerful people tied up with Árd Na Mara. They'll go to any length to cover up their scandals.' I ground my back molars on the piece of glass in my mouth.

'Jaysus, Mary and Joseph,' Mossie exclaims. 'Not that again! That may have been true twenty years ago, but not anymore. I've told ya. Nobody's interested. And you need to get these wild ideas out of your head.' He has the cheek to look at me as if I'm mad.

I crunch on the glass as it mingles with my blood. Mossie's eyes widen as I laugh out loud. 'You haven't got a baldy notion, have you? Why do you think so many people died on the island when the story broke? Do you think that journalist fell off the cliff by accident? Or did that old gossip fall down the stairs and break her own skinny neck? I've been protecting this island all my life, and I am not about to let the likes of you and yours ruin it again.' I watch the shock register on his face and I swipe at the blood trickling down my mouth. The pain is nothing compared to my fury right now. 'That's right!' I roar against the storm. 'And your precious Isla isn't exempt, either. Do you think she fell down those lighthouse steps on her own?' The rain is hammering now, like icy nails on my skin.

'You wouldn't hurt Isla. I don't believe you!' Mossie replies, but the look in his eyes says different. The sea bashes white froth at the feet of the lighthouse as the storm picks up.

'I couldn't risk her shaming the island by confessing to an Englishwoman, no less. I told her she had to keep quiet. But frightened people rarely hold their tongue. It was just a little push.' I'm smiling now, satisfied, as he takes it all in. 'The police never came out, did they? Why do you think that is, Mossie? Because they know what secrets need to be kept.'

'You mad fecker!' Mossie squeals against the wind. Then, all at once, he drives his fist and tries to punch me in the face. I meet it with some amusement as I swiftly duck out of the way. He's not a heavy man, but when I manage to pick him up, he squeals like a pig. 'Get the feck off me!' he squawks. 'Let me go!'

'I will in a minute,' I laugh. 'Don't you worry, I'll let you go alright.' I head for the cliff edge. It's time to put an end to Mossie's gossiping once and for all.

CHAPTER 46

CLAIRE

'The babies died that night . . .' Daniel says, with a tremble on his breath. 'Martina's babies.'

'Babies?' I wonder at the plural.

He swallows loudly and I hear his throat click. The wind is streaking through the house now. The night has closed in, dark and wet, and I'm grateful for the warmth of the bedroom. Daniel's talking about Martina. The woman who's been on his mind ever since he got here. 'Daniel?' I gently encourage him to carry on.

'Martina was a resident here. She came to stay twelve months before Mam and Da died.'

'Tell me about her.' I want to build up a picture in my mind. We are at the tail end of a tiresome day. I sense Daniel is finally ready to offload. Moments pass as he gathers his thoughts.

'She was tall, slim, graceful. She had long black wavy hair and very defined features. Her skin was like porcelain, and she had beautiful rosebud lips.' I listen as Daniel describes her like a piece of art. She is, truth be told. Because, given his description, the woman in the basement painting is her. 'She told me she moved to

Dublin to get away from her family, who came from the backend of nowhere.' He smiles, meeting my eyes. 'Her words, not mine. She used to work for the local parish priest and played the clarinet in her spare time. But her voice was her real gift. At first, I couldn't understand how she ended up with us.'

His smile turns cold on his lips. 'Our parents tried to protect us. They didn't tell us what happened to some of the women when they were here. Everyone got a clean slate when they came to Árd Na Mara. But some of them were rough. They'd shout and swear and spit. Others were violent and had to be restrained. Some were addicted to drugs. But Martina . . .' He pauses, his gaze flicking wistfully towards the window. 'She was so sad all the time. Da moved her from the basement to the upstairs room because she wouldn't eat. She used to stand by her window, staring out at sea. At night we'd hear her singing . . .'

'"My Bonnie Lies Over the Ocean"?'

Daniel responds with a nod. 'Night after night. Her voice was so haunting, her words used to fill the corridors. It drove Mam mad. But Da hadn't the heart to take her out of that room. She loved the sea almost as much as Isla . . . at least, I thought she did. But it was all a ruse, so we'd help her escape.' He leans against the headboard, unable to meet my gaze. 'I used to smuggle her in trinkets from the beach. Shells, seaweed, feathers. I was a teenager back then, and smitten with her.'

'What did she do to be sent to Árd Na Mara? Did you ever find out?' I've waited so long for the truth. All my earlier annoyances have been forgotten.

'Are you sure you want to know?' Daniel cautions. 'It's in the past, after all.'

I can see from his expression that the truth is ugly, but it's definitely not in the past.

'Tell me,' I say, impatient.

Daniel presses his lips together, as if he's trying to contain the words.

'She drowned her newborn baby. Brought him to Sandymount Strand in Dublin and waded into the sea. The father had ended their relationship. She claimed she was suicidal, but I think she did it out of revenge. She was dragged out of the water, but the baby was a wee thing and didn't make it. Rumour had it the father was an archbishop. Very high up in the Catholic Church.'

'Of course he was,' I say quietly, because there is a theme of powerful men paying to have their dirty secrets hidden from view. They didn't care about these women, only that they were hidden away from the glare of society, where they could do no harm. At Árd Na Mara. The thought makes me angry and I hate this place even more. But then I think of Martina's baby and how devastated I was after my misdiagnosis when that little girl died . . . How could someone purposely snuff out a new life? Daniel is watching me intensely, and I drag the blanket to my chest as coldness seeps in.

'Árd Na Mara became the place to hide all manner of dirty little secrets,' he continues. 'But I'd never met anyone like Martina. She was just twenty, but she seemed wise for her years and had a way of making you feel like you were the only person who mattered in the world.'

I don't want to hear about how wonderful Martina was or wasn't anymore. 'She had more babies?'

Daniel nodded. 'Everything changed when she became pregnant for the second time. I guessed that Da was the father. I knew he'd spent time alone with her. I couldn't look him in the eye after that. Months later, I got up the courage to tell Ma.'

I try to comprehend the situation, but I can't imagine what it was like. 'What did she say?'

'She already knew and said we mustn't speak about it again. Then she said they'd have to take away Martina's babies because she was a danger to them both. That's when I found out that she was expecting twins. I couldn't believe they could be so cruel, but Mam was adamant that it was too risky to leave her with them. That's when she told me what Martina had done to her previous baby.'

I shake my head, unable to conceive the strange family dynamics Daniel grew up in.

'Martina was manipulative. She knew how to get what she needed from each one of us. I shouldn't have told her about Mam and Da's plans to take her babies, but, well . . .' He gesticulated. 'She got it out of me. Every day, she'd beg me to help. She was desperate to escape from this place. She made out that she wanted to start a new life on the mainland with her babies, but she was just using them like she used us. She knew I'd never risk helping her escape. But every night she sang that song, I believed she was calling out to the baby she'd lost.' The house shudders around us as it is battered with wind. I draw my knees to my chest and hug them.

'And Isla and Louis? What about them?'

'Martina told Isla that the selkies took the babies that were born in Árd Na Mara. She said that if she looked hard enough, she could see them swimming with the seals. Isla's not stupid, but she took to the story and used to draw pictures of the babies for her. As for Louis . . .' Daniel frowned. 'He was very insular back then. It was always him and Da. I don't think he cared about the patients. Louis spent as much time as he could on the mainland or out with his friends. He didn't bother with me.'

My own upbringing was so different from my husband's. My sister and I did everything together. It's why the death of her child hit me so hard. I make a mental note to arrange to call her again. Our relationship has been strained, but I miss her so much that it hurts. I tune back into Daniel's voice as he continues raking over the embers of his past.

'I was wasting my time with my parents, trying to persuade them not to take Martina's twins. I tried to reason with Teresa. You know what it's like when you're a teenager, all that hormone-driven angst? Well, you can multiply it tenfold. But Teresa said they'd already arranged to give them to good people who couldn't have babies of their own. She warned me that Martina was manipulative, but I wasn't ready to listen. Not back then. I was head over heels in love.'

Daniel has always been a sensitive soul, and I imagine him as a teenager, his thoughts consumed with saving his first love. I watch him stare up at the ceiling, as if invoking ghosts of the past.

'The night Martina gave birth, Mossie took me and Louis out to the cinema. By the time we got back, the twins were gone. Martina was delirious, out of it. Mam and Da were out at sea. There was nothing I could do. Louis was furious.'

'Louis? Why? I thought he wasn't involved.'

Daniel gave a strange, bitter laugh. 'It turned out that Martina had been flirting with him too. That's when I saw her for what she was: not a real person but a mirror. Martina could see into your soul and reflect it back to you to get what she needed at the time. Louis had been spending all his pocket money to buy her chocolate treats. With Da, she played up to his ego, acting like she was in love with him. With Mam, she gave sympathy, telling her she deserved better than Da, and how she wished she'd had a mother like her.'

'And you?'

Daniel exhales a long breath, regret carrying on his words. 'We talked about art and travel, and she spoke about running away with me and starting a new life far removed from the island. Little did I know she was saying the same thing to Louis. Isla was taken in too.'

I nod. Isla is a trusting soul.

'Teresa saw right through her, though. She put me straight when I was open to hearing it.'

I gently guide my husband to the core of his story. 'So Martina gave birth to twins and your parents took them to the mainland for adoption?' I'm being generous with my estimation. Judging by the secrecy surrounding Árd Na Mara, it wouldn't surprise me if Gabriel was taking advantage of some of the vulnerable women in his care.

'My father was no angel,' Daniel counters, his handsome face twisted in bitterness and shame. 'He sold those babies for cash.'

'Oh God, Daniel that's . . .' I shake my head, because despite my suspicions it's a shocking, vile practice. 'That's awful.'

'That's why they kept Isla – because Da knew he couldn't sell her on.' Daniel touches the scar over his mouth as he sometimes does when he's stressed. His cleft lip may have been corrected in surgery, but it could have been enough to deem him as imperfect when it came to a quick sale. I say none of this, as his admission seems difficult enough.

'My parents went out in *Éireann Rose* to take the twins to the mainland, but they never made it,' Daniel continues. 'The boat capsized.'

'And Isla was with them?'

Daniel nods. 'Mam couldn't manage the twins on her own. One was strapped into a papoose on her chest, and Isla had the other. But then a sudden storm came in and the boat capsized. Isla was lucky. She barely escaped with her life.'

'And the babies . . . ?'

Another weary shake of the head. 'I think it's why Isla finds such comfort in the legend of the selkies. A part of her wants to believe the babies are still out there in the waves, that their spirits live on.'

'That explains all the drawings.' I'm thinking aloud as I recall the images on Isla's walls. 'How many babies were born in Árd Na Mara?'

Daniel shrugs. 'I don't know for sure. No more than a few. They became good at hiding it. Security in the home was tight back then. People couldn't just walk in and out like they can now. There were bolts on the doors, and shutters on the downstairs windows. Anyone who knew what they were up to was paid to keep their mouth shut. We weren't allowed near the basement as that's where the pregnant women were kept. They only allowed Martina upstairs because she refused to eat. She had us all under her spell. But as soon as Mam found out Martina was pregnant, she didn't talk to her after that.'

'I daresay she didn't,' I muse, wondering how Mary had put up with her husband's infidelities for so long. 'What about the shackles?'

'A necessity. They were only used on the women who were determined to self-harm.'

I sit in silence. The sound of a screeching fox outside makes for a chilling backdrop. The whole thing was an abomination. 'It must have been awful for Isla. What age was she when it happened? Has she ever had any counselling?'

I'm not surprised when Daniel shakes his head. 'She was the same age as Martina, barely twenty years old. It's not something we like to talk about. Best to leave these things in the past.'

'Judging from her bedroom, she has a lot of unresolved issues around what happened that day. Maybe after she settles in again, I'll be able to help.'

'Maybe,' Daniel says quietly, staring into nothingness. Rain lashes against our windowpane, but we are lost in our own little world. Then a thought occurs.

'What happened to Martina?' I wait patiently for Daniel to answer. As his face contorts with emotion, I can see how it's upsetting him. 'Didn't she kick up a stink about her babies? Was there an investigation?'

'She screamed bloody murder when she found out the twins had drowned. But Teresa brought her down to the basement room and sedated her.' He exhales with a sense of finality.

I shake my head as a memory of the roses bloomed in my mind. 'What happened to her after that? Because from what you've told me about Martina, she wasn't the sort of person to let things lie.'

'She died from an overdose.' Daniel's eyes are moist, his head bowed. 'She'd been storing up her drugs. She had them hidden in her clothes. After the babies . . . she took them all at once.'

'Are you sure?' I have to ask because I am not convinced.

'I don't know. I don't *want* to know. I'd just lost my parents. Isla was traumatised. We all were. Mossie and Teresa saved us all. If it weren't for them . . .' He swipes away a tear. 'All I know is that one minute Martina was there, and the next her body was being taken away. I didn't ask questions. I couldn't cope with the grief of losing her on top of everything else.' He turns to me and takes my hands. 'If Mossie and Teresa had been arrested, what would have happened to us? How would Isla have coped? She needed Árd Na Mara. She needed a stable home.'

He stares at me until I get what he's trying to say. That I should stop with the questions and let things lie. I rub a thumb over the back of his hand. 'You should have told me.'

'When?' Daniel replies with an edge to his tone. 'When we first met, or the day we arrived here? Because I hate it, all of it. It makes me sick to think of what went on.' He slaps another errant tear away as his frustration mounts.

I press my palm on his back to calm him down. 'Hey, I know this hasn't been easy. You've had a very unconventional childhood and there's a lot of stuff to work through. Let's get some sleep, eh? We'll pick this up tomorrow.'

I give him a squeeze and he gratefully kisses me goodnight. But my mind is racing as I switch off my bedroom light. Was Martina

211

murdered? I can't imagine Teresa or Mossie deliberately hurting anyone. They'd given up their lives to care for Daniel and his siblings. Martina was only young. But then I recall what Daniel said about her screaming. Perhaps she'd been over-sedated to the point of no return.

What a hell-hole Árd Na Mara has turned out to be. I'm not a superstitious person but it feels like this place is cursed. I stare at the high ceiling and to the shifting shadows caused by the quivering ivy leaves. I imagine Mary staring at this ceiling, filled with despair. A tear trickles down my face and nestles in the cove of my ear. I feel sorry for her, because while I didn't know her, I feel a sense of empathy. Selkie Island can be bleak, and it can't have been easy, rearing a family along with caring for the women imprisoned in this soulless house. I want to check on Kitty, but the baby monitor beside our bed is silent. I'll hear if she as much as sniffles in the night. I lie in the dark, listening to the patter of rain, as the storm begins to ease.

CHAPTER 47

DANIEL

I listen to Claire's breathing, and I can tell that she's still awake. Like me, her thoughts won't let her have a peaceful passage into sleep. We face away from each other, silence stretching between us. The bed is a double, but there's a chasm between us right now. I've told her as much as I can, but I knew she'd trip me up with questions. She was right to doubt my account of Martina's death. I feel like I'm physically shrinking as I think about what happened. Each night, nightmares attack my body as remorse swarms my brain.

Before I met Martina, I was a hormonal teenager with little experience of the outside world. It wasn't until I began secondary school that I truly appreciated just how weird my home life was. I tried to distance myself from the women in Árd Na Mara, but contact was inevitable as I carried out my chores. Everything changed the day Martina arrived. Like the siren call of the mermaids, her voice drew me in. I was speechless when I saw her. To me, she was the most beautiful creature I'd ever seen. Her wavy hair framed her face, her eyes large and expressive as she caught me peeping through the door hatch.

'Don't go,' she'd said, as I'd slammed it shut, my cheeks flushed. It was the command whispered with the slightest hint of affection that made my heart race. Da used to laugh and ruffle my hair when he found me peeking at the women. Mam would tell me off and banish me to my room. 'Please,' Martina continued. 'I'm scared. Nobody will tell me what's going on.'

She was sitting on her bed, hugging her knees. She hadn't yet been put in the regulation tracksuit that my mother made all the girls wear. I remember Martina's clothes so clearly: the white linen blouse and slim-fitting pale blue jeans that revealed her slender form. All sorts of emotions were stirred up within me that day.

'Are you alright?' I'd said, hesitantly reopening the hatch.

Martina seemed touched by my concern, and so unlike the other women as she approached the door. Every word spoken through her lips felt like a gift. She had an uncanny way of knowing what another person was thinking and exactly what they needed to hear.

In time, we became friends. At least, that's what I was led to believe. But she'd flirted with Louis too. He was a year younger than me, but broader in stature and closer to what Da wanted in a son than I could ever be. I don't think he liked what he saw when he looked at me. I was self-conscious of the thin white scar from my cleft lip that marked me as different. The nicknames I picked up in school tore my confidence apart, making me feel like an outsider. Even the islanders referred to me as 'the boy with the hare lip' – as if I didn't have a name. But Martina saw me differently than everyone else. She called it my battle scar and said it made me strong. She was right, as I strove for success and couldn't get away from small-minded island thinking quickly enough.

As the wind rises outside, I am reminded of that awful night when my parents died. I have not been completely truthful with my wife. Mossie *had* taken me and Louis out to the cinema, but we came home early from the mainland because of the choppy crossing back.

Mam and Da had planned to take the *Éireann Rose* and bring Isla to help transport the twins. It angers me to think that they involved my sister like that. Mam always underestimated how deeply Isla felt things. They should have found another way. I knew the moment that we got back to Árd Na Mara that Martina had given birth. She was out of it by then, drugged by my father before he left with her twins. She rambled something about the sea. Under Teresa's watch, I sloped off to my bedroom, but not before I remembered my promise to Martina that I would bring her babies home. Within minutes, I was breathless, dodging the rocks on the cliff path that punched into the thin soles of my shoes. Teenage angst drove me on with reckless abandon. I wasn't the only person sneaking out that night. Louis was ahead of me, sprinting into the night. He swore at me to go home, but even he realised that we could do more together than alone.

'I know where there's a boat,' he'd said, as the wind howled around us. 'They're not getting away with this.' Only then did I realise that I wasn't the only person in love with Martina, and willing to do whatever it took.

But what started off as good intentions soon ended with tragedy. My parents didn't die because of the storm. They were killed. The twins didn't belong to Da. He just took the blame. As I said, I lied to Claire. Everything that happened revolved around that night, and by the time we got back to Árd Na Mara, Martina was gone.

CHAPTER 48

MARY

Then

I stood in my kitchen, ready and calm. I decided not to ambush my husband when we were alone in our bedroom, as I'd done countless times before. I had another plan. Gabriel and I were going to walk the length of the island as the kids ate their breakfast. When I say kids, both our boys now towered over me. While Isla was accepting, my sons were asking questions about what we did for a living, and I didn't want to take in errant women any more. Louis was like his father and looked at the women with a curiosity that didn't sit easy with me. This would be the last time I'd tell Gabriel that enough was enough. Today, I wouldn't be put off, cajoled, manipulated, or blackmailed. I felt too old, too guilty, too depressed to carry on with it all. Gabriel must have paid off his debt. The years were catching up with me, but I had made plans. There was a house coming up for sale near the bay. It would be perfect for us, and there would be no treks across the precarious cliff edge on the way to the pier to catch the ferry. It came with a couple of spare rooms that I could use for a B&B. It would mean selling Árd Na Mara, but it would put an end to Gabriel's scheming when it came to the women in our care.

As my husband searched for his boots, I cast an eye over my boys, who were sitting at the kitchen table eating the breakfast that Teresa had made. Even on Saturdays, they had to get up early to do their chores. A late breakfast was their reward. The pair of them were like chalk and cheese. Despite his French name, Louis was Irish through and through. He loved the island and, like me, knew every inch of it. He was his father's shadow, and God knows why, but he looked up to him. Danny was a dreamer and wanted to travel the world. When he was born, I immediately took to him, and while Gabriel drew back in shock, Teresa knew exactly what was wrong. She watched him closely and advised us on the surgery needed to repair his cleft lip. But while it could be fixed, the boy wasn't perfect enough to warrant selling on. Gabriel knew another baby would keep my silence, and he'd always wanted a son. For months after Danny was born, I expected his mother to reclaim him, but she never did. A pale, good-looking boy, Danny's slender frame and soft hands were never meant for hard manual work. They both liked to paint, but Danny was a better artist. Louis's work was raw and natural. He painted quickly and moved on. Danny got lost in a painting and every brushstroke was well thought out. His mother was not a bad soul, but she was adamant from the start that she didn't want her baby. She just wasn't capable of motherly love.

Louis preferred to play football with his friends than hold a paintbrush most days. Gabriel once told me that he loved Louis more because he came from both of us. There was no shame involved in his conception, which I considered a minor miracle. But I loved all my children the same.

A hairdryer turned on upstairs, signalling that Isla was back from her swim. My little island baby was blossoming into a beautiful young woman. A solitary girl, she preferred the company of wildlife to people. She passed all her exams with reasonable grades, and working at Árd Na Mara gained her valuable experience. As Gabriel tied his laces, I grabbed my rucksack from the kitchen counter. I packed a picnic because I had every intention of being gone for a while. At least the weather was favourable.

'We'll be back in a couple of hours,' I said to Teresa, who was sweeping the floor. She'd banished Mossie to the garden, demanding that he paint the wrought-iron fence before it rusted away.

'I'm sure we can manage without you.' She waved me away like an errant fly.

Then we were off, Gabriel and I, quietly walking the path bordering the cliff edge and taking in the view. I filled my lungs with sea air, and we marvelled at a rare sight of the white-tailed eagle as it glided through the cloudless sky. It was almost like old times as Gabriel and I enjoyed our nature walk. Skye, my beloved dog, was no longer with us, but I could imagine her bounding ahead, barking as she disturbed his photoshoot. If it hadn't been for her, we might never have met as we did. I wonder if that would have been a bad thing.

'This is a good spot,' I said, as I found a flat piece of rock that offered beautiful views over the bay. I lay down my rucksack, and Gabriel took the blanket from his bag. He'd been telling me about his travels to the mainland – the sanitised version, I'm sure. He looked tired, and I wondered if he would ever slow down. I waited until we were settled on the blanket before I mentioned it. I'd brought a nice bottle of red – his favourite any time of the day, a flask of tea for me, along with some crusty baguettes, olives and cheese which I'd bought from a deli on the mainland the day before.

'You've gone to a lot of trouble.' Gabriel uncorked the wine with a pop. 'Have I missed an anniversary?' His recent trip back to France strengthened his accent, and I told myself to stay focused.

'We need to talk about Árd Na Mara.' It was our one bone of contention, but I barely got the words out when Gabriel interrupted me.

'I know what you're going to say.' He flashed his usual charming smile. 'But you don't need to worry. Everything will be just fine.'

'No, Gabriel,' I said sternly, waving away his offer of wine. 'It's far from fine. I've stood by you through thick and thin, but it's going to take more than a picnic on the island to fix what's wrong. The boys are getting older. They're *noticing* the girls. It's not healthy to have them around so many immoral young women.' My face flushed as I relayed the speech I'd practised all week. I'd been to confessions and taken Father Hennessy's advice on board. It had felt so good to offload. 'Let me finish,' I said, as Gabriel opened his mouth to speak. 'Because I'm only going to say this once. This has got to end. People are talking. They're calling Árd Na Mara a knocking shop. I want those women out.'

I launched into a tirade about the boys and how it was only natural that they would develop crushes, given how few young women there were of their age on the island. They weren't meant to talk to our patients; it was against the rules. But what sort of example had their father set? Not only did he openly flirt with the women, but he was unapologetic with it. As for the rest of it . . . Árd Na Mara had experienced its fair share of tragedy over the years. From escape attempts to drownings to suicide. Two of the women managed to go missing and never turned up again. Any other establishment would have been under scrutiny, but not here on this isolated island. I tried to make their lives comfortable, and some served their time and moved on, but other women did not fare so well. Losing Catherine had been hard and not a day passed that I did not feel guilty for benefitting from her death. I will never forget the day that she took her own life, and the part we played in facilitating it. It had happened too often since then.

Gabriel's attention was waning as he tore off another piece of baguette, so I issued an ultimatum. 'I've been to see a solicitor on the mainland. I know my rights, Gabriel. You can't take Árd Na Mara from me.'

I watched his expression change, and his methodical chewing came to a halt. The mention of a solicitor shocked him. His days of shady dealings were numbered. I put this to my husband. Then I told him about the house coming up for sale and my plans of starting a B&B.

'*Mon amour*, I have plans too. Just one more crossing . . .' His voice flowed like caramel as he bargained. 'Then I swear, that's it.' Then he said what a bonus it was that Martina was expecting twins, as if she were some kind of brood mare. He leaned across the blanket and took my hand. 'I've found a wealthy couple who will raise the twins as their own, and give us enough money to set up your B&B.' I was ready to disagree, but he wasn't finished. 'Believe it or not, I'm tired of this too. I want to be there for the boys. You're right, I need to set a better example for them. We'll bring the twins to the mainland after they're born. Then we'll make plans. Good, wholesome plans, yes? So we can sleep easy in our bed at night.'

I monitored his expression, trying to decipher if he was placating me or telling the truth. But regulations were tightening. Institutes like ours were being monitored. It was only a matter of time before we were found out.

'Alright,' I said with a weary sigh.

We arranged for our boat to be ready. A twin birth was something we'd never encountered before, but Teresa was confident she could manage it. I should have been worried about Martina and the effect she was having on my boys. The woman was a devious bitch. Soon, our world would come crashing down.

CHAPTER 49

CLAIRE

The slamming of the front door has awoken me. I've been in the middle of a dream where I'm swimming in the sea, searching for Kitty. I inhale a sharp breath. My nightdress is damp with sweat and there are tears drizzling down my face.

'What . . . what's going on? Daniel?'

I switch on the light. My watch reads 2 a.m. and my husband is sitting on the edge of the mattress, pulling his socks on. For a moment, I wonder if he's in the midst of a night terror, but then he speaks.

'One of the doors is banging downstairs,' he says quietly, standing to put on his jeans. 'Mossie must have come home and left one unlocked.' A slamming door punctuates his sentence. 'It'll come off its hinges at this rate.'

I thought the storm was abating, but now the windows and doors creak and groan against the force of the wind and rain. I watch as he tugs on his jumper and heads out the room. This isn't the sort of house where you walk about in your pyjamas, or bare feet, for that matter. The only way to get the place properly insulated will be to replace all the wooden windows with PVC. But my renovation concerns are overshadowed by fear as my husband fails to return. Mossie is security conscious. It's been drummed into him over the years. The sound of raised voices downstairs fills me with dread. Something is very wrong. They're going to wake up Kitty. I swing my legs from the bed and pull on my dressing gown. The baby monitor is silent, but I can't go downstairs without checking on my daughter first. I stride across the landing, wasting no time in getting to her room.

Now I'm staring into her empty cot, my heart fluttering in panic.

Steady, I tell myself. *Remember your breathing.* She probably woke up in all the commotion and Daniel's taken her downstairs. I don't know, though. He's never been that attentive and, now that I think of it, I haven't heard a peep from her all night. I trot down the stairs, my hand skimming the banisters, my heartbeat in line with my feet tapping against wood. A sense of dread clambers up into my throat as I enter the kitchen.

Teresa is standing there, her damp hair sticking to her face, her skin reddened from being out in the storm. She's talking to Daniel and they freeze at the sight of me.

'It's Isla,' she says, not waiting for me to ask the inevitable question. 'She left a note in her room. She's taken our boat to the mainland. That girl . . . once she gets something into her head, there's no stopping her.'

'That old thing? Why?' I say, knowing *Éireann Rose*, the little boat kept as a relic of that tragic night, is in need of repair. I scan the room. The downstairs travel cot is empty, as is the high chair. 'Where's Kitty? She's not in her room.'

Daniel is at the back door when he comes to a halt. 'Isla's got her.' He raises a hand to reassure me, but as I stare at him, bewildered, I'm far from reassured. 'It's OK. Louis has gone after them. She won't have got far.'

I clutch the back of a chair for balance. I can't breathe. I feel like somebody has punched me in the gut.

'Call the coastguards,' I manage to say.

'I've already done it,' Teresa replies. 'They're out to sea helping a trawler that's in trouble. God knows when they'll be free.'

'I'll be fine,' Daniel says, and now he's pulling on his wellingtons as he prepares to catch up with Louis. 'She's not gone long.'

'Gone to the bottom of the sea, on a night like this,' I cry, fear engulfing me in its icy grip. That old sense of cold terror envelops me. There's going to be another death. I cling to my husband's jacket as he tries to leave. 'You're not going without me! Kitty will freeze on a night like this!' I'm screaming now. I've heard these sounds before.

'No, you're not,' Daniel says firmly. 'And every second we spend here arguing, Isla is going further out to sea. Stay here. I'll call as soon as I find her.'

'What about Kitty?' I shout after him into the night, but Teresa pulls me back inside. 'What are you doing?' I squirm beneath Teresa's grip. She has a strength I didn't know she possessed, and something tells me she's done this before. Teresa has her arm around me and is chiding me to sit down. I rush towards the door but discover that it's locked. 'What's going on?' I say, rounding on her.

'You'll only slow them down,' she says resolutely. 'It's for the best.'

'But I feel so helpless,' I said, staring out of the windows at the sea.

'Then pray,' she says, pulling a string of rosary beads from her dressing-gown pocket. 'For all our souls.'

But I'm not satisfied with the power of prayer alone. I go into the pantry and take the binoculars from the shelf. The staircase feels twice as long as I run to the top floor. A gust of icy wind and rain greets me as I tug open our bedroom window and train my binoculars on the bay. My heart is pounding now, the binoculars shaking in my grip. In the distance, I see the waves crashing against the shore. A lone figure rows a boat. It's Isla. It must be. I blink, clearing my vision before pressing the heavy binoculars to my eyes. Is that my papoose strapped to her chest?

I try to steady my breathing, but the air feels so thin. The hairs prickle on the back of my neck as I realise that Teresa is standing in the doorway, watching me. Is this what it was like for the women who stayed here years ago?

'Why is Isla taking Kitty out on a night like this?' I scream. 'Stop her! I want my baby back!'

But she's just standing there, staring at me. Panicked, I grab for my clothes, pulling on the first thing that comes to hand. Thick socks. Jeans. A jumper. But even if I run, what can I do? Isla's out on the water.

'Oh God,' I utter, feeling like I'm about to throw up. I pick up the binoculars and focus them in time to see Isla resting the oars on the boat. I watch her bob about on the dark, restless waters while curious seals approach. 'Where's Louis?' I croak. 'I can't see him.' But my questions are left unanswered as they echo around the walls of the room. The sudden strobe of the lighthouse leaves me in no doubt. It *is* Isla out there on the choppy waves, and she's removing Kitty from her papoose. 'No!' I cry, my intestines twisting with fear.

I shout, even though Isla can't hear me. 'What are you doing? No, Isla! Please stop!' I turn to Teresa. 'Do something!'

'Sit down,' she says with a calmness that terrifies me. 'Take it easy. You're getting yourself all worked up. Isla won't come to any harm. She's well used to these waters, and the storm is easing off.'

But it's not Isla I'm worried about. It's Kitty, and I can't bear to look. She's giving her to the selkies, just as she did with the twins the night they died.

'It was her, wasn't it?' I say, tears streaming down my face. 'It was Isla who made the boat capsize.' I see the guilt on her face. 'Now she's doing it again, only this time with Kitty. She's offering up my baby because she thinks we're cursed!'

I know it sounds crazy, but it's the only conclusion I can come to as to why Isla would want to harm my child. Then I catch movement behind Teresa and I can't believe my eyes as Daniel stands in the doorway. 'What . . . what are you doing back?'

'Louis has gone too far ahead. My place is here with you.'

'Are you crazy?' I'm fumbling with the binoculars. My hands are shaking so much that I can't hold the binoculars steady or focus them anymore.

But Daniel is at my side, guiding me away from the window. 'It's alright,' he says. 'Everything's going to be alright. Isla's taken Kitty away from you, because Kitty has caused nothing but arguments between us. Isla's just trying to help.'

Frustration burns like a fire inside me and I want to punch that calm smile off his face. This isn't the man I married. This is Danny from the island with his strange, unnerving gaze.

'I need my phone,' I say, my words shaky. 'Give me my phone. I'm calling the police.'

But Daniel doesn't move.

A thought rises. The basement. There's a phone in the basement. The one I found in the drawers. I'll call the police from there. But Daniel blocks my exit as I try to escape.

'There's no point,' he says, as Teresa joins his side.

'Why not?' I scream. Fear twists my insides because I know what he's going to say.

Daniel clamps a hand on my shoulder. 'Because Kitty is dead.'

CHAPTER 50

MARY

Then

Everything changed with Martina. The other women thought they were in love with my husband, but it was never reciprocated. Martina was the opposite. She had a way of drawing people to her, like moths burning their wings on a flame. I hated her for it, because I could see it in his eyes. Not love exactly, because he loved nobody but himself, but interest. Perhaps it was a meeting of minds. She was the first woman to arrive at the house who ever worried me, and it was only later that I could see how much she affected my children too. She was at the root of our deaths. She and her manipulating ways.

Initially, I was taken in too. She exploited my love for Selkie Island and its mystical tales. I brought flowers to her room, and she hung on my every word as I arranged them in a plastic vase. She always had a smile for me, saying how wonderful it must have been growing up surrounded by God's great bounty, while explaining how the mainland was a cesspit of degradation which had brought her nothing but pain. She repented for her sins, explaining she hadn't been a well woman, and she even had confessions with the priest.

As someone who believed in forgiveness and salvation, I swallowed it whole. I put a cross in her room, and a picture of the Virgin Mary. She told me everything I wanted to hear and more. But it was only when I overheard her talking to my boys that my attitude hardened towards her. She told Danny how amazing he was, and how his scar made him even more attractive in her eyes. She talked of the famous art galleries she'd visited in various countries, coming across as a young, cosmopolitan woman of the world. I listened from around the corner as he said he was an artist, and the next day she was thrilled when he showed her his work through the hatch in the door. She took advantage of his kind nature to get what she wanted. Even if it was an extra biscuit, a warm blanket – just the smallest things were worth the charade.

I listened on another occasion to her talking to Louis, complimenting his strong physique, how like his father he was, yet brighter, funnier and misunderstood. She talked about all the sporting events she'd attended and the famous sportspeople she'd rubbed shoulders with. Calculated lies passed her lips as she reached out through the gap in the door and stroked his face. My precious boy fell hook, line and sinker. And why wouldn't he? She was an exotic creature in a gilded cage.

Gabriel could not do enough for her, eventually allowing her to move to one of the upstairs rooms so she could gaze out to sea every night, singing. That melancholy song of hers used to drive me insane. I was hardly surprised when she fell pregnant. The boys were furious, because by then they were old enough to understand what was going on.

'How do you put up with it?' Danny asked me one night, his face red with anger. He had tears in his eyes, still so young, fighting these grown-up emotions he couldn't get hold of.

I explained that he was to think of it as a business transaction, and that Martina knew perfectly well what was happening and was a willing participant. She provided a baby, and we gave her the best of care, with a recommendation to the board that she be released early when the time came. It was hard to say those words, but I needed him to know exactly the sort of man his father was.

It didn't stop me from feeling awful when the time came to take the twins away from their mother. It was the first time I saw any genuine emotion in Martina.

When I made big decisions, I did so with a limited view. I realise that now. My perception of the world was skewed. I was under-educated, having spent much of my childhood helping my parents when I should have been in school. I knew nothing but the island, and my head was easily turned. I allowed myself to be manipulated every step of the way. There was love in my heart, but sadly love can make you do foolish things. I deserved what came next. We both did.

CHAPTER 51

CLAIRE

I barely remember getting from the bedroom to the kitchen as Teresa and Daniel guide me downstairs. For one awful moment, I thought I'd be locked in the basement, just like the women before me.

'She's in shock,' Teresa said. 'She needs a cup of sweet tea.'

My legs were like jelly. Daniel was on the phone talking to Louis. He told me that Isla was safe.

Now I sit at the kitchen table, unable to comprehend what's happened. Sweet, trusting Isla has taken Kitty from her papoose and thrown her into the icy sea. The room spins around me, and a cup of tea is forced into my shaking hands. I can't drink because I'm unable to swallow. I barely manage to utter the words.

'She's not dead. I won't let it happen. Louis . . . Louis will find her in time.'

Daniel takes the cup from my grip as tea spills over the edges. 'It's too late for Louis . . . It's too late for anybody to help our daughter now.' He's staring at me, unblinking, and I'm frozen in this moment as my brain feels like it's shutting down. 'God!' he exclaims. 'This isn't easy for me either. I've been trying to do this gently, hoping that you'd see it . . . praying you'd work it out. But Isla has done what I've not been brave enough to do myself.'

I feel sick to my stomach because a small part of me knows what he is going to say. I don't want to face it. I'll never be ready to accept the truth. I'd rather die. Then I'm back at the window in London, on that ledge as I prepare to jump. The memory flashes before me, telling me what I need to know. I'm engulfed in a wave of grief as I think of my suicide attempt. I didn't want to die. I just wanted to stop the pain.

I flinch as Daniel touches my arm, bringing me back to the present day.

'Our daughter Kitty died from meningitis over a year ago,' he says. 'You couldn't live with yourself because you were accepting an award the night she took a turn for the worse.'

I back away from my husband, his words steel pins being pushed into my heart.

'You're mad,' I cry, still fighting it. 'Why . . . are you doing this to me?'

Daniel kneels before me, and only now can I see the grey hairs on his temple, and the lines on his face which have been etched by grief.

'I thought if I brought you here, it would give your mind a chance to heal. You're strong, Claire. But that was half the problem. You couldn't cope with falling apart.'

I am shaking. I don't feel strong, not now.

'No. Kitty's alive. Do you hear me? As real as you and me . . . or are you telling me you're a ghost too?'

I look to Teresa for something, anything, to back me up. But she's standing there, arms folded and hands tucked into her armpits as if she's watching the aftermath of some awful car crash.

'I'm no ghost . . .' Daniel continues. 'And neither is she. It's just your mind trying to protect itself. You tried to kill yourself.

Then your subconscious kicked in. It was an act of self-preservation. Your psychiatrist told me not to force things. She said you'd find your own way in time. But I can't have you thinking that any of us would hurt you. You need to face the truth. I can't do this on my own anymore.'

I can barely stand the pain as I am pulled into Daniel's orbit. It is a place of torment and suffering, of the realisation that my daughter is never coming back. I try to stand, pressing my palms against the table as dizziness weakens my legs.

'But I heard screaming . . .'

'That was you. We lost our little girl.'

The edges of my memories are fuzzy. My sister was with me in the hospital when I broke the news. I thought that her little girl had lost her life. Then the screaming. It came from me? I'd received treatment in an institution. But it wasn't like Árd Na Mara. I'd been allowed to come and go. Has it really been a year? I remember taking my medication. The pain being unbearable at times. But then . . . a baby . . . all this time here, didn't I have a baby in my arms?

'Get away from me!' I said, but my voice is shrill, dislocated from my body, just as it had been that day. I was so wrapped up in work that I did not spot the signs that took my child's life. Lunging towards the kitchen door, I escape out into the night air, screaming at my husband to leave me be.

A calm voice follows, telling him to go back inside. Teresa is here.

A warm shawl is placed around my shoulders, but it fails to ease the pain.

'It's not true . . .' The words are ghostly on my lips. 'It can't be.' A thought crosses my mind. I cling to hope wherever I can find it. The tiniest grain. 'You saw her.' I swipe away the tears dripping from my jawbone. 'Teresa, you saw my baby. You held her . . . changed her nappy.'

'I did what had to be done to get you well.' She sighs. 'Danny told me what happened . . .' Even she is finding the truth of our loss hard to put into words.

'And you went along with the lie?' I say, disbelieving.

'I'd crawl across broken glass for that boy if he asked me to.'

I nod. Of course she would. Like everyone else on this island, their loyalties lie with their own. But it's not true. It can't be. I feel my hair prickle on the back of my neck as I recall the sounds of Kitty's cries. The tiny, inaudible burps. The sniffles in the night.

'Didn't you hear her?' I cry. But all I see is pity reflected at me.

'It's a doll,' Teresa said sadly. 'Sure enough, the most lifelike one I've seen. It's weighted, with fine hair, and eyes that open and close. It's made of silicone so it feels real. It even has that baby smell. When you're out and about with the pram, people can't tell the difference, as long as it's tucked safely away.'

It. The sound of that word makes my stomach roll. But this time I'm seeing what I was blind to before. Daniel never reacted when Kitty cried in the night. Her sounds were exclusively for me because they had been in my head all along. But still, instinctively, I answered because I couldn't bear to be in a world without her.

'When Danny called me, he was in a bad way,' Teresa continues. 'He'd lost his little girl, and he almost lost you. Then you went through a course of treatment. It brought you back to yourself, because your mind tricked you into believing it was your niece who died.'

'You make me sound so weak.'

But Teresa is shaking her head. 'It's like Danny said. It's because you were strong that you couldn't cope. All your life, you've found a way around things. But this time there was nothing you could do. Danny thought it would be easier to give you some time. Let your mind rest. This is a healing island. Many before you have discovered that for themselves.'

'But Kitty's still here. I can feel her,' I whisper, as the wind ruffles my hair.

Teresa nods. 'I know. You're not the only person in the world to lose a child. But in time, the sound of her cries will fade. You'll never get over it, but you'll find the strength to carry on.'

'What if I can't?'

The silence between us is loaded as Teresa's features become stern. 'You've got to. The living need you more than the dead.'

The weight of my grief falls once more on my shoulders as her words hit home. I look behind her to see Daniel standing in the doorway of Árd Na Mara. Teresa follows my gaze.

'Best I'll leave you to it. You two have a lot to talk about. You don't need me anymore.'

I lower my head, biting my bottom lip. She is right. Isla is on her way back and she needs Teresa more. A cold breeze curls around me as if in warning of the tough times ahead.

'I'm sorry,' Daniel says softly, as he takes Teresa's place. 'I . . . I couldn't face losing you too.' Only now can I see the suffering that I was previously blind to. 'That day . . . on the window ledge. You asked me to join you. Sometimes when the pain was too much, I regretted not taking your hand and jumping when we had the chance. But then when you came out of the institution, you reverted to thinking Kitty was alive. It seemed like such a nice place to be, cushioned from the pain, if only for a while.'

'That's why you weren't interested in Kitty. You wouldn't take her from her cot or feed her at night.'

'I tried, but I couldn't kiss that cold, lifeless doll and act as if it were real. Neither could I press a bottle to its mouth. It didn't come close to what we had with Kitty: looking into her face during our night feeds, her little gurgles and coos when she held my fingers tight. The doll felt like an insult to her memory. I couldn't stand to look at it.' He shook his head. 'We tried to stretch out the time that

233

you spent away from Kitty, so you could see outside the bubble. But it was hard. Isla has hated lying to you. She's badgered me from the start to tell you the truth. I guess that's why she took things into her own hands tonight.'

Of course. I recall the first time I met her, and the curious glances she gave to the 'baby' in my arms. Then, when I was locked in the basement, nobody seemed to care that Kitty had been left on her own. Isla wasn't giving Kitty to the selkies. She was trying to break the spell I was under, make me see the truth.

'It's why your family hasn't been in touch,' Daniel continues. 'They wanted to have you committed, but then Kim Chéng got in touch. You remember her, don't you? You shared a room with her when you went to university. She read about your suicide attempt and wanted to help. She admitted you in for treatment and you took to it so well.' He tries to explain further, and I'm listening through the haze of grief. 'The experimental treatment stemmed from a neuroscientist who treated phantom pains in people who suddenly lost their limbs. They were desperate for relief, but doctors couldn't treat something that wasn't there. Then they came up with the idea of a mirror, which reflected the patient's existing leg or arm, tricking the mind into thinking it was still here.' He pauses for breath. 'In a way, the doll was your mirror. It reflected what you needed to see to help treat the pain. Do you understand?' He scratches his temple. 'It took me a while to wrap my head around it, but you saw what you needed to see in order to survive.'

'Transitory object therapy,' I say. I've heard of it before. As crazy as it sounds, it's beginning to make sense. Slowly, memories of the treatment creep back into my mind. A doll being pressed into my arms. Me, holding it close to my chest. Plump tears fill my eyes. 'I just can't believe she's gone.' But deep down, I have always known.

I step back, the swell of panic making my chest hurt. I shudder as I think about the ferry. The whispers and funny looks down the pub. No wonder Aoife couldn't face me. She must have thought I was mad, yet everyone has been kind in their own way.

'Does *everyone* know?' I say, my cheeks burning from humiliation.

'Only those who need to. Nobody's judging you, Claire. They know what we've been through, and it's something every parent dreads. Aoife and Orla . . . they just want to help.'

'I need to be alone.' I brush past him and walk into the house, glancing over my shoulder to ensure he's not following. 'I won't do anything stupid, before you ask.'

But he's standing there, his face a picture of concern.

'I just need five minutes,' I add, unsure of how to feel. I should be furious at his deception, but he was trying to help.

Then I'm up the stairs and in Kitty's old bedroom. I touch the wooden cot, my heart heavy with grief that has been waiting in the sidelines all along.

Why did he have to tell me? I wish I could take back everything I know. I pick up the ruffled pink dress that my 'baby' would never outgrow.

Surely living in a world with the ghost of my daughter is better than nothing at all?

I hear the front door open, and Isla's voice rises from the hall. How can I face any of them again?

CHAPTER 52

DANIEL

Perhaps the grief of my daughter's loss has made me irrational, but all I wanted was for me and Claire to be a happy couple again. When she tried to commit suicide, it wasn't a cry for help. She was serious. The first time, she asked a colleague to get hold of the drugs she needed to send herself into oblivion. I'm grateful that they came to me instead. The second time, I caught her in the bathroom, with a tub of warm water and a razor blade on the side. Her letter was written, her financial affairs in order, and she had even paid for a funeral plan. After that, I shadowed her every movement, but all along she'd been biding her time. She convinced me that she was getting better. Then she jumped from our window ledge. In reality, she didn't believe that she deserved saving when she hadn't been there for our child.

I admit, there were times when I resented her for not picking up on the illness that claimed our daughter's life. I never spoke the words aloud. Perhaps she saw it anyway, in a look, a touch, or the way I withdrew. But that ugly seed of animosity withered and died in the face of her insurmountable pain. Now she knows the truth and as I stand outside the bedroom door, it feels like I'm starting all over again. But this time I'm not alone. Downstairs, Teresa is fussing over Isla as she comes home.

'Claire?' I push open the bedroom door. 'Isla's back.'

I still can't believe that she did it. I imagine her, stealing the doll from the cot and creeping out into the night. Most people would never return to the sea after what Isla had been through. But the dark waters that surround us are part of her very soul. Isla must have thought that I'd never get around to telling Claire the truth.

My wife is a pitiful sight as she stares at the empty cot, but at least she responds with a nod.

'Will you come downstairs and see her? Give her a chance to explain?'

Another nod of acceptance. But first, she goes into the bathroom and washes her face. She drags a brush over her hair and blows her nose. After checking herself in the mirror, she joins me and we take the stairs. She's doing this for Isla, so my sister won't feel bad about what she's done. This has been so challenging for her, being part of our conspiracy. I thought hard before asking her, Teresa, and Mossie to come on board. In the end, Louis did too.

The treatment that my wife received in the psychiatric unit had worked to an extent. Dr Kim Chéng had felt like a lifesaver at the time. It helped that there was a strong bond of trust before the treatment began. Clare put herself in the hands of her old friend. But it was never meant to go this far. When Claire came home with the doll, Kim recommended that I ease her back into the truth. She wasn't meant to leave her flat. I took that upon myself and planned it meticulously. We took the ferry instead of a plane and kept our distance from other people. Teresa spoke to Orla and cleared it with her, although we never brought the doll as far as the pub. Wrapped up in clothes, it looked just like any sleeping infant. Kim warned me that it could be a bad idea, changing Claire's routine. But I believed that taking Claire to Selkie Island was the best way to protect her. The project of renovating Árd Na Mara took her focus away from our child. A fresh start. I still love the island. I am a part of it, shaped by it, just like my siblings. But maybe I was wrong to expect Claire to feel the same.

I am shocked at the sight of Isla as I descend the stairs. The moment takes on a surreal quality as she stands there, dripping wet, with the papoose strapped to her chest, just as she did years ago. But this time it is empty. She dropped the doll into the sea to shock my wife into accepting the truth. She could see the arguments that it was causing and knew Claire would never recover as long as it was around.

'Are you sure you're alright?' Teresa wraps a towel over Isla's shoulders. 'What were you thinking, going out there at this hour?'

Louis stands next to her, his hair damp as he takes off his coat. 'She fell over getting out of the boat. She didn't go out far. Just far enough to throw the . . .' He pauses, looking at me uncertainly. 'Well, you know. She threw it into the sea. But apart from that, she's grand.' He glances over at Claire, looking awkward. 'Alright?'

Claire can barely look him in the eye. She gives him a tight nod before approaching Isla. 'Thank you,' she says, taking her by the hand. 'For having the strength to tell me the truth in the best way you knew how.'

Isla smiles, her face relieved from the stress of lying. 'She's with the selkies now.'

CHAPTER 53

CLAIRE

I turn away from Teresa, trying to absorb my new reality. She's in my bedroom, staring out the window as Daniel and Louis go on the hunt for Mossie, who still hasn't come home. To think, just hours ago I was banging on that glass, crying out for my baby. Now the sea twinkles like black diamonds as the moon reflects the dark waters beneath.

Teresa said she's here because our room offers the best view of the cliff paths below. She's looking out for Mossie, but I know she's also babysitting me. What a crazy, messed-up night it's been. At least Isla is tucked up, warm and comfortable in bed. 'How did you do it?' I'd said to her. 'Go out at night in a boat after everything that happened with your mam and da?' My heart was aching for what I'd lost, but I couldn't be the only one. Isla had to be traumatised too.

But her gentle smile was like the sun breaking through the darkest of clouds. 'The sea is my happy place, not bad,' she simply said. 'They're with me in the water. They all are. Why would I be scared of it?'

She gives me hope. Because if she can get through this then so can I. I hugged her, we wept, and I left her in no doubt that by getting rid of the doll, she did the right thing – but there were to be no more surprises from now on. The last thing I want is for her to be hurt.

There is one more person I need to talk to, from outside the bubble I've been living in. I'm in my pyjamas now, but I'll never sleep on my own – not when there's an empty cot in the next room. I'm exhausted, physically and mentally, and soon it will be dawn. I want to swallow the sleeping tablet that sits on my bedside table and zone out. But first I have a call to make.

'Where are you going?' Teresa asks as I rise from the bed.

'To use the phone. And don't pretend that you don't have one. I know there's one in the basement. I know a lot of things.'

Teresa pales, suddenly unsure of herself. 'Please, pet. Don't call the police.'

I frown. As if I'd do that now. What would I say? That I've been in therapy for the last year, thinking the doll was my baby? Or that Daniel's parents once made a side hustle out of selling babies every now and again? Or perhaps I could ask what happened to Martina while she was here. The thought of hauling Daniel's family over the coals makes me turn cold. What good would that do now?

'We've been through enough. I just want to speak to my sister.' I watch Teresa's features relax as I speak in a reassuring tone.

Teresa's tied herself up in knots because Mossie still isn't home. She trains her binoculars on Daniel and Louis as they search the cliff paths for him. Seconds pass before she breaks away from watching, slips her hand into her dressing-gown pocket and pulls out a Nokia phone. Sheepishly, she hands it over.

'Daniel thought it best if you didn't contact the outside world. He didn't want you to find out about your treatment that way.'

Teresa is no stranger to lies, having spent the best part of her life in Árd Na Mara. But her concerns come from a good place. Sighing, I take the phone.

My sister's number is committed to memory and my hands are trembling as I hold the mobile to my ear.

'Hello?'

'Susan, is it true? About the doll?' I blurt the words the moment I hear her sleepy voice.

The silence between us is deafening and confirms what I already know. Memories are filtering in slowly, but this time I'm coping.

'I've been expecting this question.' Her voice is heavy with sadness. 'I thought I'd know what to say, but I don't. Are you OK?' I hear a door close in the background, and the sounds of the streets fade away.

'No, I'm not OK,' I say softly. 'I'm not sure if I'll ever be OK again.'

'If you're alive, then you're better than you were. Don't be cross with Daniel. The treatment was a last resort.'

I'm surprised by her reaction. Susan has always been on my side, but she seems resolute as she speaks. 'He had to do something. You couldn't live with the pain.'

'I thought I'd killed your baby.' My voice shudders into the phone. 'I had a memory of your face, you crying . . .' Then I relay my distorted memories.

There is only a year between us in age. Susan and I did everything together . . . went to the same university, got married the same year, even got pregnant at the same time. But her daughter lives while mine died.

'Your memories of me crying were real,' Susan replied, and I hear the rush of water from a tap as she pours herself a drink. 'You were in shock. I'd just arrived at the hospital. You told me what happened. I cried . . . we both did. Then you broke down.' There's a crack in Susan's voice as her emotions get the better of her and I feel a familiar stab of pain.

Now I know for sure that the screaming on a loop in my memory is mine. 'But Daniel lied . . . How could he lie to me? I feel so humiliated.' I speak in a low voice, aware that Teresa is listening, and her allegiance will always be with him.

'Sweetheart, you were in bits. You wanted to die, but you were quiet about it, shuffling around, trying to find a way out. Daniel had to watch you twenty-four/seven while coping with devastating grief. Then Kim found out what happened, and she persuaded you to accept treatment. You were a test case, so you didn't have to pay. It was amazing. We got the old Claire back.'

'But it was under the guise of a lie.' I shift on the bed, my head bowed.

'It gave you time to breathe. To heal, just enough hope to carry on. Therapy has changed. Exposing your pain to the light isn't always the best way. Sometimes it's better to deal with a little at a time. It's like swallowing a bottle of poison. If you do it over the course of a year, it's not going to cause as much damage as all in one go.'

A hint of a smile touches my face. These are Kim's words. I've heard them before. She always had a knack of explaining things simply in a way that laypeople could understand. Susan is still talking.

'I was as much involved as Daniel in this. The drugs, the therapy . . . and the doll . . . they worked, and I encouraged it all.'

A memory returns. Kim, telling me that I would find a purpose again. Then a hazy conversation about medication and props as I withdrew into myself. Drugs clouded my vision long enough to fall into a world in which I could safely live.

'You took to it so well,' my sister's voice continues. 'Much better than anyone expected. But you couldn't stay at the centre for ever. The plan was to get you off the meds and gradually separate you from the doll.'

'And that's when Daniel brought me to the island,' I say, as the pieces slot together. But how did he pass the baby off as ours? Then I think about how lifelike she . . . *it* was, always swaddled, rarely exposed.

'I'm coming to see you.' Susan interrupts my thoughts. 'I'm checking flights now.'

I don't try to stop her. I don't know how I feel about Daniel right now, but I need my sister here. Despite her being in on everything, she's the only person I fully trust.

'I've missed you so much,' I say, unable to stop the tears.

'Oh, honey, I've missed you too. So many times I've wanted to come over, but I didn't want to disrupt your treatment. I know it's going to be hard. We've always known. But you're stronger now. Small steps. Just keep moving forward and you'll be fine.'

After a teary goodbye, I put down the phone and see Teresa rest the binoculars on the window ledge. She turns to me, her face pale with worry.

'Danny's back.'

I follow her downstairs to find my husband walking into the kitchen, closing the back door behind him.

'We found Mossie,' he says, breathless from what can only be bad news. I study his face for answers because Mossie isn't here. Then he turns to Teresa and my stomach churns as he utters the doom-laden words. 'You might want to sit down.'

CHAPTER 54

MARY

Then

If I can get through the next twenty-four hours, then everything will be OK.

As Martina went into labour, it became my mantra. Teresa had explained that twins usually deliver early, so I wasn't to worry about her inducing the birth. I don't know how she got her hands on the oxytocin, but she'd been having secret meetings with Gabriel as they planned it all out. Mossie and I stayed out of it, instead focusing on getting through the day. During times like those, I missed my parents. Had they been alive and in their full health, they would never have allowed such a thing. When it came to Gabriel, I lacked a backbone, but at least this would be our last trip.

I'd tried to relocate Martina to a basement room, but Gabriel wouldn't allow it, calling it 'inhumane'. His lack of awareness often floored me. Couldn't he see what everyone else did? All the care I strived for meant nothing if one of those women became pregnant under our roof. Martina pandered to his ego, and her beauty gave him pause. I tried to view her with compassion, reasoning that whatever she'd been through to get her to this point must have been truly awful. The fact that she'd drowned her first baby was unimaginable. It took some time for me to see it, but Teresa had her figured out from day one. Yet she allowed us all to pander to her, most likely seeing us as fools. But the day she went into labour, Martina let the mask slip. There was truth in pain. Agony demands full attention and lies fall away. I didn't want to be left alone with her, but Teresa insisted that she didn't need outside help. I'd assisted with births before, but the memory of Catherine falling to her death was always at the forefront of my mind. But Martina wasn't Catherine. She wasn't screaming, she was seething as her true feelings were exposed.

'Get your dirty fat fingers away from me!' she spat, as I approached with a cold, damp cloth. We didn't need to restrain Martina because there was nowhere for her to go.

'Now, now, I'm just trying to help.' I glanced over at Teresa, who was preparing for the babies' arrival. Two clear Perspex hospital cots were set up, along with everything she needed to deliver them safely into the world.

'Bitch! Stupid fat cow!' Martina spat, bubbles of saliva gathering in the corners of her mouth. I refused to give her a reaction as she slapped the facecloth away. 'Do you know what your boys get up to when everyone's gone to bed?'

I turned away as her words hit home. Martina's pretty face contorted with pain, her damp black hair clinging to her face as she hissed one abusive word after another, spewing swearwords I'd never heard of until that day. It felt more like an exorcism than a woman giving birth.

I was emotionally exhausted by the time the twins arrived. I wished they'd been given a better start in life, but Árd Na Mara was yet to witness a peaceful birth.

I wondered if Martina would ask to hold her babies, because she knew we were taking them away. Gabriel had come to some sort of deal that I insisted on staying out of. But she was sleeping by the time we'd cleaned up.

'Just a sedative,' Teresa explained, and I was grateful for it.

I didn't want to think about what state Martina would be in when she awoke.

We didn't have time to dwell, as the boys came home from school. Mossie was taking them out to the cinema to clear the path for us to make the crossing to the mainland. They didn't need to know about the births, we tried to shield them as much as we could from the distressing aftermath. A storm was forecast for later on, but we had to go tonight. The Lynch family had struck the deal and wouldn't take kindly to being let down. It was the best thing for everyone. So why was I filled with dread?

CHAPTER 55

CLAIRE

'Jesus, Mary and Joseph,' Teresa utters beneath her breath. 'What an awful state of affairs.' Her face is shrunken with worry, her limp more pronounced. The last twenty-four hours have taken their toll. I feel guilty that I have contributed towards it. Teresa should be at home taking it easy, but instead we're back on the mainland and she's pacing the hospital corridors, waiting for news once more. Louis has gone home for a change of clothes while Daniel hasn't left my side.

A doctor I've come to recognise appears. 'Claire. I didn't expect to see you again so soon.'

'Looks like we can't get enough of this place,' I joke. 'How is he?'

And I'm back, in the real world, coping well as I carry the underlying sadness that will always be a part of me. We discuss Mossie's injuries. He'll be out of action for a while. His leg is fractured in several places, and he's got some badly bruised ribs. If Daniel and Louis hadn't found Mossie when they did, he may not have survived the night. I nod solemnly, thanking the doctor for his time.

'Can we go in?'

'Of course.'

I allow Teresa to go ahead of me as we approach the ward. I want to link arms with her and tell her everything will be OK, just as she's done with me. But Teresa's a proud woman, and strides through her limp to reach Mossie's bed. He's sitting up, his leg in a cast, a cup of tea on the table and a smile touching his face.

'You old fool,' Teresa says, shaking her head. 'What were ya playing at? Frightened the life out of me, you did!' Her eyes are shiny with tears but she doesn't kiss or hug him, just pulls a chair close and sits next to his bed. There is love in Mossie's eyes as he watches his wife take a seat. Some signs of affection don't have to be big or flashy. For Teresa and Mossie, just being there is enough.

'How are you feeling?' I ask, peeping at his chart.

'Like I've been run over by a truck . . . twice.'

'I thought you knew those cliff paths. What happened? How did you fall?' I rest a packet of Kimberley biscuits on his table. Daniel places a bottle of Lucozade next to it – the Irish cure for everything.

Mossie had been barely conscious when Louis found him, moaning weakly as he clung on to a tree root jutting off the cliff. Louis stayed with him, waiting for the air ambulance, while Daniel ran home to inform us.

Now Mossie looks from left to right, taking in each of our faces. 'I didn't fall,' he says. 'I was pushed.' He speaks in a conspiratorial whisper as we gather around the bed. 'And you're not going to believe who by.'

CHAPTER 56

THE ISLANDER

They're coming for me. I knew the moment that Mossie was found that the jig was up. I stand in my room, staring out into the distance. Why didn't the little bastard die, like those who went before him? It was the Englishwoman's fault. She knocked everything out of kilter, coming here with her ridiculous fake baby wrapped up as if it could feel the cold.

I remember the day she got off the ferry with it strapped close to her chest. Always checking, always touching, kissing, petting, fussing. And she was meant to be some award-winning doctor. Is the woman insane? I had every intention of taking her precious baby and making it disappear. The joke was on me when I locked her in the basement and found a doll in the cot. At first, I thought I was wrong, that a toy had been put there in the baby's place. But then I spied through the window later on and saw Teresa throwing it into the travel cot by the leg. Then I remembered Isla going for a swim and leaving the pram at the bay. I couldn't fathom why such a caring woman would neglect her own niece like that – until I found out more.

The fact that the Englishwoman was grieving her child left me dumbfounded. When someone has lost everything, how do you frighten them after that? They've already faced the worst. Pain is their constant companion. I took my frustrations out on Mossie. He's always been an irritant, and I no longer had use for him. It had felt good to offload, but I took it too far when I told him the truth about the people who died. In the end, he knew too much, and the scandal of Árd Na Mara's history would taint the island for ever. The auld eejit wasn't meant to survive.

All this time, I've carried out my duties without fear of reprisal. I've kept the islanders safe – not that I'd get any thanks for it if they knew. I've kept our reputation intact. Ensured they could sleep soundly in their beds. Rid us of any undesirables, including the women from the institute who tried to escape. And now, after all of that, it's weaselly little Mossie Nikolic who will take me down.

I watch the coastguards through my binoculars as they make the crossing to our island. There's a detective on board, as well as uniformed police. Their faces are determined. They won't take any nonsense from me. I knew the little bastard would squeal. I became complacent. I should have gone back and checked that I'd finished the job.

I glance at my treasures, all laid out on my windowsill. I swear I can hear my stomach rattle with everything I've swallowed over the last few days. My gut feels distended, and not all the items that I've swallowed have reappeared as they should. Yet I'm unable to stop. Each time I feel trapped, I swallow something else. It started with an engagement ring, all those years ago. I'd just returned from the mainland, and had it nestled in my pocket when Mary called to say we needed to talk. I'd presumed we were on the same page and that marriage was on the cards. I didn't see it coming when she said she didn't love me anymore. She may as well have punched me in the gut.

That day I stood on the cliff edge, ready to throw the ring into the sea. I held it up in my hand and it glinted in the sun. A madness seemed to overcome me as I put it in my mouth. With one swallow, it was gone. Tears streamed from my eyes as laughter shook my body. It was the beginning of a dangerous compulsion, but now it's come to an end. There's no point in running. You can't escape from the island. You either sink or swim – literally.

I caress a smooth grey pebble, one I picked up from the beach. It's more of a stone than a pebble. It's as big as a marble and almost as round, smoothed away by the ebb and flow of the tide. I've never swallowed anything this size before. I took it from the beach the night Mary and Gabriel died. But I was simply a watcher that night. Who would have thought they would end up being drowned by one of their own?

The police have pulled up to the pier, and my heart beats faster than is comfortable. I rub my stomach, thinking of my family and what they will say. The islanders will stand behind me. It's all in my diaries – the good work I've done. But my family . . . I imagine their judgement and the thought burns a hole within. I am an outcast now, but it pains me just the same. I pop the stone into my mouth, but today my compulsion offers little relief. The floorboards creak beneath my weight as I tread back and forth. The stone is too big to roll over my tongue. It's a hard ball that lodges against the roof of my mouth. I'm sweating, my nostrils flaring as my breath accelerates. I clench my fists by my side as the police approach the house. If they want a fight, by God, I'll give it to them.

They're here, speaking loudly as they update their radios of the time of their arrival. Bastards, the lot of them. Once there was a time when a word from my father was enough to make them back down. But Mossie was right about one thing – the people in power are long gone, as much as I hate to admit it to myself. The front door is opened. I lock my bedroom door. I'm not going to make this easy for them.

Bastards, I think again. *Fecking, interfering—*

I cough as the stone moves, instinctively swallowing it back. I gag, trying to bring it up. It's too big . . . I didn't mean to . . . but my breath won't come. There's nothing. No air. Just a firm blockage in my throat. Now there are footsteps clattering through my house, shouting and disarray as they approach.

My door handle is rattled back and forth with loud commands to open the door. I clutch my neck. The stone won't budge. I need to get it out.

'Open up!' the Gardaí shout, announcing themselves.

My eyes roll in their sockets as I try but fail to breathe.

Jesus, if I can just let them in.

But I instinctively grapple with my throat. My mouth opens and closes like a trout pulled from the river. I punch myself in the throat, trying to dislodge the object. Why did I lock the door? They're banging now, and I drop to my knees, shoving my fingers down my oesophagus in an attempt to make myself sick.

The edges of my world become fuzzy and their shouts ring in my ears. My vision is tinged in red as my blood vessels burst and my lungs burn for the want of air. After three sharp pounds, the door swings open, and the last thing I see are police officers' boots clattering against the floor as they rush towards me. My world begins to fade in a cacophony of shouting as they try to figure out what's wrong.

'He's having a heart attack!' one man shouts.

'Out of my way, he's choking!' someone else bellows, as they grab hold of me.

Then the voices fade, and the colours dissolve as darkness falls, heavy, like a cold, sudden night.

CHAPTER 57

DANIEL

Six months later

Thank God for the sun. It can make the worst of times a little more bearable. It has a healing quality about it, and even the air smells better when you feel its warmth against your skin. A light spray of foam speckles my face as I ride the ferry, watching Selkie Island come into view. It's the strangest thing, but my seasickness has vanished. Now I feel nothing more than slight nausea as I make the journey across. So much has happened, it's a miracle we're all still here.

All but one.

'Are you OK?' I say to my female companion, who has also come off the mainland.

Aoife travelled over with Isla this morning but is going home early, so her mother's not left alone for long. She nods thoughtfully, but I need to hear her say the words. Pain isn't always obvious. It folds in on itself like origami, bestowing a thousand internal cuts. I raise my voice against the hum of the outboard engine.

'No, really. Are you alright? Because if you need to talk . . .'

I haven't seen much of her since the funeral, and I feel bad about that. There's been a lot to organise due to our change in circumstances, but I want to make things right.

She turns to face me, pushing her fringe back off her face. Her hair has grown longer, and her skin is summer tanned.

'I'm getting there. It was hard, losing Dad on top of everything else . . . Well, you know. I'm going to stay on the island for another while, help Mum through it all.'

'If there's anything you need, you know where we are.'

And I mean it, because Aoife has been a true friend. I have taken over running the online side of things as she finds her feet. At first, our only guests were murder tourists and journalists hanging about in the hope of a better story. But like always, we chose to remain tight-lipped. Our families have history that spans decades, and we won't allow her father's actions to taint it.

Aoife nods because there's not much more she can say. She doesn't blame Mossie for calling the police when he did. It was Kieran's mental health issues that led to the disorder that took his life.

Police revived him long enough to get to the hospital, where he was later pronounced brain dead. The contents of his stomach were the talk of the hospital staff room, according to Claire. Coins, marbles, pins, stones, even shells were found in his stomach during the autopsy. But nothing as big as the stone that blocked his windpipe.

I'm surprised at how little we knew about the man who came to live on Selkie Island with his mother when he was a boy. He never mentioned his father, only that he'd once lived in Dublin, but his parents had separated after his mam found out about his affair.

How must he have felt, being trapped in a house fire, barely managing to escape with his life? I've pictured him as a child living on the mainland, watching his family home go up in flames. But we didn't know that Catherine had been the one who pushed the flaming petrol bomb through their cat flap.

How ironic that she would be sent to an institution on the very island where Kieran's mother chose to start again.

Or was Catherine's fate pre-determined? Did she really throw herself from the top floor of Árd Na Mara, or was she pushed? How long had Kieran known of her existence?

It was hardly any wonder that he viewed our family with such disdain – we were the people who took in the woman who had burned his family home to the ground. He was swept away from his city life and private school to the remoteness and desolation of Selkie Island with a depressed mother whose mental health was fragile at best. His life changed immeasurably after the fire.

No wonder my father kept Isla's birth a secret. How would things have ended had Kieran known that she was his half-sister? The result of his father's scandalous tryst.

So Aoife is Isla's niece – of sorts. Only now do I see the resemblance – the same sandy freckles and auburn hair. They've developed a natural bond over the years. But she's not ready to know. Not just yet.

Kieran's diaries made for shocking reading, according to Orla. If the contents are true, many people have died at his hands. I'm just glad Orla hid the diaries from the police. The last thing we needed was them looking into our family history.

It's time for a fresh start. You never really know what goes on behind closed doors. To the world, Orla and her family had it all. A successful business, a beautiful home, and a close-knit family loved by all. But in reality, the business was paid for by an inheritance left by Kieran's father, who was not just corrupt, but a crook.

Kieran lived in the loft room on the top floor of his new home, his marriage crumbling due to growing mental health issues that he refused treatment for. He insisted he was the shepherd of Selkie Island and the people who lived there, who he regarded as his flock.

When he wasn't in the bar, he was roaming the cliff edges, obsessed with watching my family's business and the babies born under its roof. I only hope that wherever Kieran is now, he has found some peace. Dark shadows move in the sea and I realise that we're not alone. The seals have come out to play.

'Look!' Aoife points. 'They're saying hello.'

I lean over the side of the ferry, watch them effortlessly glide through the waters as they escort us home.

CHAPTER 58

MARY

Then

The storm came in quickly the night I died. We were stuck between the island and the mainland, riding each surge while praying our little boat wouldn't capsize. It was as if God was pounding the waves in anger and it was utterly terrifying.

Gabriel had to shout over the noise. I didn't know it back then, but it was the last coherent sentence that he would speak.

'It's rough, but we'll get there soon enough!'

How I wanted to believe him. But that night felt different. You can only inflict so much damage on the world before it catches up with you. We held those newborn babies tightly, stealing them away into the night.

The lights of the mainland were mesmerising, and I blinked against the spray, willing a safe crossing. I smiled at Isla to reassure her, but her expression left me cold. I have never in my life seen such a quiet display of rage. Another wave hit the boat with force and I clung on to the side. I could not bring myself to look at my husband because I was caught in Isla's gaze.

I should have given her more credit. She didn't just disapprove, she hated us for what we were doing. I couldn't bear it, because I knew in my heart that she was right. What had I done?

There was another loud boom as a thunderous wave hit our boat. Finally, I looked to Gabriel, but he was staring ahead, his expression fixed as he guided us towards the mainland.

What then? I thought, peeping down at the baby in my care. She and her twin had been ripped away from their mother's embrace. What sort of person sells babies for the highest price?

'Sorry,' I whispered to the angelic infant, but my words were whipped away by the wind.

'No!' Isla screamed, her utterances louder than mine. She was judging us with a fury that rose with the waves.

I tried to ask her what was wrong, but her eyes burned with a hatred that chilled me to the core.

'No more!' she shouted, standing now. I didn't know how she was keeping her balance against the wind, but she was. The baby was strapped in the papoose to her chest, her life jacket strewn over her back. But on this freezing-cold night, these poor wee things needed to be inside. What had we been thinking, coming out during a storm? All because Gabriel felt it safer to travel at night when everyone else was sensibly tucked away.

'Isla, sit down!' I cried, unable to stand because I was too scared of falling on top of the baby.

Gabriel shouted something incoherent as he signalled at her to sit down.

'No more!' Isla exclaimed, and I made out the words 'not . . . your . . . babies!' leaving her lips.

I gripped the seat of the boat as she purposely rocked it from side to side. I wanted to scream, but my breath was stolen away. The lighthouse cast another beam upon us, and I watched her expression soften as she stared out to sea. The seals . . . there were dozens of them either side of the boat, with large black saucer eyes as they bobbed, unperturbed by the frothy waves.

'Isla . . . !' Gabriel shouted as he rose from his seat. They tussled as he tried to control her, and she pushed him aside with a force of strength.

I cried out as Gabriel lost his balance and hit his head against the side of the boat with a sickening thud. Seawater mingled with blood as it drizzled from the side of his face. He lay, shaking, unable to find his feet as Isla continued to rock the boat.

I had no time to help him as we were hit by another wave. With nobody to steer it, the boat was unbalanced by the waves. I gasped for breath as we were thrown into the sea and the seawater slapped against my body with the force of a train. I clawed the water for purchase as I desperately scrambled for air.

Where was Gabriel? Isla? And . . . holy mother of God, what about the wee ones?

With horrific clarity, I realised that we weren't going to make it home. Then I was crying, spluttering, convulsing as shock grasped my body, turning it cold. The cruelty of it, forcing a death like this upon me, with a baby strapped to my chest. I tried keeping the poor mite above the surface, but I'd swallowed too much water and the icy sea was turning my body numb. My last living breath was taken as the seals gathered round. I touched their glossy skin before slipping into the depths of the sea.

◆ ◆ ◆

I was there when Teresa and Mossie found my body. It was a small mercy that I had been reasonably well preserved. The current dragged me back to the island, my charge still nestled in the

259

papoose strapped to my chest. I'm glad they were the ones to find me. They didn't deserve to be spared the horrors of what we'd done.

I know they tried to protect Isla, but they were just as instrumental as I was in the deaths of those newborns. Teresa should have spoken up when she realised what was going on, but she treated those fragile new mothers with little compassion. They weren't inherently bad people. Everyone makes mistakes, but a good person changes direction when they know their course is wrong.

That was my Isla. She saw what was happening and decided enough was enough. Either way, she knew what I had denied for so long. Gabriel was never going to stop. Not for me, not for her, not for anyone. Because there would always be another scheme at someone else's expense. All she wanted was for us to turn around and put our shameful excursions to an end. I know that she tried to speak to Teresa, but like everyone who did his bidding, Gabriel had something on them. It was his way of bending them to his will.

Teresa was arrested for stealing drugs from a hospital on the mainland. There was a lucrative market for such a thing, and Mossie was also arrested, for selling them on. Lucky for them, my husband had friends in high places – the politician in the Dáil, Kieran's father. He made the charges go away, while Gabriel provided the couple with a home – as long as they kept their mouths shut. They could never have known that when they came to live on the island they would end up being our children's guardians. They might have only served a couple of years in prison, but they've given their whole lives to the island instead.

Did they regret their choices? I know I did. Gabriel used our children like a weapon, and I was powerless to utter a word. Each time, he'd promise me that this was our last journey across to those shores. Over the years he sold so many babies – at least nine that I know of – and most were his own flesh and blood. We hid it as much as we could, which meant we couldn't take on many staff. Three of the women in our care died on the cliffs trying to escape.

Orla knew. Most of the people on our side of the island were aware of what went on at Árd Na Mara. In the end, it was everyone's secret to bear. Nobody wanted Selkie Island to become tainted by our crimes – least of all Kieran. To think how envious I was of Orla's happiness, when all along her husband was just as disturbed as mine. I thought I knew the man – hell, I almost married him. But Kieran never opened up about his past. Perhaps I was destined to be attracted to bad men. Such was my life's course.

Gabriel was found weeks after me. He was such a good swimmer, almost as good as Isla – but he couldn't save himself after his head injury.

I came to learn of my boys giving chase much later on. I hadn't known who was in the boat behind us at the time. I had too much on my mind. It was only after I died that I saw Louis steering the outboard motor, with Danny directing him. Their faces white with shock, they pulled Isla from the water, but Gabriel and I had been dragged under by the waves. I don't know why they chose to keep it a secret that they were there. Perhaps they were trying to protect their sister from what she had done.

Now I get to swim with Isla as she takes another dip in the sea. I think she senses I am among the seals, along with all the souls who lost their lives in these waters long before their time. It is both a blessing and a curse.

CHAPTER 59

CLAIRE

The award hangs in my office, a testament to what I have overcome. It would have been so easy to leave Ireland and never return. My old job was open to me in London and the flat that I missed so much was still being leased. I have my own money. I have always remained financially independent, and we haven't spent that much on the house.

On that awful night when Isla rid me of the doll, I took off my wedding ring and left it on a dresser in the bedroom.

Perhaps Daniel had meant well, but at the time I couldn't see how I could trust a man willing to engage in such a colossal lie. I felt betrayed and shockingly humiliated as I relived my grief all over again. As if that wasn't bad enough, he'd dragged other people into the lie too.

Now, as I look back with a clear mind, it all makes sense. Daniel wasn't an absent father, he was no father at all, because our baby had died. Perhaps I had been a project to distract him from his own pain. We have talked and I understand his defence that he'd only wanted what was good for me. But I can't live with Danny until we regain a level of trust. Because there's one thing I've come to realise. He's not Daniel. That part of him only existed while he turned his back on his true self. He's Danny, who belongs on Selkie Island, painting pictures and holding classes in Árd Na Mara while supporting a family I barely knew up until a few months ago.

But yet, I'm unable to completely let go. The island still calls to me. I haven't gone far. I stride down the hospital corridor, my stethoscope around my neck. It feels incredibly rewarding to be in this new role. I'm the head of paediatrics in Cork Hospital, and my team is amazing. They were so welcoming the first time I came here, and after several meetings and interviews, I took the job.

The one good thing about my unorthodox treatment is that Kim kept it under wraps. According to her, I was there for grief counselling, and the results of the study are anonymous. At least here I can start again. I'm just Claire, the award-winning paediatrician, not the mentally ill woman who believed a doll was her baby.

I can see myself living here permanently and I suppose that means I'm not ready to let go of Danny just yet. There are other people here that I care about too.

I smile as I approach my lunch date. She's sitting by the window in the hospital canteen. Not the most glamorous of settings, but we've been meeting here once a week since I took up my new role. I am proud of how Isla has bounced back, and this time away from Árd Na Mara is good for her. I'm one of the few people that Danny has told about Isla's biological father and we've agreed that unless she asks, we'll keep it to ourselves for now.

I'm staying in a flat on the mainland and it's been nice, living by myself. There are pictures of Kitty on the wall, and my sister visits from time to time. Work keeps me sane, although I've developed an aversion to dolls. They make my skin crawl.

Isla chats about island life and makes me promise to visit soon. She tells me about Danny's art classes, and how well he and Louis are getting on, especially now that Danny has come clean about *The Drowning Man*. His agent freaked out at the sight of the brothers' joint social media video revealing the truth about the painting. It could have backfired massively, but after it went viral, sales of Danny's paintings went through the roof. He makes more money from the prints now than from the original works of art.

As for Árd Na Mara, it's still a bit rough around the edges, but it's comfortable and clean. The art students and writers who stay accept its unique atmosphere as part of the island's charm.

Danny's art classes keep Teresa and Mossie in work and give something back to the community, just as the art students help to keep Orla's business afloat.

Isla asks me how I am and I tell her some titbits about work. I make her smile with happy stories of children at the hospital who have got better and been able to go home. It's nice to see her free of the stresses of before. I've apologised to her a thousand times, even though it's not my fault. It was hard on her having to act as if the doll I was carrying around was real. No wonder she felt uncomfortable and ran away from it at times. She was the only one brave enough to show me the truth in the end. I will never forget the sight of her standing there sopping wet, with that empty papoose strapped to her chest.

Not long after that, Danny filled in the details about the night Mary and Gabriel drowned. He and Louis had stolen a nearby boat, furious at their parents for kidnapping Martina's twins. But they hadn't gone far when Isla stood up in the boat, pushing her father so hard that he'd ended up concussed. After the boat tipped over, they managed to get to Isla and drag her on board. But they couldn't save the babies, or their parents, by the time they were found. A part of me imagines her standing up and screaming at Gabriel to turn around. I wonder, how could someone so gentle hold so much anger inside? She stood by her convictions because, in her heart, she knew what her parents were doing was wrong. But nobody would listen to Isla so she took it upon herself to make things right. The same way she took action the night she threw my doll into the sea. But had Isla been arrested the night her parents died, the police may not have seen it that way. It seemed safer at the time to leave Isla in the clear and say she'd been at home. It's a tragedy, whatever way you look at it. I want her to put it behind her and start her life afresh.

'He misses you,' Isla says, relishing her chocolate cake. She's talking about Danny. I'm touched that Isla likes me enough to want me to return to Árd Na Mara.

'I miss him too,' I reply. 'And I'll be here for you every day, any time, anything you need.'

'Ditto,' she says with a smile, returning her attention to her cake.

It's the best I can offer for now.

'So you're not coming back?'

'One day.' I smile.

'You should tell the truth.'

I barely catch the words as Isla utters them.

'Sorry?'

'I know stuff,' Isla replies. 'You don't need to hide things.' She pushes her plate aside, and I don't know how to respond. 'I know that Kieran was my brother. I know that Mammy Catherine jumped out the window after I was born. I know that Danny was the twins' daddy, too.'

'What?' I glance around the canteen, checking there were no witnesses to these revelations that have come out of the blue.

'Aoife told me some of it. Teresa the rest. You shouldn't hide stuff from me. Not when *I* tell *you* the truth.' She's presuming I know about Danny fathering the twins, but I'm stunned. He was only fifteen back then. I didn't have a clue.

'Oh . . . right, sorry,' I say, trying to compose myself. 'It's just . . . that's a lot to take on board. How do you feel about it?'

She shrugs. 'It's OK.' She checks her watch.

I need to be getting back to work myself. As we rise, I open my arms for a hug.

'Don't be a stranger,' Isla says, as we part.

'I won't,' I reply. 'Send Danny my love.'

And I mean it, because it's hit me that I've been living in my own bubble all this time. Straight-talking Isla has made me realise that I'm not alone in my pain.

As I watch her leave, I remember something Danny once said: 'I can't do this on my own. Not again.' I'd presumed he was talking about grief, and the loss of his parents. But now I see he was referring to the other children he'd lost. How self-centred I've been.

I slide my phone from my pocket and type out a text. *Fancy a drink tonight?*

It's about time I got to know my mysterious island man. He doesn't have to go it alone anymore.

CHAPTER 60

TERESA

I breathe a sigh of contentment as I stand on top of the landing, duster in hand. Árd Na Mara is safe again. I have kept this place running through the good times and the bad. It's not that I love the building, I just cannot live anywhere else. Keeping the family together is the most important thing in my life.

Gabriel and Mary's marriage was rocky from the start. Even before I met Mary, I could tell that Gabriel was only with her out of convenience. He spoke about his business, about the potential of the institution, and the type of women he took in. But he hardly spoke about Mary, and when he did, he had nothing good to say.

When we first came to Árd Na Mara, we were barely inside the door when Mary ran from the place, angry and upset. I knew I wouldn't be in for an easy time, but it was better than the prison sentence that faced us on the mainland. Back then, Gabriel was a guardian angel of sorts. When he offered us bed and board in Árd Na Mara, we snapped his hand off. Even now, despite everything, I wouldn't change a thing. The story of us dealing drugs was the palatable version of what really went on. Árd Na Mara wasn't the only place that got rid of unwanted women. If you knew what to administer and gave the right amount, you could do it in a hospital setting too. I was well paid at the time, but when the third woman died under my care, it was safer for me to move on.

The sound of Daniel's voice carries in the air. He's on the phone to Claire. From what I can gather, they're arranging to have a drink. I've always known those two would get back together, but just as I predicted, Claire would gravitate towards the mainland. They deserve some happiness after everything they've been through.

Kieran's death came as a shock to us all, but sure I'm glad he's dead. He made Orla's life a misery and ruled his children with a rod of iron. Few people knew what the man was really like. But then Selkie Island has always been good at keeping secrets.

Kieran wasn't the only one who wanted to keep it safe. I did what was needed to keep our patients in line. Most could be controlled by drugs, but others, like Martina, needed taking in hand. Mary was good with Isla, but too naïve to deal with the realities of our harsh world. Gabriel and I had a special relationship, not that you'd think it to look at me now. I wasn't always like this. When I worked at the hospital, I was shapely and not unattractive. My long, dark hair tumbled as far as my waist when I let it down.

Over time, Gabriel and I became close. At night, we'd plot together, making plans for Árd Na Mara. He was generous when he could be and often gave me a cut of the proceeds. I knew too much of his shady dealings for him to let me go. One night, we lay together in one of the basement rooms. It happened only the once, and while it meant nothing to Gabriel, I was disgusted with myself. How could I do that, with Mary and Mossie under the same roof? But nothing was more enticing to Gabriel than forbidden fruit.

I loved my husband like a brother. So when I told him I was pregnant, he knew the child wasn't his. He gave me an ultimatum. Get rid of the baby, or he would leave the island for good. He never suspected Gabriel. He believed my story when I told him I'd met an old flame on the mainland during a rare trip away. Back then, Mossie drank himself into a stupor every day. It wasn't hard to pull the wool over his eyes. I didn't want to rear the child. A part of me wasn't capable of intimacy. I'd always known that I was different in that way.

Then Daniel was born. His small deformity put paid to Gabriel's plans. The couple he had lined up wouldn't take what they considered to be a 'damaged' child. That's when Mary stepped in, and I was grateful for her to do what I wasn't capable of. She never understood why Mossie and I rejected a child she believed to be our own flesh and blood, but she had always wanted a little brother for Isla, although we were all surprised when Louis came along.

If Mary favoured Louis, she never showed it. What she lacked in common sense, she made up for as a mother. I may not always demonstrate my emotions, but I was devastated when she drowned. That night broke my heart, not least of all because Isla was involved.

I'll never forget the sight of Isla, standing drenched in the hall with the papoose strapped to her chest and that poor little dead baby inside. We buried the baby beneath an apple tree in the church graveyard and changed the story of that night to protect Isla and the boys. We told people it was a tragic accident. There was no mention of the poor little twins. I consoled myself that such innocents were in the arms of the Lord. When Danny told me that he was the father, I have never felt fury like it. How dare Martina seduce my son – a fifteen-year-old boy!

Nobody knew that the babies existed. Nobody except us and Martina. It's why I couldn't afford to let her live. Gabriel may have taken the blame for her pregnancy, but justice had not been served.

Martina didn't die by suicide. I ensured that she had a long sleep. The boys believed me when I put her death down as an over-dose. We kept our silence for Isla, because we couldn't afford for the truth about Gabriel and Mary's baby-selling business to get out. It took a firm hand to ensure the coroner's compliance. No mention was made of the fact that Martina had recently given birth and we scattered her cremated ashes under the graveyard apple tree. The notorious Lynch family were good at cleaning up messes, and they did so on the condition that we take our secrets to the grave. The woman knew too much and I don't regret a thing.

For years, Selkie Island has carried the burden of its curse. But now, as I reflect on the past, I believe we have paid our debt in full. I snap out of my thoughts as Danny smiles up at me from downstairs. He tells me that the kettle is on and invites me to join him for a brew. I shake my head and tell him that *I'll* be the one making the tea. It's funny how I have ended up being a mother to my son. He may not know it yet, but I will always be here for him – whatever it takes.

AUTHOR'S NOTE

(SPOILER ALERT: Please don't read this letter before you've finished the book, otherwise it will ruin the ending for you.)

The Islanders is such a special book to me that I've been moved to write this little afternote. *The Islanders* is the twentieth book I've written, and I am hugely grateful to have got this far. I honestly couldn't have done it without you, the person who has picked up my book and is interested enough to keep reading right up until the last page. When I write, it's always with the reader in mind. I'm known for writing twists and turns and when I was plotting my twentieth book, I had to come up with something special.

If you've read my previous books, you'll know that Ireland is very close to my heart. I often feature at least one colourful Irish character to keep us entertained. I grew up in a remote but lovely place called Gallen in County Offaly. There's a strong sense of community in Gallen and the neighbouring town of Ferbane. A sense of protectiveness from the outside world. People genuinely care, not just about each other but for the place as a whole too.

During my childhood, my mum would take me to Bere Island to visit her sister Chrissie, who lived there with her husband and two sons. It's a tiny island at just seven miles long, situated off the Beara Peninsula in County Cork. Chrissie and her family always made me feel so welcome, even allowing me to climb onto their temperamental donkey, who would soon have me flat on my back. I used to help Chrissie feed the chickens, and later we'd drink milk which originated from their cows and eat fresh crab brought in from the boats that day. In the hazy summer evenings, we'd walk around the island with her sons. Chrissie would tell me about the old stone forts and the smugglers' coves. I reflect on those times with such fondness, which is why I've always wanted to set a book there. I created a fictional sister island, because Bere Island is far too nice a place for such dark deeds to occur.

That explains the setting. But what about the twist? As with all my books, parts are inspired by my personal experiences, either from my time in the police or beyond that. It may surprise some to know that I once owned a gift shop called The Gift Boutique, and sold collectable Ashton Drake dolls. When they first came on the scene, we sold them in record numbers, and they created quite a fuss. As they were displayed in their bassinets, they were so amazingly lifelike that people used to tap on the shop-window glass to check they weren't sleeping babies. I even ended up in the local newspaper as they ran a story on me. The dolls were usually sold to adults, and the reasons behind the expensive purchases were often heart-rending. Some women collected them for fun, but many had a sadder story, having experienced the loss of a child. The dolls provided comfort, filling their empty arms as they tried to come to terms with their loss. Some women pushed them in pushchairs. Others strapped them into car seats and brought them shopping. These weighted dolls with their silicone 'skin' even had their own range of clothes. Car windows were sometimes smashed because people thought the 'baby' left alone inside was neglected and overheated. I explain this to demonstrate that the ending of *The*

Islanders is not as implausible as you may think. If you're tempted to look up Ashton Drake dolls, go one further and search online for 'reborn' dolls and 'one of a kind'. It really is eye-opening – and given how much I love a twist, I couldn't let that go without putting it in a book.

I hope you enjoyed it. If you're new to my work, do check out my backlist, especially *The Village*, which is in a similar vein to this book. If you've read them all, thank you so much. Here's to the next twenty!

Caroline x

ACKNOWLEDGEMENTS

I always struggle to write the acknowledgements because a simple thank you is never enough. I'm always afraid that I'll leave someone out because so many people have helped me along the way. I'll start with my agent, the wonderful Madeleine Milburn, and her team. They are such an inspiring, hard-working collective that I am hugely fortunate to know. I've always felt valued at the agency, and no question is too stupid or email too long. Thanks to my publisher, Thomas & Mercer, and the amazing editors I've had the pleasure of working with along the way. In particular Victoria Haslam, who commissioned this book, and Kasim Mohammed, who has championed it from beginning to end. I'd also like to thank structural editor Ian Pindar, who I have been fortunate enough to work with on several occasions now. He knows my dark side well. Thanks also to the proofreaders who helped polish the manuscript and weed out any continuity errors I may have left behind. I'm also hugely grateful to everyone involved in marketing this book and also to Lisa Brewster for doing such a great job with the cover.

A very special mention goes to my dearest friends, Mel Sherratt and Angela Marsons. These inspirational authors have been with me from the start of my writing career and are of invaluable support.

I'd also like to thank the ladies from the First Friday Club. It sounds like a cosy crime novel, but they're real. I've recently moved to Lincoln and was so fortunate to be taken under their wing. A special shout out to Jo Hillas-Smith, who buys all my books and discusses them with gusto every time we socialise. A special mention also goes to Teresa Nikolic, who generously donated to charity in order to win the bid to have a character named after her in this book. As always, a special thank you to my family, Paul, Aoife, Jess, Ben and my husband, Neil. I work long hours and spend most of my day in a dream world, but they have always been of huge support. I'm also in gratitude to the author Facebook groups which have been invaluable during the course of my career. Also to the book clubs and book bloggers who have shared and reviewed my work. Last but not least, thanks to my readers for buying this book. I do hope you've enjoyed your visit to the island.

ABOUT THE AUTHOR

 A former police detective, Caroline Mitchell now writes full-time.

She has worked in CID and specialised in roles dealing with vulnerable victims – high-risk victims of domestic abuse and serious sexual offences. The mental strength shown by the victims of these crimes is a constant source of inspiration to her, and Mitchell combines their tenacity with her knowledge of police procedure to create tense psychological thrillers.

Originally from Ireland, she now lives in a woodland village in Lincoln.

You can find out more about her at www.caroline-writes.com, or follow her on Twitter (@caroline_writes) or Facebook (www.facebook.com/CMitchellAuthor). To download a free short story, please join her VIP readers' club here: https://books.bookfunnel.com/carolinemitchell.

Follow the Author on Amazon

If you enjoyed this book, follow Caroline Mitchell on Amazon to be notified when the author releases a new book!
To do this, please follow these instructions:

Desktop:

1) Search for the author's name on Amazon or in the Amazon App.
2) Click on the author's name to arrive on their Amazon page.
3) Click the 'Follow' button.

Mobile and Tablet:

1) Search for the author's name on Amazon or in the Amazon App.
2) Click on one of the author's books.
3) Click on the author's name to arrive on their Amazon page.
4) Click the 'Follow' button.

Kindle eReader and Kindle App:

If you enjoyed this book on a Kindle eReader or in the Kindle App, you will find the author 'Follow' button after the last page.

Printed in Great Britain
by Amazon